P9-DBY-418

the QUILTER'S DAUGHTER

Daughters of Lancaster County 2

WANDA *&* BRUNSTETTER

BARBOUR BOOKS
An Imprint of Barbour Publishing, Inc.

© 2006 by Wanda E. Brunstetter

Print ISBN 978-1-63409-219-7

eBook Editions:
Adobe Digital Edition (.epub) 978-1-63409-396-5
Kindle and MobiPocket Edition (.prc) 978-1-63409-397-2

All rights reserved. No part of this publication may be reproduced or transmitted for commercial purposes, except for brief quotations in printed reviews, without written permission of the publisher.

All scripture quotations are taken from the King James Version of the Bible.

Scripture quotations marked NIV are taken from the HOLY BIBLE, NEW INTERNATIONAL VERSION®. NIV®. Copyright © 1973, 1978, 1984, 2011 by Biblica, Inc.™ Used by permission. All rights reserved worldwide.

All Pennsylvania Dutch words are taken from the Revised Pennsylvania German Dictionary found in Lancaster County, Pennsylvania.

This book is a work of fiction. Names, characters, places, and incidents are either products of the author's imagination or used fictitiously. Any similarity to actual people, organizations, and/or events is purely coincidental.

Cover design: Müllerhaus Publishing Arts, Inc., www.mullerhaus.net

Published by Barbour Books, an imprint of Barbour Publishing, Inc., P.O. Box 719, Uhrichsville, Ohio 44683, www.barbourbooks.com

Our mission is to publish and distribute inspirational products offering exceptional value and biblical encouragement to the masses.

ecpa Member of the
Evangelical Christian
Publishers Association

Printed in the United States of America.

Dedication

To my friend Katherine Baar,
who has walked through the
fire and come out victorious.

To Betty Yoder,
a special friend with a spirit for adventure.

And to Donna Mae Crow,
a dear friend who is always there
when I need a listening ear.

When thou passest through the waters,
I will be with thee; and through the rivers,
they shall not overflow thee:
when thou walkest through the fire,
thou shalt not be burned;
neither shall the flame kindle upon thee.

ISAIAH 43:2 KJV

Prologue

A dark cloud hovered over Abby Miller's bed, pressing on her from all sides. Blinking against stinging tears, she drew in a ragged breath. An invisible hand pushed against her face, and she flung her covers aside. "*Ich kann nimmi schnaufe!* I can't breathe!"

Meow. Meow. Somewhere in the distance, Abby heard the pathetic cry and knew she must save the poor kitten. With a panicked sob, she rolled out of bed, but the minute her bare feet touched the floor, she shrank back from the intense heat. Paralyzing fear wrapped its arms around Abby, threatening to strip away her sanity. She lifted her hands to her face and rubbed her eyes, forcing them to focus. "Where are you, kitty? I'm coming, kitty."

Suddenly, she realized that her room was engulfed in flames—lapping at the curtains, snapping, crackling, consuming everything in sight. As the smoky haze grew thicker and the fire became an inferno, Abby grabbed the Lone Star quilt off her bed and covered her head. Coughing, choking, gasping on the acrid smoke, she stumbled and staggered toward the door. "*Feier!* Fire! Somebody, please help me save the kitten!"

∞

Abby bolted upright in bed. Droplets of perspiration dripped from her forehead, trickling onto her hot cheeks. Goose bumps covered her arms, and her cotton nightgown was soaking wet.

A howling wind rattled the windows. Rain pelted the roof like a herd of stampeding horses, while roars of thunder pounded the night air.

Huddled under her patchwork quilt, Abby drew in a deep breath and tried to still her racing heart. She ordered herself to sit up and light the kerosene lamp on the small table by her bed. As the room became illuminated, she was able to see the cedar chest that had belonged to her grandmother at the foot of her bed. The wooden rocker Dad had made for her thirteenth birthday was positioned between the two windows, and her dressing table stood across the room where it always had. She'd been dreaming.

"*Jah*, that's all it was—the same horrible nightmare I've had before." Abby clutched the comforting quilt and wrapped it around her shoulders. "Oh Lord, what does that night terror mean?"

Chapter 1

Abby opened the front door of her quilt shop and stepped onto the porch. A gentle breeze caressed her face, and she inhaled deeply. She hadn't slept well after waking from that dreadful nightmare, the one she'd had several times over the last few months. Fire and smoke. Unable to breathe. Paralyzing fear. What was the meaning of the dream, and why did she have it so often?

Abby remembered an article in *The Budget* some time ago about a young Amish boy in Indiana who'd been trapped in his father's burning barn. Could that newspaper article have stuck in her brain and caused the recurring nightmares, or was there something more to it? And what about those pathetic cries of a kitten she'd heard in her dream? Had there been a cat in the barn with the boy that day? She didn't remember all the details of the article and had long since thrown that issue of *The Budget* away.

Abby retrieved a stack of letters from the mailbox. *These thoughts aren't good for me. Lester Mast and I have finally set a date for our wedding, the sun is shining, spring is in the air, and my business is doing better than ever. There's so much to be thankful for.*

"Anything good in the mail?" Lena asked when

Abby reentered the shop.

Abby smiled at her sister-in-law and held up the stack of envelopes. "Looks like a note from Mom." She placed all of the mail but her mother's letter on the desk and reached underneath to grab her metal lunchbox. "It's a beautiful day, and I think I'll go out to the picnic table so I can read Mom's letter and eat lunch. Can you handle things on your own for a while?"

Lena nodded and repositioned a blond tendril that had slipped from under her small white head covering. "Jah, sure, I've already eaten my lunch, and we aren't so busy at the moment."

Abby nodded and hurried out the back door. She got situated at the picnic table and tore open the envelope. Mom had enclosed a white handkerchief with the initials *A. M.* embroidered in one corner.

"I'll bet this is for my hope chest. Either that, or Mom thinks I've come down with a cold."

Laying the hankie aside, Abby read the letter:

> *Dear Abby,*
>
> *The enclosed handkerchief is a gift from Mary Ann for your hope chest. She said she was glad you're engaged to a man with the same last initial as yours. That way, if you decide not to marry him, you can still use the hankie.*

Abby chuckled. "Leave it to Mary Ann to say something like that. Never know what my youngest stepsister might come up with."

She continued reading:

*Things are going well here. Naomi's doing
fine with her second pregnancy, and I think
she and Caleb are hoping for a boy this time
around. Samuel and Mary Ann are growing
like weeds, and Nancy, who turned fifteen
last month, is talking about courting and
such. 'Course her dad would never allow
it—not until she's sixteen.*

*Matthew, Norman, and Jake continue
to help their dad on the farm, and my dear
husband has never seemed so content.*

*I have some news of my own, which I
hope will bring you as much joy as it has me.
Abraham and I are expecting a baby.*

Her mother having a *boppli*! Abby's eyes
flooded with tears, causing the words on the page
to blur. Could this be true? After all these years,
was Mom, at age forty-seven, really going to have
another baby? Using the new hankie to dab her
eyes, she read on:

*Since Lena is helping you at the quilt shop,
I thought you might want to share the news
with her and your brother.*

*Other than a queasy stomach, I'm feeling
pretty good. As you can imagine, Abraham is
thrilled about this. Who would have thought
after being barren for so many years, the
Lord would bless me with another child?*

*I know you're busy planning your
wedding, but I'm hoping you can be here
when the baby is born. Since that will
happen in late October, and your wedding*

*is not until the end of November, it
shouldn't interfere with your big day. With
Lena there to help in the quilt shop, maybe
you can come a week or so before the baby is
born and then stay a week or two after? I'm
sure I'll be able to handle things on my own
by then.*

*Looking forward to hearing from you
soon.*

*With love,
Mom*

Abby thought about the day her widowed *mamm* had left Ohio for Pennsylvania. It had begun as a weekend trip to visit her cousin Edna. But then Mom ended up staying to help Abraham Fisher at his store, because his oldest daughter had run away from home soon after his son was kidnapped. It didn't take long for Mom and Abraham to fall in love and get married. Now, after four years of marriage, they were expecting a baby. Such a miracle it was!

"Abby, are you done with your lunch yet?" Lena called from the back door of the quilt shop. "A busload of tourists just showed up, and I could use some help."

Unable to speak around the lump in her throat, Abby merely nodded and stood. She would have to wait until the tourists left to share Mom's unexpected news with her sister-in-law.

❧

"You look tired today, *Fraa*. Are you doin' too much?"

Naomi Hoffmeir released a weary sigh. "Jah,

Caleb, this wife of yours is a bit tired." She patted her bulging stomach. "This one's draining my energy more than Sarah did."

Her husband nodded toward their two-year-old daughter, toddling around the store, checking out everything within her reach. "I'd say our little girl's more than makin' up for her quiet ways when she was a *boppli.*"

Naomi nodded. "You're right about that." She bent over and scooped Sarah into her arms. "I love you, sweet girl, even if you are a handful at times."

"Want me to put her down for a nap?"

"Sure, that's fine."

Caleb extended his arms, and Sarah reached out her hands. "Jah, that's right, come to your *daadi.*"

"I hope she cooperates and falls asleep right away," Naomi said as father and daughter headed for the back room, where they kept Sarah's playpen and a few toys.

"I think she will. Already her eyes are droopin'," he called over his shoulder.

Naomi sighed. *Sarah reminds me so much of Zach—full of energy and eager to investigate new things. How proud Mama would be if she were still alive and could see the precious granddaughter named after her.*

Naomi's gaze went to the calendar hanging near the counter by the front door. In just a few weeks it would be Zach's sixth birthday. Had her little brother been missing five years already?

A lump lodged in Naomi's throat as she reflected on all that had happened since the boy's kidnapping. She had run off for a time, unable to cope with the blame she felt for Zach's disappearance. Then shortly after she returned home, Papa had married Fannie Miller. Naomi and Caleb's wedding took place soon after he'd injured his hand, and ever since their marriage, they'd been working at the store that had been in Naomi's family a good many years.

Despite the fact that Naomi led a busy, satisfying life, she often found herself thinking of Zach, praying for him, and wondering if he was happy and safe. Except for that one notice they'd read in *The Budget* shortly after he was taken, there had been no word on her little brother.

Naomi lifted her gaze to the ceiling. *Thank You, Lord, for the healing You gave our family during such a difficult time. And bless my little brother, wherever he might be.*

"How's business today?" Fannie asked, stepping into the store from the adjoining quilt shop.

Naomi turned to face her stepmother. "No customers at the moment. How's it going with you?"

"Things are fine at my shop." Fannie tapped her stomach. "But my insides are still pretty unsettled."

Naomi nodded, for she knew exactly how Fannie felt. She had been sick for the first six months when she carried Sarah, but this pregnancy was different. Not one day of morning sickness so far, and since she only had four months until the baby came, Naomi figured she was in the clear. Her only complaint was frequent fatigue. "Have you told Abby your exciting news?" she asked Fannie.

"Jah. Sent her a letter a few days ago. She should have gotten it by now."

"I'm sure she'll be as thrilled as we all are."

Fannie's hazel-colored eyes filled with tears.

"It's such a miracle, me bein' in my late forties and gettin' pregnant after all these years." She gave Naomi a hug. "I'm glad our little ones can grow up together."

"Jah. God is good, isn't He?"

"That's for certain sure."

"Papa's beside himself over this, ya know."

Fannie crossed her arms over her ample chest, and her forehead creased with concern. "This babe won't take the place of your missing brother. I hope you realize that."

Naomi sucked in her lower lip. "I know." But even as the words slipped off her tongue, she wondered if she believed them. *Would Papa be so caught up with the baby that he'd forget he'd ever had a son named Zach?*

"Your *daed* deserves this chance with another child, don't ya think?"

"Of course he does, and so do you."

An English woman entered the store just then. "I'll let you get back to work," Fannie whispered. "And I've got a Log Cabin quilt that needs to be finished."

"Talk to you later then." Naomi turned toward the customer and smiled. "May I help ya with somethin'?"

∽

Linda Scott aimed the digital camera she'd recently purchased and snapped a picture of her son. Jimmy had been playing in the sandbox, but he'd decided to try out the slide.

Jimmy takes after his dad, she mused. *He's not afraid of high places. Maybe he'll be a painter someday, too. I'm glad he's not like me—afraid of so many things.*

"Do you mind if I share your bench?"

Linda slid over as a woman with dark hair cut in a short bob took a seat beside her.

"I'm Beth Walters, and that's my son Allen."

Linda's gaze went to the dark-haired boy climbing the ladder behind her son. "My name's Linda Scott, and my boy's name is Jimmy."

"Do you and Jimmy live nearby? I don't recall seeing you at the park before."

"Our house is a few blocks away. We normally come here after Jimmy gets home from morning kindergarten. But since there's no school today, he wanted to play as soon as he finished breakfast."

"My son is in afternoon kindergarten, so mornings usually work best for us." Beth glanced at her watch. "We've only been living in Puyallup a few months, and my husband has a night job at a lumber mill in Tacoma. I try to occupy Allen with quiet games at home, or we come to the park so Eric can sleep."

Linda stared at the camera clasped in her hands. She couldn't imagine having to plan her and Jimmy's lives around Jim's work schedule. Since her husband owned his own painting business and had several employees, Jim could usually come and go as he pleased. Although, lately he'd been working so much, he was seldom at home. Linda figured he might be using his job as an excuse to avoid her and their frequent arguments. She and Jim hadn't gotten along well since they'd adopted Jimmy five years ago.

"Looks like our boys are making friends," Beth said, her words pulling Linda's thoughts aside.

She looked up. Allen sat on one of the swings, and Jimmy stood behind him, pushing.

"Be careful, Jimmy. Don't push too hard or too fast."

"Allen will be fine," Beth said with a nod. "He always hangs on tight."

Linda lifted the camera and snapped a few pictures of the children. *This should prove to Jim that I'm letting our boy make new friends.*

"Jimmy looks small to be in kindergarten. How old is he?" Beth asked.

"He'll turn six in a few weeks."

"Allen celebrated his sixth birthday in February." Beth smiled. "Since we both live in the same neighborhood, I guess our boys will be starting first grade together this fall."

Linda nodded, remembering how Jim had wanted her to homeschool their son but changed his mind shortly before Jimmy started kindergarten, saying he thought it would be better if the child went to public school where he could play with other kids.

"Your dubious expression makes me think you're not looking forward to sending Jimmy to school all day. Is he your youngest?"

"Jimmy's our only child," Linda said, feeling tears prick her eyes. She'd wanted to adopt another baby as soon as Jimmy was out of diapers, but Jim flatly refused. He'd said one child was enough and reminded Linda that since they argued so much it wouldn't be good to bring another child into an already troubled home.

"Eric and I have two older boys," Beth commented. "Ricky's eight and Brett's ten. Having three kids so close in age was hard when they were little, but now that they're older, it's gotten easier."

As the boys moved from the swings to the teeter-totter, Linda snapped a few more pictures.

"Maybe we can both bring our boys to the park next Saturday," Beth said. "It will give us all a chance to get to know each other."

The thought of making a new friend was pleasant. Linda hadn't made any real friends since she and Jim moved from Boise, Idaho, to Puyallup, Washington, several years ago. Maybe it was time to reach out to another person. She and Jim certainly weren't good friends anymore.

Chapter 2

Anxious to read the letter she'd just received, Fannie closed the door behind Samuel and Mary Ann. She'd sent the two outside to weed the flowerbeds. They had been arguing ever since they got home from school, and she knew the only way to have any peace and quiet was to find something constructive for them to do.

Fannie reached for the pot of herbal tea brewing on the back of the propane stove and took a seat at the kitchen table. Then she poured herself a cup of tea and tore open Abby's letter.

Dear Mom,

The news of your pregnancy was quite a surprise—a pleasant one of course. How thrilled you and Abraham must be, and I'm certain the rest of his family is happy, too.

I told Lena and Harold about the baby, and they're as excited as I am. Lena said she would get a note off to you soon, because you know how Harold is when it comes to writing letters.

I can't help but worry about you, Mom. Please take care of yourself and be sure to get plenty of rest.

In answer to your question about me

coming there when the baby is born—I'd be happy to come. Fact is, you couldn't keep me from being there when my little brother or sister is born.

Things are fine here in Berlin. The quilt shop is doing well, and Lester and I have been talking about our upcoming marriage and where we will live. Since I've been staying with Lena and Harold since you moved to Pennsylvania, our old house has been sitting empty when it's not had renters. So, if you have no objections, Lester and I would like to buy your house and live there.

Give my love to Abraham and the rest of the family. Please write back soon, for I want to know how you're doing. I'll be praying for both you and the baby.

Love,
Abby

Fannie clicked her tongue. "Silly girl. I wouldn't dream of lettin' you buy that old house. It'll be my wedding present to you and Lester."

Her eyes misted as she thought about her daughter getting married in November. Abby and Lester had been courting for four years and probably would have been married by now, except two years ago Lester's daed passed away unexpectedly, leaving Lester, the only son in his family, to care for his mamm and run their blacksmith shop. It had taken him awhile to get to the point where he felt ready to take on the responsibility of marriage.

Fannie smiled through her tears. *At least they've finally set the wedding date for November, although*

Abby could have had it sooner, since weddings in Holmes County aren't restricted to November and December the way they are here in Lancaster. But Abby's a thoughtful daughter, and she knows that by the end of November the harvest will be done and Abraham and the boys will be free to leave their work and accompany me and the girls to Ohio for the wedding.

Fannie placed her hand against her stomach and massaged it gently. She bowed her head. "Heavenly Father, please bless this child I'm carrying. Thank You for the miracle You've given Abraham and me. Let our little one be healthy, and grant me good health as well." Tears slipped out from under Fannie's lashes and rolled onto her cheeks. "Lord, You know how much Abraham has gone through, first losin' his Sarah, and then Zach. I pray for Your mercy, and through me and this babe I'm carrying, I ask You to restore to my husband all he lost after his first wife and youngest son were taken."

A door slammed, and Fannie opened her eyes.

"I'm sorry. I didn't realize you were prayin'," Nancy said as she moved toward the kitchen sink.

Fannie wiped the tears from her cheeks and smiled. "It's all right. I was about done anyhow."

Nancy crossed the room and laid a hand on Fannie's shoulder. "I couldn't help but hear part of your prayer, Mama Fannie. But I wasn't eavesdroppin'. Honest. I just got done workin' in the garden and came inside for a glass of water."

Fannie patted Nancy's hand. "It's okay. I wasn't sharing anything with God that I'm ashamed of."

Nancy pulled out a chair and sat down. "Papa's

doin' all right now. Even before he found out you were gonna have a boppli, he was dealin' with things pretty well."

"I know, but this babe will be like a reward for his patience and faithfulness. Kind of like Job in the Bible when he lost everything and God gave him even more in the end." Fannie reached for her cup of tea. "Of course, I'm not saying me and the child I carry could ever replace your real mamm or your little *bruder* who was kidnapped."

Nancy nodded, and her chin quivered. "I know."

"How'd you get so smart for a girl of fifteen?"

"Maybe it's from bein' around you so much."

A ruckus broke out on the back porch.

"*Ach*, my! It must be Samuel and Mary Ann scrappin' again." Fannie pushed her chair back, ready to deal with the problem.

"Want me to tend to it?" Nancy asked.

"Would ya mind?"

"I'd be happy to. You just sit there and relax. Have yourself another cup of tea. I'll start supper as soon as I get things straightened out between the *kinner*."

Fannie appreciated her stepdaughter's willingness to help out. Nancy was a good girl, and a pretty one, too, with her light brown hair offset by a pair of luminous green eyes. Now that Naomi was married and had a family of her own, it was nice to have another pair of capable hands she could rely on, even though Nancy did tend to be a bit headstrong at times.

She yawned. "I think I'll take my cup of tea into the living room and stretch out on the sofa a few minutes. Call me when you need help in the kitchen, okay?"

Nancy nodded and scurried out the door.

∽

Abraham blotted the sweat from his forehead, while he stomped his dirt-crusted boots against the steps on the back porch. He and the boys had accomplished a lot in the fields today. Much of the planting was now done. He'd sent Norman home to his bride, Ruth, whom he had married last fall. Jake and Matthew, still single and living at home, had gone to the barn to put the mules away.

When Abraham entered the house, he found Fannie slouched on the sofa in the living room with her feet propped on a leather stool. Her head leaned against a pillow, and her eyes were closed, but she opened them as soon as his boots touched the hardwood floor.

"Were ya sleepin'?" he asked, tossing his straw hat onto the coffee table.

"Just restin' my eyes."

He leaned over and kissed her forehead. "Did ya work at the quilt shop today?"

"Jah, only until two though. Then I did a little shopping in Paradise and came home."

"You be sure to rest whenever possible," he said, taking a seat beside her.

She reached for his hand. "You sound like Abby. She's worried I'm going to do too much and said in her letter that I should get plenty of rest."

"Abby's a smart woman," Abraham said with a nod. "Takes after her mamm."

Fannie nudged him in the ribs with her elbow. "Go on with ya, now. I'm gettin' too old to be taken in by such a flattering tongue."

"That'll be the day. And ya ain't old neither." Abraham gently patted Fannie's stomach. "You think you'd have a boppli in there if you was old?"

Her cheeks turned pink, and she looked away. It made Abraham feel kind of good to know he could still make her blush. He rested his head on her shoulder and whispered, "I love you, Fannie Mae Fisher."

She brushed the top of his head with her lips. "I love you, too."

"You've made me so happy, and I know you'll make a *wunderbaar gut* mamm."

"I hope I'll be a wonderful good mom. I've wanted another boppli for such a long time, but I had given up hope that it would ever happen."

"God is full of grace and miracles, ain't it so?"

"Jah," she murmured. "He truly is."

∽∞∽

Abby glanced at the small clock on her desk and frowned. What was keeping Lena? She should have been here by now.

Since Abby lived in the same house with Harold and Lena, the two women usually rode to work together in one buggy. This morning, however, Lena had said she was tired and wanted to stay in bed a little longer. She'd told Abby she would hitch up one of their other buggies and try to be at the quilt shop by ten o'clock. It was almost eleven now, and there was still no sign of Lena. Had her buggy broken down along the way? Could she have been in an accident?

Abby drew in a deep breath and tried to relax. There was no point in worrying. "Most things one worries about never come to pass," Mom had often told her.

She pushed her chair away from the desk and stood. "Maybe I should go look for Lena." Her gaze came to rest on the clock again. At eleven thirty several ladies from their Amish community would show up at the shop, ready to work on a quilt and eat lunch together. Abby didn't want to leave the place unattended, so she decided to wait awhile longer. If Lena didn't arrive by the time the women did, she would go looking for her.

The bell above the front door jingled, and Abby's friend Rachel entered the quilt shop.

"I'm a little early," Rachel said cheerfully, "but I thought if I came over now it would give us a chance to visit before the others get here."

Abby smiled. "I always enjoy chatting, but I'm wonderin' if you could do me a favor."

"I will if I can. What is it?"

"Lena was supposed to be here by ten o'clock. As you can see, she's not. So, I'm thinking I should head in the direction of home, in case she's broken down somewhere or has been involved in an accident."

Rachel's forehead wrinkled, and concern showed in her dark eyes. "You think she's been hurt?"

"I hope not, but I'd feel better if I went to check on things. Would you mind watching the store while I'm gone?"

"Sure, I can do that." Rachel glanced around the spacious room. "I see there are no customers at the moment either."

Abby nodded. "Things have been slow this morning, but if someone does come in, I'm sure you can handle it."

Rachel grinned, her cheeks turning slightly pink. "I'll do my best."

"Hopefully, I won't be gone too long. But if the others show up before I get back, please tell them to begin working on the quilt." Abby grabbed her black shawl and matching bonnet from the shelf under her desk and headed for the back door. "See you soon, Rachel. And please say a prayer that everything's okay with Lena."

"I surely will."

Abby murmured her own quick prayer and hurried out the door.

Chapter 3

Abby's heart pounded when she discovered Lena's buggy, with a gentle mare hitched to the front of it, sitting in the front yard. She'd been relieved when she hadn't run into her sister-in-law on the road. But now, realizing Lena hadn't even left home caused her a different concern. Was she still sleeping? Could she be sick? This was so unlike Lena.

Abby took the steps two at a time and entered the house through the back door. "Lena! Are you here?"

Silence.

Abby peered into the kitchen.

The room was empty.

Her next stop was the living room, but Lena wasn't there either. *Where could she be? Surely not still in bed. Why would the horse and buggy be out front if she were sleeping?*

Abby climbed the stairs to the bedrooms. "Lena!"

"I'm in here" came a muffled reply.

Abby hurried to Lena and Harold's room. The door was ajar, so she felt it would be okay to step inside. She found Lena fully dressed, lying on top of the bed. Her face looked pale, and dark circles shadowed her pale blue eyes.

"What's wrong? Are you sick?" Abby rushed to the bed and placed her hand on Lena's forehead. She felt relief to discover that it was cool.

Lena moaned. "I've been throwing up all morning."

"You must have the flu, although I'm sure you don't have a fever. Want me to get a cup of mint tea to settle your stomach?"

Lena shook her head. "It's not the flu."

"It couldn't be food poisoning. You, me, and Harold all had the same thing for supper last night, and I feel fine."

Lena pushed herself to a sitting position, leaning her head against the pillows that were propped against the headboard. "I—I think I'm in a family way. I missed my monthly, and for the last week I've felt awfully nauseous." She slowly shook her head. "Although today's been the worst."

Abby's mouth dropped open. She lived under the same roof with Harold and Lena and hadn't suspected a thing. How could she be so unobservant? Maybe those terrible nightmares she'd been having were making it hard for her to focus.

She sank to the edge of the bed, too numb to say a word. It didn't seem possible that Naomi, Mom, and now Lena were all expecting *bopplin* so close together.

"I thought the queasiness would pass and that I'd be able to come into work. But soon after I got the horse hitched to the buggy, I had another round of vomiting." Lena gripped her stomach and drew in a deep breath.

Abby stood. "I'll go downstairs and fix you some mint tea. Maybe some saltine crackers would help, too."

"Danki." Lena offered Abby a weak smile. "I'm planning to see the doctor next week, but I'm almost certain I'm pregnant."

"Guess I'll have to get busy and sew some little blankets," Abby said. "Between you, Mom, and Naomi, there will surely be a need for many baby things."

"Harold and I have been married a little over five years, and we were about to give up hope of ever having any kinner." Lena smiled. "This is such a happy surprise, and it seems like God is really blessing our family these days."

"Jah, I believe He is." Abby left the room and headed downstairs to the kitchen, but a shadow of fear crept into her soul—the same one she'd been fighting since she got the news of her mother's pregnancy. Now she had the worry of her sister-in-law, too.

The words of Psalm 55:22 filled Abby's thoughts: *"Cast thy burden upon the Lord, and he shall sustain thee: he shall never suffer the righteous to be moved."* She drew in a deep breath. "I will not worry but will trust God in all things."

❧

When Abby returned to her shop some time later, things were really busy. The women who had come to help with the quilt had already eaten their lunch and were hard at work in front of the quilting frame, exchanging stories and comparing thimbles. Abby noticed that some of the women's fingers had turned green from their skin interacting with the metal of their thimbles. Mary Kaulp had a hole in her thimble and said it had worn through from so much use. "Sometimes the needle sticks through it, and that's sure a big surprise," Mary quipped.

Abby flinched as she thought of how many times she had pricked her finger while working on a quilt. Still, she wouldn't trade the work for anything. She glanced over at Lester's mamm, Deborah. The dark-haired woman sat in front of one of the treadle sewing machines, pumping her legs up and down as she folded over the lining of the quilt she was working on in order to stitch down the binding. Everyone kept busy, and several customers were milling around the store. Three English women stood in line behind the counter, waiting for their purchases to be rung up. Rachel's cheeks were bright red, and her forehead glistened with perspiration.

"I'm glad you're back," she whispered when Abby slipped behind the counter. "Things have been kind of hectic."

"Sorry for taking so long, but I found Lena at home, and she wasn't feeling well." Abby helped her friend fold the Rose of Sharon quilt that an English customer had purchased. "I'll tell you more about it later."

"Jah, okay."

For the next hour, Abby and Rachel waited on customers, and in between they worked with the women on the Dahlia pattern quilt. At two o'clock, Lester entered the store.

"I came by earlier hopin' to take you to lunch," he told Abby, "but Rachel said you'd gone lookin' for Lena because she didn't show up for work this morning."

Abby nodded. "I was getting worried about her."

"Did ya find her? Is she okay?" Lester's deep-set

blue eyes revealed concern.

"She was still at home, not feeling well." Abby didn't think it would be right to tell Lester that Lena suspected she was pregnant when it hadn't been confirmed yet.

"Sorry to hear that. Is she gonna be okay?"

"Jah, I'm sure she will."

"Glad to hear it's nothing serious." Lester removed his straw hat and raked a hand through his wavy blond hair. "Have you eaten yet?"

She shook her head.

"Then why don't we go over to the Subway?"

"What about your blacksmith shop? Shouldn't you be there right now?"

"My helper is takin' care of things, and we're pretty well caught up." Lester snickered. "Besides, I'm the boss. I can take off whenever I want, now that I've got Seth workin' for me."

Abby smiled, then glanced around the store. Only a few customers remained, and the quilters were doing fine on their own. Even so, she didn't feel right about imposing further on Rachel.

As if she could read Abby's thoughts, her friend spoke up. "Things are slower now. I'll be happy to stay and wait on customers if you'd like to have lunch with Lester."

Abby tipped her head, as she considered the offer.

"We won't be gone long," Lester coaxed. He glanced across the room. "My mamm's here, and I'm sure she'd pitch in to help Rachel if it was needed."

Rachel smiled. "That's right. I can ask any of the ladies if I get real busy, so go on now, and take your time."

"All right, then." Abby stepped out from behind the counter, and Lester steered her toward the front door.

"I'll have her back within the hour," he called over his shoulder.

A short time later, Abby and Lester were seated at a booth inside the Subway restaurant, sharing a large turkey hoagie.

Leaning against the seat back, Abby began to relax. It was the first time all day that she'd really felt calm, but then she knew why. She always felt good whenever she was with Lester. She had known since their first date that she could spend the rest of her life with him. He was kind, gentle, and hard working, the way her daed had been when he was alive.

Lester reached across the table and took her hand. "Your eyes are sure pretty, ya know that? I always did like the color of sweet, dark chocolate."

Abby smiled, despite the blush she felt cascade over her cheeks. Lester always knew the right thing to say. "Danki," she murmured.

"Is your family still plannin' to come to our wedding in November?" he asked.

She nodded. "I hope so. But it will depend on how well Mom's doin' by then."

Lester stared at her strangely. "What's wrong with your mamm?"

"I got a note from her the other day, saying she's expecting a boppli near the end of October."

Lester's jaw dropped. "Really?"

"It would seem that God has given Mom and Abraham a second chance."

He let out a low whistle. "That is great news.

If the baby's due in October and we're not gettin' married till late November, then there shouldn't be a problem with them comin' to Ohio for the wedding, do ya think?"

"I'm sure there won't be." Abby toyed with her napkin. "I am concerned about Mom though."

"How come?"

"She's not so young anymore. A lot could happen." She took a small bite of her sandwich, chewed, and swallowed. "When the time gets closer to Mom's delivery, I'll need to go to Pennsylvania to help out. Then I'll have to stay until after the boppli comes and I'm sure Mom can handle things on her own."

Lester grabbed his cup of iced tea and gulped some down. "We've waited a long time to get married, Abby. I sure hope you're home in plenty of time for the big day."

"Oh, I will be," Abby assured him.

"Will Lena run the quilt shop in your absence, or do you think you'll have to hire a second person to help out?"

Abby nibbled on the inside of her cheek. Should she tell Lester about Lena's suspected pregnancy or wait until she knew for sure? "I'm hoping Lena can mind the store, but if that doesn't work out, I'll have to think about hiring someone else."

Lester stared at Abby as he swirled his straw around the inside of his cup. "I can see by your solemn expression that you're worried. Is it leavin' Lena in charge of the store, or are you frettin' over your mamm's condition?"

"A little of both," Abby admitted. "Mostly, I'm worried about Mom."

"Is she doin' okay so far?"

"Jah, but she's having some morning sickness."

"That's pretty common."

"True, but—"

Lester held up his hand. "Abby, please try not to worry. Women have been havin' babies for thousands of years."

She chuckled softly. "I know. Ever since Adam and Eve. But this is my mamm we're talkin' about."

He nodded with a look of understanding. "She'll be fine; just pray."

"I am and shall continue to do so."

~

"Daddy, Daddy, guess what?"

Jim Scott set two paint buckets on the floor of his garage and turned to face his son. "What's got you so excited, Jimmy?"

"Me and Mommy went to the park again today. I saw my friend Allen there."

"Is Allen the little boy in the picture Mommy took last week?" Jim asked.

Jimmy's dark eyes gleamed as he bobbed his head up and down. "Me and Allen had ice cream."

"You did, huh?"

"Yep. Big chocolate cones."

Jim ruffled his son's chestnut-colored hair. "That's nice. I'm glad you've made a new friend." *And I'm happy my overprotective wife is finally giving you a bit of space to grow and learn.*

"Mommy said we could go to the park again soon."

Jim's cell phone rang. "I've got to get that, Jimmy. Find something to do until I'm off the phone."

"Okay, Daddy."

Jim flipped the phone cover open. "Scott's Painting and Decorating. Yeah, sure, Hank. What can I do for you?"

Absorbed in his conversation, Jim almost forgot about Jimmy until the boy wandered out of the storage closet holding a scrap of material. At first Jim thought it was a paint rag, but then he realized it was multicolored, not white.

"I've got to go, Hank. I'll call you back." Jim clicked off and turned to face his son. "What have you got there, Jimmy?"

When Jimmy opened the piece of fabric to its full length and held it out, Jim felt the blood drain from his face. It was a baby quilt—the same one Jimmy had been wrapped in the day Jim snatched him off the picnic table in an Amish family's yard.

"Where'd you get this?" Jim's hands trembled, but he tried to keep his voice calm as he moved toward his son.

Jimmy pointed to the storage closet at the back of the garage where Jim kept some of his painting supplies.

"You'd better let me have that."

The child stood there, unmoving.

"Give it to me, now!"

Jim barely realized he'd shouted until Jimmy's eyes filled with tears.

"Please, don't start bawling."

Jimmy sniffed and handed Jim the quilt.

I should have thrown this thing out years ago instead of stashing it away with my paint rags. If Linda ever sees the quilt, she'll start asking questions, and then I'll have some serious explaining to do.

"Jimmy, I want you to go inside the house and tell Mommy I'll be ready for lunch in a few minutes."

"Okay." Jimmy hesitated a moment, then pointed to the quilt. "Can I have that, Daddy?"

"No! And don't mention it to your mother. Is that clear?"

Jimmy blinked, and for a moment Jim thought the boy was going to give in to his tears.

Jim held the quilt at his side as he squatted in front of his son. "This is just an old rag. It's nothing you'd want to play with. Understand?"

Jimmy nodded soberly, then turned toward the door leading to the house. His shoulders were slumped, and he hung his head as though he'd lost one of his favorite toys. Jim felt like a heel, but he couldn't let Jimmy have the quilt. "I'll be in soon," he called to his son's retreating form.

As soon as Jimmy was out of sight, Jim made a beeline for his work van. He snapped the back door open and stuffed the quilt inside, burying it under a canvas tarp. When he returned to work after lunch, he would ditch the incriminating piece of evidence.

"Out of sight, out of mind," Jim mumbled. But even as the words tumbled out of his mouth, he wondered if he would ever be free of his deception. Jimmy wasn't legally theirs, and no matter how hard he tried, Jim would never forget the day he had kidnapped the boy.

Chapter 4

Abby stretched her tired neck and shoulder muscles as she sank onto the wooden stool behind the counter where she waited on customers. For the past week she'd been working at the quilt shop alone. Lena had gone to the doctor, and her pregnancy had been confirmed. Since her morning sickness was not any better, Harold insisted she quit helping Abby at the store. He had asked his mother-in-law, Esther, to help Lena with some of the chores at home, saying that he wanted his wife to rest as much as possible.

Abby had talked with Rachel about the possibility of her coming to work in the quilt shop, but her friend had just gotten word that her application at the Farmstead restaurant had been accepted. None of the women who regularly made quilts to be sold at the store seemed interested in working full time, and Abby wondered if she would ever find someone to take Lena's place. Soon it would be summer, and then even more tourists would flock to Holmes County, which meant her shop would often be full of people.

The bell above the front door jingled, and Abby glanced up to see who had come in. It was Lester, carrying a paper sack and wearing his usual cheerful smile.

WANDA E. BRUNSTETTER

"I knew you wouldn't be able to go out to eat today, so I brought you some lunch." He placed the sack on the counter and smiled.

Abby was happy she was betrothed to such a considerate man. "Danki. That was thoughtful." She reached for the sack. "What'd you bring?"

"Got us an order of fried chicken, coleslaw, and some hot potato salad from the Farmstead restaurant. Saw your friend Rachel waiting tables."

"She started working there a couple days ago." Abby peeked inside the sack, and the pleasing aroma of warm chicken caused her to lick her lips. "*Umm. . .*it sure smells good."

"Want to eat here, or would ya rather go out to the picnic table in back of your store?" Lester asked.

"I guess we'd better stay put in case a customer comes in."

"Jah, okay." Lester pulled another stool over to the counter, sat down beside Abby, and took her hand. They bowed for silent prayer; then he reached into the sack and withdrew their lunch.

Abby unfolded the napkins and placed the plastic silverware beside their paper plates, while Lester poured cups of iced tea from the insulated jug he'd brought along. They ate in companionable silence, until Lester wiped his mouth and announced, "My mamm's comin' by later on."

"Does she need some quilting material?"

He shrugged and gave Abby a quick wink.

"You're up to something. What is it?"

"I ain't up to nothin'."

Abby was sure Lester was teasing and would tell her if it was anything important, so she didn't press the issue.

A short time later, as they were clearing away the remains of their lunch, the front door opened and Deborah Mast walked in. *"Wie geht's,"* she said with a cheery wave.

"Good day to you," Abby replied. "What can I help you with?"

Deborah smiled and stepped up to the counter, casting a quick glance in her son's direction. "Lester tells me you're in need of a helper here."

Abby nodded. "Lena had to quit because she's got the morning sickness real bad. She and my mamm seem to be going through the same struggles right now."

Lester cleared his throat. "Uh—guess I'd best be gettin' back to work." He gave Abby's arm a gentle squeeze. "See you later."

"Have a good day," she said.

"And don't work too hard," Lester's mamm called to him.

When Deborah's son waved and disappeared out the door, she stepped up to Abby. "I was pleased to hear that your mamm's in a family way. She must be real *hallich*."

"Jah, she's happy as a springtime robin, and so is the rest of the family."

"I guess Lena must be excited about her pregnancy, too, since she and Harold have no kinner yet." Deborah leaned on the counter. "Speaking of Lena. . . Since you haven't found a replacement for her, I was wondering if you'd want to hire me to take her place."

Abby's lips curved into a smile. "I know you often help the ladies on their quilt project, but I didn't think to ask if you'd consider coming to work here."

"I would be happy to, if you think I'd be useful."

"Of course, you're a wonderful quilter."

Deborah grunted. "That doesn't mean I've got a head for business."

"I'm sure you'll do fine. You're friendly and outgoing, and that's what matters most when it comes to waiting on customers."

"Since I've been widowed these last two years and all my kinner but Lester are out on their own, I've got time on my hands." Deborah smiled. "How soon would you like me to start work?"

"How about right now?"

"That sounds good to me. Where do you want me to begin?"

∞

Abraham wiped the sweat from his forehead using a damp rag he'd left hanging on the pump behind the house. He and his sons had worked hard in the fields all morning, and he was more than ready for their noon meal.

"Sure hope Nancy and Fannie have lunch on the table," Jake commented. "I'm hungry enough to eat an old mule."

"Jah, me, too," Matthew agreed.

Abraham stood off to one side, watching the two brothers as they took turns washing up. Norman had gone to his own place for lunch, saying he wanted to spend a few minutes with his wife. Abraham knew about that "in love" feeling; he'd been blessed with it twice. Even now, after being with Fannie four years, he felt like a lovesick schoolboy whenever she smiled at him in a certain way or said something to make him feel special.

"Hey, watch what you're doin', Jake!" Matthew's

usual calm voice rose a notch, driving Abraham's musings to the back of his mind.

Jake grunted. "I'm washin' up; what do you expect?"

"I expect you to keep the soap and water on yourself, not on me."

Abraham shook his head. It was hard to believe Matthew was almost twenty-six years old and Jake had recently turned twenty, since they both were acting like a couple of children. "You two had better knock it off, or I'll make you eat in the barn."

Matthew grunted. "That'd be a good place for Jake, since he already smells like one of the sweaty horses."

Jake wrinkled his nose and slapped the wet rag against Matthew's arm. "You don't smell like no rose garden yourself. No wonder ya can't find a wife."

Matthew's ears turned crimson, but he made no reply.

"I think the real reason you're not married is 'cause you're scared," Jake taunted.

Matthew flicked some water in his brother's direction. "Let's drop the subject, okay?"

"I agree." Abraham nodded toward the house. "We'd best not keep the women waitin'. I'm sure they have lunch on the table by now."

"First one to the house gets two helpings of dessert!" Jake hollered as he took off on a run.

Matthew shook his head. "I wonder if he'll ever grow up."

Abraham thumped his eldest son on the back. "Why don't you try to set him a better example?"

"*Humph!* A lot of good that would do."

Abraham wondered if something was eating at Matthew, but he figured in time his boy would come to grips with whatever it was, so he said nothing as he strode toward the house.

～

Fannie placed a platter of ham on the table and yawned. She'd been unable to go to the quilt shop this morning because of her queasy stomach, and even though her nausea had subsided some, she felt too tired to do much of anything. All she really wanted to do was get the men fed, then collapse on the sofa awhile.

"Want me to ring the dinner bell again?" Nancy asked as she headed to the refrigerator to fetch a jar of pickles.

"I think I hear our menfolk comin' now," Fannie replied.

Sure enough, the thump, thump of men's boots could be heard on the back steps. A few seconds later, Abraham, Matthew, and Jake entered the room.

Fannie nodded at the table. "Everything's ready, so take a chair and eat yourselves full."

Abraham gave her a peck on the cheek and then pulled out his chair at the head of the table. Once everyone was seated, he bowed his head for silent prayer, and the others did the same.

Fannie folded her hands in her lap, and when the prayer was over, she stared at the food set before her. Thick slices of the ham she had carved earlier, a heaping bowl of macaroni salad, deviled eggs, tangy pickled beets, dilled pickles, and a basket of fresh homemade bread for sandwiches filled the table. None of it appealed, but for the sake of the baby she carried, she knew she must eat.

"You okay, Fannie?" Abraham asked with a look of concern.

She forced a smile and nodded. "Fine and dandy."

"You look awfully *mied*. Are you still feelin' sick to your stomach?"

"Just in the mornings now, but you're right, I am a bit tired."

Abraham glanced over at Nancy, who sat beside Fannie. "After lunch, I want you to clear away the dishes and clean up the kitchen while my wife takes a nap."

Nancy nodded. "Okay, Papa."

"I take it you're not goin' to the quilt shop this afternoon," Matthew said around a mouthful of macaroni salad.

"Guess I'd better not," Fannie replied.

"I'm thinkin' we might need to close down the shop or find someone else to run it for a time," Abraham said.

Fannie sighed. It would be a shame to close the quilt shop. Many women in the area made quilts and sold them in her store. And what of the tourists who liked to shop there?

"Naomi's not up to working at the store and minding the quilt shop as well," Abraham went on to say. "She's got her hands full taking care of little Sarah, not to mention her being in a family way again. Once her boppli's born, she won't be able to work at the store for a while either."

"If you didn't need me in the fields, I'd be happy to work at the store while Naomi takes over Fannie's quilt shop," Matthew said.

Jake spoke up for the first time since they'd

begun the meal. "Yeah, right. I can see my big brother tradin' in his plow for a broom and sittin' behind a cash register all day instead of workin' the mules out in the fields."

"It would be a sight better than puttin' up with the likes of you," Matthew shot back.

Abraham held up his hand. "Don't start scrappin' again. I've already had enough of it today, and I'm sure the womenfolk aren't in the mood to hear it either."

"Maybe I'll pay Edna a visit this afternoon," Fannie said, deliberately changing the subject.

"I thought you were going to take a nap."

"I'll go after I've rested awhile."

"Why do you want to travel all the way over to Edna's place in Strasburg?" Matthew asked.

"Cousin Edna's always full of good advice. Maybe she can come up with some idea to solve my dilemma."

Abraham grunted. "The only thing that fun-lovin' woman can come up with is a good joke or two."

Fannie shrugged. "That might be exactly what I need today."

Chapter 5

Abby smiled as she watched Deborah wait on the English customer near the front of the store. She had been working at the quilt shop a few weeks now and was doing a fine job. The pleasant expression on the woman's face and the exuberance with which she went about her tasks let Abby know that Lester's mamm thoroughly enjoyed her work.

It was almost time to close for the day, yet she was still pleasant and energetic. *She responds well to the customers, too. She also enjoys quilting and is good at it. I'm sure Deborah will be a wonderful mother-in-law.* Not everyone was blessed with a sweet mamm like hers and an easy-going *schwiegermammi*, like Deborah Mast would be.

Shortly after the last customer left the store, Lester showed up, informing his mother that he'd come by to give her a ride home.

"I'll be ready in a few minutes," she said. "Just need to put a couple things away."

"That's all right, Deborah," Abby was quick to say. "You've worked hard today, and if you want to head home, I can take care of anything else that needs to be done."

Lester moved in front of the treadle sewing machine where Abby sat. "Such a thoughtful daughter-in-law my mamm will be gettin'."

Abby smiled. "And how about you, Lester Mast? What kind of wife do you think I'll be?"

He chucked her under the chin and winked. "A mighty fine one, I'd have to say."

"I'll surely try, but you know I'm not perfect," she replied, taking pleasure in the feel of his calloused fingers against her skin.

"You're even-tempered, kind, considerate, and pretty. What else could a man ask for in a wife?"

Before Abby could reply, Lester leaned closer. "Say, how about you and me goin' out to lunch tomorrow? Maybe we can eat at the Farmstead restaurant this time."

Abby pursed her lips. "I'd like that, but things have been busy here all week. It's only May, yet every day we've had lots of customers. I wouldn't feel right about leaving your mamm alone when things are so hectic."

"I can manage," Deborah called from across the room. "You two have yourselves some fun. You deserve it."

Abby deliberated a few seconds. "I'll tell you what. How about I bring a lunch basket for us to share out back at the picnic table? That way I'll be close, in case your mamm needs help."

"Sounds fine to me." Lester grinned. "And I'll bring the dessert."

∽

"Hey boss, where'd ya put that box of mudding tape?" Ed Munson called to Jim, who had just descended a six-foot ladder. Part of his crew had been painting the outside of a new apartment complex, while the rest of the men mudded and taped the new Sheetrock walls.

"The tape's in the back of my van." Jim wiped his hands on the paint rag protruding from his back pocket and glanced at the gray paint splattered all over the front of his white overalls. "If my wife could see me now, she'd have a fit."

Linda didn't approve of him working side-by-side with his paint crew, but when they got busy, they needed his help. At other times, Jim had to pick up supplies, bid jobs, or do paperwork, so the painting was left to his six employees.

"What's this?" Ed shouted to Jim. "You usin' some fancy paint rags these days?"

Jim's heart palpitated when he realized what Ed held in his hands. It was that baby quilt—the one he'd forgotten to dispose of. "Uh. . .it's just an old baby blanket," he stammered.

Ed's reddish-brown mustache twitched when he smiled. "You and Linda plannin' to adopt another baby?"

"This was something I picked up on our vacation to Ohio a few years ago." Jim snatched the quilt from the man who had been working as his foreman for the last two years. "I'm planning to get rid of it."

"I'm thinkin' my wife would like it," Ed said. "She's into quilts and that kind of thing. So if you're just gonna pitch it, I'd be happy to take it off your hands."

If it had been anything other than the Amish baby quilt, Jim would have let Ed have it. But this was the one piece of tangible evidence that linked him to the kidnapping of an Amish baby. If he gave it to Ed, and Ed's wife said something to Linda,

Jim would have some serious explaining to do.

"I've. . .uh. . .already promised it to someone else," Jim lied. "In fact, I'll be taking the quilt to them as soon as I get off work today."

Ed shrugged and turned away. "Guess I'd best go back to the van and get that mudding tape."

Jim glanced at his watch. It was only two o'clock. Too early to call it quits for the day. However, this was something he felt couldn't wait, so he decided to take a drive to Tacoma, where he purchased most of his paint and supplies.

"I'm going to Parker Paint," he called to Ed as the man closed the van door and headed back with the box of mudding tape. "Make sure the guys stay on course while I'm gone."

"Sure thing, boss," Ed yelled over his shoulder.

A short time later, Jim drove into downtown Tacoma. When he spotted a thrift store, he pulled into the parking lot, grabbed the quilt, and rushed inside.

The middle-aged woman at the front desk was busy waiting on a customer, so Jim stood off to one side until they had finished with their business. When the elderly gentleman left, Jim stepped forward and plunked the quilt down for the clerk's inspection. "Would you be interested in this?"

She slipped on her reading glasses and studied the covering intently. "Why, this looks like an Amish quilt."

"Yeah, it is."

"Since the items we take in here are on a consignment-only basis, why don't you tell me how much you would like it to be sold for?"

Jim frowned. "Can't you just buy it from me outright?"

"Sorry, but that's not our policy."

This isn't going so well. I thought it would be easy to get rid of my albatross. He deliberated a few more seconds and finally pushed the quilt toward the clerk. "I guess you can have it then."

Her dark eyebrows rose a notch, and she squinted at him. "What?"

"I said, you can have the quilt, free and clear. I just need—I mean, I want to get rid of the silly thing."

The woman pursed her lips as she fingered one edge of the covering. "This is a very nice piece, sir. Are you sure you want to leave it with no payment in return?"

"I'm positive."

"Very well then. Let me write you a receipt."

Jim transferred his weight from one foot to the other. "No, no. That won't be necessary. Do whatever you want with the quilt, and I'll be on my way." He whirled around and rushed out of the store, feeling as though a heavy weight had been lifted off his shoulders. The only evidence linking him to a missing Amish baby was gone, and he never had to worry about it again.

∽∾

Linda lowered herself onto the park bench, anxious to read the romance novel she'd recently purchased. It helped to immerse herself in someone else's complicated life, even if it was only fiction.

She glanced up at Jimmy to be sure he was okay. No other children were at the park, so she hoped he would play happily by himself. Relieved to see that he seemed content to play on the slide, she opened her book to the first page. She'd only read a few lines when the sound of children's laughter pulled her attention away from her book. She looked up and saw Allen rush over to the slide where Jimmy was playing while his mother headed her way.

"Sure is a nice day. Won't be long and summer will be here," Beth said as she seated herself on the bench beside Linda. She took a sip from the Styrofoam cup in her hand. "Umm. . .this mocha latté is delicious. I would have bought two if I'd known you were going to be here."

"That's okay," Linda replied. "I prefer tea over coffee anyway."

"Have you ever tried an iced herbal raspberry tea?"

Linda shook her head. "I usually drink plain black or orange pekoe."

"Mommy, Mommy, watch me go down the slide on my belly!" Jimmy shouted, interrupting their conversation.

Linda stood and cupped her hands around her mouth. "Be careful, Jimmy! I don't want you to get hurt."

"I'll be okay!" The boy flopped onto his stomach and skimmed down the slide, giggling all the way. When he came to the bottom, he grabbed the edge of the slide and did a somersault to the ground.

"Boys will be boys," Beth said with a chuckle.

Linda inhaled deeply and blew out her breath in a quick puff. "I wish I could wrap Jimmy in a bubble and keep him safe from any harm."

"That would be nice, but think of all the fun our kids would miss if we shielded them in such a way."

Linda dug her fingernails into the palms of her hands. Was she selfish for wanting to protect her child? From the first day they'd adopted Jimmy, Jim had accused her of being overprotective. She tried not to be, but Jimmy was their only son, and she loved him so much. When Jimmy turned six on April 15, in his excitement to see his cousins Cameron and Pam, who lived in Idaho, he'd fallen off the porch and sprained his ankle. Linda had felt the child's pain as if it were her own.

"I'm glad I ran into you today," Beth said, breaking into Linda's thoughts. "I've been wanting to tell you about the vacation Bible school our church is having next month. I was hoping you would let Jimmy attend."

Bible school? Linda had attended vacation Bible school when she was a young girl, but she only went then to please her friend Carrie who lived next door. She'd been ten years old at the time and had received a Bible for memorizing five scripture verses and being there every day. *I wonder whatever happened to that old Bible? Did Jim throw it out after we got married, or is it buried somewhere on our bookshelf in the living room?*

"Anyway," Beth continued, "the sessions will be from ten in the morning until noon during the third week of June. We'll have Bible stories, crafts, puppets, and snacks."

Linda was prepared to tell Beth that she didn't think Jimmy was ready for Bible school, when Beth added, "The classes are for preschool kids all the way up to the sixth grade. Since Jimmy and Allen are both in the same grade, they'll be together."

"I don't know—"

"If you'd like to come along, that would be great. We're always in need of helpers."

"It would probably be better than sitting at home feeling sorry for myself," Linda mumbled.

Beth touched Linda's arm. "Is something troubling you?"

Linda's only response was a slow nod.

"If you'd like to talk about it, I promise it won't be repeated."

"I. . .I appreciate that." Linda's voice shook with emotion, and she clenched her teeth. "My marriage is a mess."

"Would you care to explain?"

"Jim and I are unable to have children of our own. We adopted Jimmy five years ago, and ever since then our marriage has been strained." Linda shifted on the unyielding bench. She didn't know why she was unloading on a near stranger, but there was something about Beth's gentle voice and compassionate expression that prompted her to reveal what she had.

"Didn't your husband want to be a father?"

Linda's gaze came to rest on her child, happily sharing the teeter-totter with his new friend. "I thought he did. In fact, he seemed as excited about going to Maryland to get our son as I was."

"You went all the way to the East Coast to adopt a baby?" Beth's uplifted eyebrows revealed her surprise.

"Jim's attorney set it up with a lawyer he knew in Maryland. Since Jim's folks live in Ohio, we turned the trip into a vacation."

"I see."

"Everything seemed to be okay until we got

home. Then Jim started accusing me of being over-protective of Jimmy." Linda's vision clouded with tears, and she sniffed. "Jim looks for excuses to be away from home, and to tell you the truth, I think he would rather be at work than with me or Jimmy."

Beth offered her a supportive smile. "Do you and Jim attend church anywhere?"

"No. Jim's opposed to anything religious, and I haven't been to church since I was a girl." A sharp throb cut across Linda's forehead, and she inhaled deeply, hoping to drive away the pain. She hadn't had one of her migraine headaches for several weeks, and she hoped she wasn't getting one now.

"Maybe vacation Bible school would be good for both you and Jimmy," Beth said.

"I. . .I don't see how it could do anything to help my stagnant marriage."

Beth gave her arm a gentle squeeze, and Linda felt comforted. "God can work miracles in people's lives."

"I think it would take even more than a miracle to fix my broken marriage." Linda paused, willing herself not to break down in front of Allen's mother. "I've asked Jim several times if we could go back east for another vacation, but he refuses to take us there."

"Has he said why?"

"No. He just reminded me that his folks have been out here to visit a couple of times and said there's no reason for us to make the long trip to Ohio."

"Men can be so stubborn," Beth said with a shake of her head.

"My husband can be downright obstinate. He

says he loves Jimmy, yet he refuses to adopt another child. It makes no sense at all."

"I'm glad you've shared your concerns, Linda. It helps me know how to pray for you."

"I appreciate that, and I will think about letting Jimmy go to Bible school." Linda sniffed and swiped at the tears trickling down her cheeks. She'd given in to her unstable emotions and insecurities again, but at the moment, it didn't matter. Beth hadn't condemned her the way Jim always did, and she actually seemed to understand. Maybe this new friendship was exactly what Linda needed.

Chapter 6

T he mail's here, Abby," Deborah called as she stepped into the quilt shop the following day. "I put it on your desk. Is that okay?"

"Sure, that's fine," Abby replied. She was busy placing some quilts on one of the shelves near the back of the store and would take time to go through the mail later on.

"Looks like there's a letter from your mamm." Deborah stepped up beside Abby and reached for one of the Tumbling Block quilts. "How's Fannie doing these days?"

"Her last letter said she was still having some morning sickness and felt awfully tired, but she's managed to work in her quilt shop a few afternoons a week."

"Bet she wishes you were there to help out," Deborah said as she straightened the corner of the quilt closest to her.

Abby sighed. "I wish I could be in two places at once, but it's not possible for me to run two quilt shops at the same time. Especially with one of them being in Pennsylvania."

"I'm sure Fannie will hire a *maad* to help out at home if she needs to."

"I suppose Mom could hire a maid, but she does have Abraham's two youngest daughters.

Nancy is fifteen, and I'm sure she's capable of cooking and cleaning. Even Mary Ann, who's not quite eleven, can help with some things when she's not in school." Abby frowned, as another thought popped into her head. "It's the quilt shop Mom needs help with the most."

The bell above the door jingled before Deborah could comment. "Guess I'd better see what that customer needs," she said.

"And I think I'll take the time to read Mom's letter. I really want to see how she's doing."

"Good idea."

Deborah moved toward the customer, and Abby hurried to her desk. She found the letter from her mother on top of the mail and quickly tore it open.

> *Dear Abby,*
>
> *I went to the doctor yesterday, and he seemed concerned about the slight swelling I have in my legs. He told me to avoid salt and to stay off my feet as much as possible. Nancy's here to help out, and Cousin Edna offered to come by a few days a week, so I'm sure everything at the house will be cared for. It's the quilt shop I'm worried about. Since I'm not able to work there right now, I may have to close it down. Sure would hate to do that though, since it's doing so well. But I suppose if there's no other way, I'll have to accept it.*
>
> *I'm doing some better with the nausea now but still feeling drained of energy. Sure will be glad when I'm feeling better. It's hard*

to do nothing but rest. You know me—always puttering around, and not happy unless I've got something constructive to do.

Enough about me now. How are things going for you? I hope your quilt shop is doing well, and I'm looking forward to hearing from you soon. Tell that future son-in-law of mine I said hello.

Love,
Mom

Abby dropped the letter to her desk and let her head fall forward. If the doctor had ordered Mom to rest more, and she was having some swelling in her legs, he must be concerned about her losing the baby. Ever since Abby had learned of her mother's pregnancy, she'd been anxious. Now, she was more worried than ever.

Am I being selfish staying here in Ohio when my mamm needs my help there? Even if it means closing my own shop, I must go to Pennsylvania and keep Mom's shop open. She gave up one quilt shop when she moved from here; I can't let her give up another. Abby's fingers clenched as she thought about Lester, and how much she would miss him. It would be hard to be separated, but their relationship was strong, and she prayed he would understand. Besides, she had promised her father before he died that she would take care of Mom.

With her decision made, Abby went to speak with Lester's mother. The woman she'd been waiting on had left the store, and Deborah now sat at one of the sewing machines, ready to begin a new quilt. She glanced up when Abby approached. "Is somethin' troubling you, Abby? Your serious expression makes me think you have some concerns."

Abby swallowed past the lump in her throat. "I just read Mom's letter, and she's had some swelling in her legs, so the doctor advised her to get more rest. I fear she might lose the boppli if she doesn't follow his orders."

Deborah shook her head. "Fannie's no schoolgirl. She'll be careful to do as the doctor says."

"But she might have to close the quilt shop." Abby pursed her lips and drew in a deep breath. "I really ought to go and keep the place running for her."

"To Pennsylvania?"

"Jah."

"What would you do about your shop here?"

"I—I was hoping you might be able to take over for me. Maybe I could see if one of the ladies who does quilting for us could help you a few days a week."

"I could ask my sister, Clara. She still has two children in school, but they're old enough to fend for themselves when she's not at home."

"That would be wonderful if Clara's in agreement."

"How soon do you plan to leave, and how long will you be gone?"

"I'll go as soon as possible and would probably stay until the boppli is born and Mom can manage on her own."

"I understand why you feel the need to go." Deborah's face tightened. "But I don't think my son's going to take this news so well."

"It will be hard for me, too." Abby smiled

through quivering lips. "I'm hoping Lester will understand."

"What will I understand?"

Abby whirled around. She hadn't realized anyone had come into the shop. "You scared me, Lester."

He gave her a quick hug. "I figured you'd hear the bell."

"Guess I wasn't paying attention."

"What were you two discussing?" Lester looked first at his mamm, then back at Abby. "I heard my name, so I suspect it must have somethin' to do with me."

"Actually, it has more to do with my mamm," Abby replied. "I'll tell you about it over lunch, okay?"

"Jah, that's fine." He held up a brown paper sack. "I brought the dessert, like I promised."

"I'll get the lunch I packed, and we can go out back to the picnic table." Abby turned to Lester's mamm. "Can you manage on your own for a while?"

Deborah waved a hand. "Jah, sure. You two go along; things will be fine here."

A few minutes later, Abby took a seat on the bench across from Lester, and they bowed their heads. When they'd finished their silent prayer, Abby reached inside her wicker basket and pulled out the meal she had provided—cold, golden-fried chicken; tangy coleslaw; baked beans; and fluffy buttermilk biscuits.

"What were you gonna tell me about your mamm?" Lester asked around a mouthful of chicken.

"She's having a difficult pregnancy and will

probably have to close her quilt shop so she can stay home and rest."

"Sorry to hear that."

Abby clutched her napkin, rolling it into a tight ball. "I've. . .uh. . .I think. . .I mean. . ." She paused and moistened her lips. Gathering up her courage, she began again. "I've decided that I should go to Pennsylvania to help out, and your mamm's agreed to run my quilt shop while I'm gone." There, it felt better to have gotten that out.

Lester's pale eyebrows squeezed together, and his mouth drooped at the corners. "You're leavin' me, Abby?"

She touched his arm. "It'll only be temporary. I'll be back soon after the boppli is born."

"But how are we gonna plan our wedding if you're not around?"

"We can do it through letters. And if we need to talk, we can call each other. You know, I have a phone here at the shop now, and since Caleb and Naomi took over the general store in Paradise, they've put one in as well."

Lester didn't look the least bit convinced, but he made no comment.

Abby prayed for the right words that would help Lester understand. "I'll be back in plenty of time for the wedding."

"But the boppli's not due until October. That's four-and-a-half months away."

"I wouldn't go so soon if I didn't think it was important for me to be with Mom right now. I'll not only be running her quilt shop, but I'll be at the house when I'm not working to make sure everything's going okay and that Mom's doing as the doctor says."

Lester's expression softened some. "I know you'll be doin' a good thing by goin' to help out, but I'll surely miss you."

"I'll miss you, too," she said, blinking against the tears clinging to her lashes.

Lester leaned forward, like he was about to kiss her, but a blaring siren sounded in the distance, and he pulled back. "Sounds like a fire truck."

Abby sniffed the air. "I smell smoke. Sure hope it's nothing serious."

"Think I'll run around front and have a look-see." Lester jumped up and disappeared around the side of the building.

"Whenever anything out of the ordinary happens, why is it that men always have to see what's going on?" Abby muttered. With an exasperated sigh, she rose to her feet and followed him.

Out front on the sidewalk, a group of people had gathered, pointing and chattering about the flames shooting out of the cheese store down the street.

"My friend Joe works there! I've got to see if he's okay," Lester shouted. He dashed away before Abby could stop him.

With her heartbeat matching the rhythm of her footsteps, Abby raced down the sidewalk toward the burning building. She was panting for breath by the time she reached Lester's side.

One part of the store was engulfed in flames, and smoke bellowed from the roof. Lester's eyes darted back and forth as he took in the situation. "I have to go inside and see if everyone made it out okay."

Abby grabbed hold of his arm. "You can't,

Lester. Please. It's too dangerous."

His wild-eyed expression caused Abby to worry that he might ignore her warning and do something foolish. "What if Joe and the other workers are still inside? Someone has to see if they're all right," he argued.

"That's the firemen's job. They're here now, so please let them handle things."

Lester's gaze went to the burning building, then back to Abby. She clutched his arm tighter. "If you went in and something happened to you, I would be overcome with grief. Please, Lester, please stay put."

He nodded slowly. "I guess you're right."

Four firemen rushed into the building, and Abby felt her muscles relax. A few seconds later, Joe and several other people who worked at the cheese store emerged from the other side of the building.

"Is everyone out?" one of the firemen shouted.

Joe nodded. "Jah, we're all safe."

Abby breathed a sigh of relief. Lester grabbed his friend in a bear hug. "I'm sure glad you're okay. Wouldn't want anything to happen to one of my future wedding attendants." He glanced over at Abby with a questioning look. "That is, if there's still going to be a wedding in November."

She clicked her tongue. "Of course there will be. I'll be back from Pennsylvania in plenty of time."

Chapter 7

Naomi arched her back and straightened with a groan. She'd been stocking shelves all morning and was paying the price for working too long without a break. She sank wearily to the stool behind the counter, relieved that Sarah was sleeping in the back room and she could finally have a few minutes to rest. Caleb had gone out to run some errands a few hours ago, so she'd been on her own for quite a while.

Naomi glanced at the stack of envelopes piled on one end of the counter and decided now would be a good time to read today's mail. She discovered a letter from her old English friend, Ginny Meyers, who was now Ginny Nelson. Three years ago Ginny had married Chad, the young man who ran the fitness center where Ginny worked when she and Naomi ran off to Portland, Oregon. Ginny's letter said she and Chad had moved from Portland and now lived in Puyallup, Washington, where they'd opened a fitness center they planned to remodel soon.

Naomi smiled. *Ginny always did want her own business, and now she's gotten her wish. Too bad she doesn't come home to visit more often. I know her folks still miss her.*

Thinking about Ginny and the time they'd

spent in Oregon made Naomi feel sad. Those had been stressful days, when she'd been homesick and thought she couldn't make it through another day. But God had seen her through the rough times. He'd brought Naomi home on Christmas Day, and her family had accepted her unconditionally.

Just the way God accepts wayward sinners, she mused. *He never turns anyone away who comes to Him with a repentant heart.*

Naomi had just finished reading Ginny's letter when the front door opened. She looked up, expecting to see a customer. Instead, Abby Miller stood on the other side of the counter, holding a small black suitcase.

"Abby, what a surprise! What are you doing here? Did Fannie know you were coming?"

Abby set the suitcase on the floor and smiled. "If I'd told her, she would have argued and insisted I not come."

Naomi rushed over to Abby and gave her a hug. "I'm sure Fannie will be happy to have you here for a visit."

"This is more than a visit," Abby said. "After reading Mom's recent letter and learning what the doctor said about her needing to rest more, I decided to take over her quilt shop until she's had the boppli and is ready to return to work."

Naomi's mouth fell open. "Why would you do that when you have your own shop to run?"

Abby yawned as she leaned on the counter. She was tired from the long bus ride and hadn't slept well in the uncomfortable seat. She'd had another one of her frightening dreams, which hadn't helped either. "I couldn't stay in Ohio, knowing Mom would likely have to close her shop here."

"That's so nice of you, Abby. I'm sorry to say it, but I'm not up to running both the store and the quilt shop. It'll be all I can do to keep helping Caleb until my own boppli is born." Naomi thumped her protruding stomach.

"I understand. How are you feeling? Are you doin' okay?"

"Jah. I'm healthy as a mule, but feeling awful top-heavy these days. It's gettin' to where I can barely bend over."

Abby offered her a sympathetic smile. "And how's little Sarah? Is she excited about becoming a big sister?"

"I think so, although I'm not sure she fully understands that a boppli's comin'."

"Your kinner will be only two years apart, so I'm sure she'll adjust real well."

"Probably so."

"Would you and Caleb be able to give me a ride to Abraham and Mom's place on your way home from work today?" Abby asked.

"I don't see why not. Caleb's running some errands, but he should be back soon. Then we can close the store early and head out to their place. I'm sure Fannie will be thrilled to see you."

Abby grinned. "I'm anxious to see her as well."

∞

Fannie shifted, trying to find a comfortable position on the sofa. Only a few days ago she'd been given orders from the doctor to stay off her feet as much as possible. Already she felt as restless as a cat on a hot summer day. If there was only something constructive she could do instead of sitting here wishing she could be at the quilt shop. The only thing useful she'd done all day was knit on the little sweater she was making for the boppli. She patted her stomach and smiled. *As fast as this babe is growing, I have to wonder if the child will weigh a ton when he's born.*

"Want me to start supper yet?" Nancy asked, stepping into the living room with a cup of tea, which she held out to Fannie.

"Danki. This is just what I need." Fannie took the offered cup, then glanced at the clock on the far wall. "It's not quite five, and I'm sure your daed and brothers will be out in the fields awhile, so there's no hurry gettin' things going in the kitchen."

"Even so, I think I'll start making a tossed salad, and then I'll put some chicken in the oven," Nancy said. "It can stay on warm if they don't come in by six o'clock."

"That sounds fine."

Nancy had no more than left the room when Fannie heard the back door open and click shut. She figured it was Mary Ann or Samuel coming in from their chores, so she settled against the sofa pillows and took a sip of tea.

A few seconds later, she heard voices in the kitchen, followed by footsteps coming down the hall. When Abby stepped into the living room, along with Caleb, Naomi, and Nancy, who held Sarah in her arms, Fannie nearly dropped her cup. "Abby! What are you doing here, daughter?"

Abby rushed to Fannie's side, dropped to the sofa, and gave her a hug. "I came as soon as I got your letter."

"My letter?"

"The one saying you had to rest more and that you would probably have to close the quilt shop."

Fannie's throat clogged with tears, and she couldn't speak.

"I'm here to take over the shop, Mom. And I plan to stay until the boppli's born and you're back on your feet."

"Oh Abby, you're such an amazing daughter," Fannie said with a catch in her voice. "But what are you going to do about your quilt shop in Berlin if you stay here and keep my store running?"

Abby smiled. "Lester's mamm and his aunt Clara will be minding the store until I get back."

Fannie was on the verge of telling Abby that her sacrifice wasn't necessary, when Naomi chimed in. "I think you should accept your daughter's offer and be thankful the Lord has provided her help." She touched Caleb's arm and smiled. "I surely appreciate it whenever someone helps me these days."

"That's another reason I need to be here," Abby said with a note of conviction. "When Naomi has her baby, someone will need to help Caleb at the store."

"I think Matthew might be plannin' to do that," Caleb announced. "He told me the other day that he's tired of farming and wants to try something new."

"But who will help Papa and the brothers in the fields?" Nancy asked.

Caleb shrugged. "Guess they'll have to hire someone, 'cause Matthew seems determined to get out of farm work."

Relief spread through Fannie like the warmth

of her tea. "The good Lord is workin' things out, and we should rejoice and be glad."

❧

It didn't take Abby long to get her suitcase unpacked and settled into the bedroom that used to be Naomi's when she lived at home. She took a seat on the four-poster bed and glanced around, noting the old wooden dresser on the opposite wall, with a small mirror hanging above it. The room looked similar to her room at home, only here dark green shades instead of white curtains covered the two windows. A beige-and-brown oval braided throw rug lay on the hardwood floor, and a blue-and-white Lone Star quilt covered the bed. If it hadn't been for the ache in Abby's heart from leaving Lester back in Ohio, she would have felt quite comfortable here.

"I think I'll go downstairs and see if there's anything I can do," she murmured.

A few minutes later, Abby found her mamm asleep on the living room couch, so she tiptoed out of the room and went to the kitchen. Nancy stood at the sink, peeling potatoes, and Mary Ann was busy setting the table. "Need any help?" Abby asked the girls.

Nancy smiled. "We've got things well underway for supper, but if you'd like to go outside and bring in the quilts I've got airin' on the fence, that would be a big help."

"Sure, I can do that."

Abby opened the back door and stepped onto the porch. The late afternoon air was still warm, and a chorus of crickets sang to her as she wandered into the yard. She drew in a deep breath, savoring the pleasant aroma of peppermint growing in clumps along the edge of the garden.

The *clip-clop* of a horse's hooves drew her attention to the road out front. *Things aren't much different here,* she noted as the horse and buggy passed. *The buggies are gray instead of black, and I know some of their church rules are a bit different, but otherwise the Plain life in Lancaster County is pretty much the same as it is back home in Holmes County.*

Abby spotted three colorful quilts draped over the split rail fence that separated Abraham's farm from his son Norman's place. The beauty of the quilts on the fence with the red barn and white house in the distance looked like a picture postcard. Tears sprang to her eyes as she dropped to the grass and studied the striking scene. Abby loved everything about quilts, from the comforting warmth they provided on a cold winter night, to the unexplainable joy of putting one together by hand. Each quilt was unique, whether intricate or simple in pattern, and served a purpose. She had been quilting since she was a young girl and never tired of the tedious work or longed for any other occupation. Quilting was her life, and she couldn't imagine doing anything else.

Abby's attention was diverted when she heard a woman shouting, "Katie! Katie! Where are you, daughter?"

Smoothing the wrinkles in her long, green dress, Abby stood and turned around. A young Amish woman hurried up the driveway, frantically waving her hands. "Have you seen my little girl? She was playing in the yard while I fixed supper, and when I went outside to get her, she had disappeared."

WANDA &. BRUNSTETTER

Abby's heart clenched at the thought of a child who might have wandered onto the road, where cars often went much faster than they should. "I've only been out here a short time," she replied, "and I haven't seen any children playing nearby."

"I don't believe I know you," the woman said, tipping her head toward Abby.

"I'm Abby Miller—Fannie's daughter."

"Jah, jah. Your mamm's mentioned you, but I'm new to the community and haven't met you before." She extended her hand. "I'm Irma Hochstetler. My husband, Sam, and I moved here from Indiana a few months ago with our little girl, Katie. Sam's a painter, and he's been workin' for Jacob Weaver. But Sam's not home yet. If he were, he'd be out looking for our little *schtinker*, who likes to wander off." Irma glanced around the yard. "I've caught Katie over here several times, playing in the barn or bothering Mary Ann, so I'm hoping that's where she is now."

"Mary Ann's in the kitchen setting the table for supper," Abby said. "If your daughter did wander over, maybe we should take a look in the barn."

Irma nodded. "That's a good idea."

Abby led the way, and once inside the barn, they called Katie's name and searched in every nook and cranny. Abby was afraid to think of the outcome if the child wasn't found. She knew the little girl's mother was equally frightened, because Irma's voice trembled as she continued to call Katie's name.

"I think we should get some others to help us look," Abby suggested. "Maybe Katie wandered up the road to someone else's farm."

Irma nodded, and tears splashed onto her

cheeks. "I'll never forgive myself if anything happens to my daughter. I should have been watchin' her closer—shouldn't have let her play in the yard alone, not even for a few minutes."

Abby gave Irma a reassuring hug, even though she didn't feel so confident right now. What if the child had been kidnapped? Could the same thing have happened to little Katie as happened to Abraham's boy Zach? "Why don't you go back to your house in case Katie comes home?" she suggested. "I'll run out to the fields and see if I can enlist the help of Abraham and his sons."

Irma's chin quivered. "Jah, I appreciate all the help I can get."

As Abby headed into the fields, she sent up a prayer for Katie and one for Zach Fisher. Mom rarely mentioned him in her letters anymore, but she felt sure the boy's family had not forgotten him.

Abby had only made it halfway across the alfalfa field when she saw a small figure zigzagging her way. When she came upon the little blond-haired girl, she knew immediately that it must be Katie Hochstetler.

"Danki, Lord," Abby murmured. At least one of her prayers had been answered, and now she could take the little girl home, gather up the quilts that were on the fence, and return to the house, knowing Katie's parents wouldn't have to suffer the way the Fishers had for so many years.

Chapter 8

Abby could hardly believe she had been in Pennsylvania a whole month. She supposed the time had swept by so quickly because of her busyness. She had been working at her mother's quilt shop five days a week, and when she wasn't there, she was at home with Mom, making sure everything ran smoothly and offering her assistance whenever it was needed. Each night, Abby fell wearily into bed, often forgetting to pray or read her Bible. She'd been negligent about writing letters to Lester and Deborah, too, which she had been reminded of today when a letter from Lester arrived. With a pang of regret, Abby took a seat on the edge of her bed and reread his note.

Dear Abby,

It's been almost two weeks since I've heard from you. I hope it's only because you've been busy and not because you've forgotten me. If things slow up at the blacksmith shop, I may catch a bus and come there for a few days. I miss you so much and feel the need to spend time with you. It would be nice to meet Abraham and his family, too.

Mom says she hasn't heard from you

*in a while either. She wanted me to tell
you that everything is going well at the
quilt shop. Lately, there have been a lot of
tourists in town, but that's pretty normal for
summertime, I suppose.*

*Please write soon, and tell your mamm
I'm prayin' for her and hope she's doin' okay.
Mom says she's prayin', too.*

*Always yours,
Lester*

Abby hurried to her dresser and retrieved her writing paper and a pen. Tonight she would write Lester a letter, no matter how tired she felt. She loved Lester with all her heart and didn't want him to think she'd forgotten him.

She had just finished her letter to Lester and sealed the envelope when someone rapped on the door. "Abby, are you still awake?"

"Jah. Please, come in."

The door opened, and Nancy entered the room, wearing a white cotton nightgown that brushed her slender ankles. The girl's golden brown hair hung loosely down her back, and its shiny luster offered proof that it had recently been brushed. "I hope I'm not disturbin' you, but I'd like to talk awhile, if it's all right."

Abby patted the edge of her bed. "Come have a seat, and tell me what's on your mind."

Nancy sat down with a groan. "It's Fannie's cousin."

"Edna?"

"Jah."

"What about her? Is Edna sick or something?"

"No, but she sure is bossy. The woman's always tellin' me what to do and complainin' because I don't do things exactly the way she wants 'em done." Nancy's forehead wrinkled. "Things were goin' along fine until she started coming over to help out. Can't you send her away, Abby?"

Abby knew her young stepsister was quite capable and probably felt like a failure in Edna's eyes. Even though she didn't know her mother's cousin well, from what Mom had said, Edna was pleasant and liked to kid around. Maybe she was only funning with Nancy when she said or did certain things. The girl might be overly sensitive in that regard.

Abby took Nancy's hand and gave it a gentle squeeze. "It's possible that Edna doesn't think you're incompetent. Maybe she's just teasing when she makes little irritating comments."

Nancy pursed her lips. "Why would she do that? Can't she see how hard I work? Doesn't she realize I'm doin' the best I can?"

"I'm sure she does. My advice is to simply ignore Cousin Edna's remarks."

"You think if I didn't try to stand up for myself, things would go better?"

Ah, so that was the problem. Everything Edna said to Nancy was going against the grain, and the girl defended herself in return.

"Edna is older and wiser than you, Nancy," Abby said. "You've been taught to show consideration for your elders, isn't that right?"

Nancy's reply was a quick nod.

"Even if Edna's comments aren't meant in jest, you should never argue with her; it's not the respectful thing to do."

"You're right. I'm sorry."

"I think it's Edna you should apologize to, don't you?"

"Jah. I'll do that when she shows up tomorrow."

"And you'll try harder to ignore the things she says that get under your skin?"

"Uh-huh."

Abby gave her stepsister a hug. "I'm proud of you. Being willing to apologize shows how mature you've become."

"Danki." Nancy stood and started for the door but turned back around. "Abby?"

"What is it?"

"I know you'll have to return to Ohio after the boppli comes, but if I had my way, you'd stay with us forever."

Abby smiled, wishing it were possible to be in two places at once. *At least I'll sleep well tonight,* she mused. *I've written Lester a letter and had a heart-to-heart talk with Nancy. Tomorrow will be a good day.*

❧

A mysterious dark cloud hovered over Abby Miller's bed, pressing on her from all sides. Blinking against stinging tears, she drew in a ragged breath. An invisible hand pushed against her face, and she flung her covers aside. "Ich kann nimmi schnaufe—I can no longer breathe!"

Meow. Meow. Somewhere in the distance, Abby heard the pathetic cry and knew she must save the poor kitten. With a panicked sob, she rolled out of bed, but the minute her bare feet touched the floor she shrank back from the intense heat. A paralyzing fear wrapped its arms around Abby, threatening to strip away her sanity. She lifted her hands to her face and rubbed her eyes, forcing them to focus. "Where are you, kitty? I'm coming, kitty."

Suddenly, she realized that her room was engulfed in flames—lapping at the curtains, snapping, crackling, consuming everything in sight. As the smoky haze grew thicker and the fire became an inferno, Abby grabbed the Lone Star quilt off her bed and covered her head. Coughing, choking, gasping on the acrid smoke, she stumbled and staggered toward the door. "Feier—fire! Somebody, please help me save the kitten!"

∞

Abby's eyes flew open as she sucked in a shallow breath. She was drenched in sweat, and her throat felt raw, as though she'd been screaming. She glanced around the room and, seeing everything was as it should be, realized she had only been dreaming. "It was that same horrible dream about a fire," she moaned.

Abby clambered out of bed and raced over to the window. She lifted the dark shade and jerked the window open, breathing deeply of the early morning air. The sun peeked over the horizon, its delicate shades of pink graduating into a fiery red. A burst of air swept suddenly into the room, and she shivered. "Oh Lord, why do I continue to have that awful dream?"

∞

Abraham stood outside the barn door, stretching his arms over his head and suppressing a yawn. He'd lain awake into the wee hours last night, worrying about Fannie. Most days she had dark circles under her eyes, and her ankles were still slightly puffy, even though she had been following the doctor's orders and resting much of the time. He had heard of women who developed toxemia during pregnancy and knew it could be serious. When he'd mentioned his concerns to Fannie last night, she'd made light of them, saying she had cut salt out of her diet and was sure that would help the swelling.

"If it doesn't, I'm takin' her back to the doctor," Abraham mumbled.

"What was that, Papa?" Matthew asked as he led one of their mules out of the barn.

Abraham's face heated. "Nothin'. I was talkin' to myself."

"You said something about going to the doctor. Does Fannie have another appointment today?"

"No, but I'll be takin' her in if she don't look better in a few days."

"Is she lookin' poorly?"

Abraham leaned against the side of the barn and groaned. "Haven't ya noticed the dark circles under her eyes?"

Matthew removed his straw hat and fanned his face with it a couple of times. "Can't say that I have, but then I've had a lot of things on my mind lately."

"Yeah, like quittin' work on the farm," Abraham grumbled. "If you hate field work so much, how come you never said anything before?"

"I don't hate it, Papa. To tell you the truth, until lately I didn't know I wanted to do something else."

"You think it could be runnin' a store?"

"Not necessarily, but if I try workin' there after Naomi has her baby, it might give me a better idea of what I want to be doing."

"*Humph!* You sure this change of attitude doesn't have more to do with some pretty face than it does with you not wantin' to farm?"

Matthew's ears turned pink, and he stared at the ground. "I don't know what you're talkin' about."

"Who, not what," Abraham corrected.

Matthew just stood there making little swirls in the dirt with the toe of his boot.

"I've seen the way you look at Abby when you think no one's watchin'. You wouldn't have a crush on her now, would ya, son?"

"'Course not. She's betrothed to some fellow in Ohio." Matthew slapped his hat back on his head. "Guess I'd best get the other mule out, or we'll be late gettin' out to the fields."

"Where are Jake and Norman? How come they're not here helpin'?" Abraham asked.

"Norman hasn't shown up yet, and Jake had to drive Mary Ann and Samuel to school because they spent so much time arguing this morning, they were late."

Matthew disappeared into the barn, and Abraham frowned. *Guess I'll need to have a little talk with my two youngest tonight.*

A buggy rolled into the yard, drawing Abraham's attention aside. He smiled and waved when he realized it was his good friend Jacob Weaver.

"What are you doin' out so early?" he asked as Jacob stepped down from his buggy.

"I'm on my way to the buggy shop to see if the new rig I ordered has been finished yet."

The mention of the buggy shop sent Abraham's mind whizzing back to the past. It had been a sad day when Caleb had to give up buggy making because of his injury. His two younger brothers were running the place now, having become quite capable under Caleb's tutelage. Caleb seemed content to run the general store, which he had purchased from Abraham. He could do most things there with only one good hand, and the change of occupations had allowed him to marry Abraham's daughter. Everything had worked out for the best. At least that's the way Abraham saw it.

"Looks like you're headin' to the fields," Jacob said.

"Jah. Just waitin' for Matthew to bring the other mule out."

As if on cue, Matthew showed up, leading Bossy, their most headstrong mule. "Had a hard time gettin' her out of the stall," he complained. "I think she had her mind set on stayin' in the barn today."

Jacob chuckled. "Always did prefer working with horses."

"Horses can be a mite stubborn, too," Abraham put in. "Fact is, I've had some that were just plain *mehne*."

"Jah. I've encountered a couple of mean ones over the years," his friend agreed.

"Papa, if you and Jacob want to jaw awhile, I'll head out to the fields with these two." Matthew nodded at Bossy and Barney.

"Sure you don't mind?" Truthfully, Abraham did want the chance to speak with Jacob a few minutes. His friend was always full of good advice, and if anyone could get Abraham thinking straight or help strengthen his faith, it was Jacob.

"Naw. We'll be fine, and Norman and Jake should be along shortly." Matthew grabbed hold of the mules' bridles and led them away.

"Want to sit a spell?" Abraham motioned to a couple of old barrels sitting near the barn.

Jacob nodded. "Jah, sounds good."

Once they were seated, Abraham confided, "I'm glad you stopped by, Jacob, because I need to talk."

"Figured as much." Jacob grinned. "Felt a little nudge from the Lord as I was passing by your place this morning. Thought I should drop over and see how things are with you."

"Things are fine with me. It's Fannie I'm worried about."

Jacob's bushy eyebrows lifted. "What's the trouble?"

Abraham related his concerns about Fannie's pregnancy, and ended by saying, "I want to believe God will bring her through this in good shape and that our boppli will be born healthy, but I've got a nagging feeling that something's not right." He rubbed the side of his head. "I haven't shared this with anyone, but I'm afraid something bad is going to happen to our family again." He paused and moistened his lips. "Don't think I could stand it if I lost this wife or the child she's carrying."

Jacob sat there with his hands clasped in his lap, staring at the ground like he was mulling things over. After a few moments, he spoke. "In the book of Psalms, David went through many tribulations. Yet in chapter 31, verse 14, he was able to say this to God: 'But I trusted in thee, O Lord: I said, Thou art my God.'"

Abraham nodded. "I know I need to have more faith and learn to put my trust in God, but that's easier said than done. Especially when things ain't lookin' so good."

"Which is why you should pray every day and read God's Word. That's how my faith has been strengthened." Jacob clasped Abraham's shoulder. "Take one day at a time, my friend. Commit your wife and unborn child to God and enjoy each moment you have with your family. None of us knows when our time will come or what the future holds."

Abraham blew out his breath. "You're right about that. If I'd known my boy was gonna be kidnapped, I'd have stayed home from the store that day and watched his every move." He glanced over at Jacob and smiled. "I appreciate your friendship more than you know."

"And I appreciate yours," his friend said with a nod.

⨯

"Hope you don't mind me cleanin' the living room while you rest," Nancy said to Fannie, who reclined on the sofa.

"No, no, not at all," Fannie replied from her place on the sofa. "It is hard for me to lie here and watch you work though."

Nancy shrugged. "It's nice to have your company. Edna will probably be here soon; then I'll have to let the two of you visit while I get some bakin' done."

"Humph!" Fannie scoffed. "Some company I

am these days."

"Just because you're not able to get up and work doesn't mean you're not good company. I've always enjoyed visiting with you and hearing stories from when you were a girl." Nancy gave the broom a couple sweeps in front of the rocking chair and then moved over to the couch.

"It has been fun doing some reminiscing," Fannie said with a smile.

Nancy swept under the sofa and Fannie cringed at the dust balls clinging to the broom. *I used to keep the house spotless, but Nancy probably didn't think to clean under there before.*

"Hey, what's this?" Nancy bent down and picked up an object, which she held out to Fannie in the palm of her hand.

"Looks like a wooden block."

Nancy squinted, and her forehead creased. "Why, I haven't seen this in some time. Must have been stuck under the couch."

"Whose block is it?" Fannie asked.

"It was Zach's." Nancy closed her fingers around it and slowly shook her head. "We'd best not let Papa see this."

Fannie swallowed around the lump in her throat. Was Abraham still grieving for his lost son? He rarely spoke of Zach anymore. Maybe talking about his missing boy brought back too many painful memories. Fannie figured her husband would always miss Zach, and so would the rest of the family. She squeezed her eyes shut. *Oh Lord, let this child I'm carrying heal any remaining pain in Abraham's heart.*

Chapter 9

If you're ready for lunch, maybe we can take our noon break together today."

Abby looked up from her quilting project and smiled at Naomi, who stood inside the door that separated their store from Mom's quilt shop. "Were you planning to go out or eat in?"

"Since Sarah's sleeping and things are quiet in the store at the moment, Caleb said it would be okay if you and I went out someplace to eat," Naomi replied.

"That's fine with me. I could use some fresh air to help wake me up."

"Didn't you sleep well last night?"

Abby set her sewing aside and shook her head. "I had a bad dream and couldn't get back to sleep when it woke me."

"Sorry to hear that. Some dreams can make you feel pretty rung out."

"Jah." Abby was tempted to reveal the details of her reoccurring dream, but she didn't want to bother her stepsister with it. Naomi had enough to deal with, having so much work to do at the store and another boppli coming in a few months.

"Should we go to lunch now?" Naomi asked.

"Jah, sure."

"We shouldn't be too long," Naomi said when

Caleb took her place behind the counter.

He gave her arm a squeeze. "No problem; take your time."

Abby and Naomi were preparing to leave the store when the door swung open. A handsome Amish man, his wavy blond hair peeking out from under his straw hat, stepped into the store carrying a small suitcase.

Abby's mouth dropped open. "Lester! What are you doing here?"

"Came to see you."

When he gave her a lopsided grin and reached for her hand, the faint smell of peppermint tickled her nose. She spied two pieces of candy sticking out of his shirt pocket. "I. . .I had no idea you were coming." She stared up at him in disbelief.

"Wanted it to be a surprise."

"And what a surprise it is. Jah, for certain sure." Then, remembering her manners, Abby introduced Lester to Naomi and Caleb.

"It's nice to meet you, Lester," Naomi said. "We've heard a lot about you."

Caleb's head bobbed up and down. "Jah, Abby's mentioned you plenty of times."

Abby felt the heat of a blush, but she couldn't deny it. She had missed Lester so much and often talked about the fun things they'd done during their courtship. She and Naomi had also discussed her upcoming wedding and how the Fisher family planned to go to Ohio to witness the ceremony in November.

"Abby and I were about to head out for some lunch," Naomi commented. "But now that Lester's here, I think it should be him and Abby going instead of me."

"Maybe you and Caleb can join us," Lester suggested.

Caleb nodded toward the back of the store. "Our little girl is sleepin' in the other room, so I'd better stay put. My wife can go with you though."

Naomi shook her head. "I'll stay here, and Caleb and I can eat the lunch I packed this morning."

Abby hesitated. "Are you sure you don't mind?"

"Not at all. I'll keep an eye on the quilt shop while you're gone."

"Danki."

Lester pushed his suitcase off to one side, opened the front door, then motioned for Abby to step out first.

"No need to hurry back," Naomi called.

A short time later, Abby and Lester sat at a corner table in the cozy restaurant down the street. Abby still couldn't believe he was here, and she just sat staring at him.

He stared back, looking pleased as a child with a new toy.

"How long are you here for, and how'd you manage to get away from the blacksmith shop to make this trip?" she asked, pulling her gaze from his handsome face to glance at the menu lying before her.

"Probably be here a couple of days. I hired on another man a few weeks ago, so I'm sure my two helpers can handle things while I'm gone."

Abby still couldn't believe he'd come all this way just to spend a few days with her.

"I've missed you, Abby." Lester's voice had a soft quality about it, yet he spoke with assurance, and it gladdened her heart.

"I've missed you, too." She smiled. "How are things in Holmes County these days?"

"Fine. Mom sends her love and said to tell you everything's goin' great at the quilt shop."

"I'm pleased to hear it. How are Lena and Harold?"

"Last I heard, Lena was feelin' some better, but Harold still insists she stay home and not work too hard." Lester's eyebrows suddenly drew together, a stark contrast from his usual smiling face. "I wish I could speed up the hands of time and get that bruder or *schweschder* of yours born so you can come back to Ohio."

Abby took a sip from her glass of water as a film of tears obscured her vision. "The time will go quickly; you'll see."

He reached across the table and took her hand, making tiny circular motions with his rough fingertips. "It hasn't so far. Every day since you left Berlin has seemed to drag by for me."

She nodded in understanding, because she felt the same way. "This coming Sunday is an off-Sunday from church, and there's going to be a picnic and softball game over at the Beechys' place. I hope you can stay that long, because I know how much you like to play ball."

Lester let go of her hand and drummed his fingers along the edge of the table. "Let's see now . . . . Today's Thursday, so if I hang around till Sunday and catch an early bus on Monday, that should work out fine and dandy. I told my mamm and the fellows at work I'd probably be gone till early next week."

"I'll see if you can stay with Caleb and Naomi

while you're here. They've got plenty of room at their place."

Lester nodded, and she was relieved that his smile had returned. "I'll stay wherever you say, just as long as I get to spend time with you," he said.

"I'll see that you do," she whispered as the waitress came to take their order.

❦

With a weary sigh, Linda stretched out in the middle of her bed. After lunch she'd put Jimmy down for a nap and had decided to take one herself. She was exhausted and couldn't believe she'd let Beth talk her into helping with crafts at vacation Bible school this week. But it had been kind of fun.

She jabbed her pillow a couple of times, trying to find a more comfortable position, then rolled onto her side. Her gaze came to rest on the Amish quilt covering their bed, and she thought about the morning they had visited a quaint little quilt shop outside of Berlin, Ohio, more than five years ago.

I've never understood why Jim doesn't have any interest in visiting Amish country again. I found it so fascinating. Her fingers traced the uniform, almost perfect hand stitches on the blue-and-white quilt done in the Lone Star pattern. *If I had more patience and better sewing skills, I might try my hand at quilting.*

She flipped onto her other side. *I wish I could convince Jim to take us to Ohio again. I'm sure Jimmy would enjoy the trip, and I know Jim's folks would love to have us visit.*

In an attempt to shrug away her irritation, Linda closed her eyes and pictured the beautiful Amish homes they'd seen when they were back

East. Most were neat, orderly, and devoid of weeds in their bountiful gardens.

"Amish country," she murmured. "Where life is slower, and the men come home to their families after work every night."

She squeezed her eyes tighter to keep threatening tears from escaping. It was pointless to wallow in self-pity. She'd done it too much, and where had it gotten her? Short of a miracle, Jim would probably never be the kind of husband she needed. The best thing to do was to keep busy and try not to dwell on their artificial marriage.

Maybe I should take Beth's suggestion and start taking Jimmy to Sunday school. We'd be around people, and it would be better than watching Jim snooze every Sunday until noon or sit in his recliner, focused on the TV.

Linda exhaled, as the need for sleep took over. *Jim needs church, too. He needs. . .*

❧

Jim entered the house through the garage door. Except for the steady hum of the refrigerator, everything was quiet. He slipped off his work boots and left them sitting by the door, then sauntered across the kitchen to get a drink of water. Today had gone well. They'd finished painting the outside of a newly remodeled fitness center, and the general contractor had praised Jim's work and said he was impressed with how quickly his paint crew had finished the job.

Jim opened a cupboard door and grabbed a glass. "Wonder if there's any iced tea in the refrigerator? That would taste better than water."

After filling his glass with cold tea, Jim grabbed

a handful of cookies from the ceramic jar on top of the china hutch, then dropped into a chair at the table. It was nice to come home to a quiet house for a change. Usually Jimmy had the TV blaring or ran around the house making weird noises.

He shook his head. *That kid's imagination can sure run wild. One minute, he's a police car with a blaring siren, and the next, he's some silly ice-cream truck. And then there's Linda. If she's not nagging me to fix something, she's asking me to take her somewhere. It's ridiculous that she won't drive. It's been years since she was involved in that little fender bender, and she wasn't even hurt.*

Jim bit off a hunk of peanut butter cookie and washed it down with a gulp of iced tea. He glanced at the clock. *I wonder if Linda and Jimmy are at the park. She's usually in the kitchen by now, starting dinner.*

"Oh, you're home," came a sleepy voice from the doorway.

Jim turned his head. Linda stood there, long blond hair in disarray and cheeks slightly pink. In the early days of their marriage he would have been pleased to see her. Now, he merely tried to be polite enough to avoid a confrontation.

"Have you been sleeping?" he asked.

She nodded. "I put Jimmy down for a nap after lunch and decided to take one, too. I didn't expect to sleep so late though."

"What'd you do all day that made you so tired?"

Linda joined him at the table. "I've been helping with crafts at Bible school this week, remember?"

He grabbed another cookie. "Oh yeah, that."

"You don't have to sound so disapproving.

Jimmy's having fun, and he's with other children. That should make you happy."

Her tone was mocking, and it only fueled Jim's irritation. "Don't get smart, Linda."

"I wasn't trying to be."

"Yeah, right."

She sighed deeply. "Why is it that every time I try to have a sensible conversation with you, it ends up in an argument?"

He shrugged. "Who's arguing?"

No reply.

"Since you've slept the afternoon away, when do you plan to have dinner on the table?"

"We're having sandwiches tonight, so it won't take long." She toyed with a piece of her hair but made no move to get up. "Uh, Jim, I was wondering. . . ."

He reached for his glass, which was almost empty. "What were you wondering?"

"Allen's mother invited Jimmy and me to come to Sunday school this week, and I was hoping we could go as a family."

Jim's forehead wrinkled. "You want me to go to Sunday school?"

She nodded. "I thought it would be something we could all do together."

He pushed away from the table and stood. "Count me out."

"Why?"

"Church is for weak people who are looking for something to make them feel better. It's a crutch, and if I needed one of those, I would rent a pair from Keller's Medical Supply."

"You don't have to be sarcastic."

He marched across the room and set his glass in the sink. "If you want to take Jimmy to Sunday school, I won't stop you, but it's not likely I'll step foot inside a church building unless it's for somebody's wedding or a funeral."

Jim glanced over his shoulder to gauge Linda's reaction. Her chin quivered as she stared at the table. He didn't care. She wasn't going to manipulate him with her tears or whining. She'd done that too many times in the past, and ever since the day he'd made up his mind to "put the hammer down," he'd been a lot happier.

Well, maybe not happier, but at least Linda knows who's in charge around here.

Chapter 10

Abby reclined on the grass beside Nancy and watched the baseball game in progress. Lester had just hit a homerun, and everyone cheered. She was glad the men in Abraham's family had made him feel welcome.

"Too bad Lester won't move to Lancaster County," Nancy said. "Then you could stay here for good."

Abby smiled. "It's nice to know you'd like me to stay."

"You're my big sister now, and I enjoy your company."

"Danki. I enjoy being with you, too."

Nancy sniffed. "Sure wish I could help at the quilt shop. I get tired of stayin' home all the time and doing nothing but housework and cooking."

Abby knew Nancy worked hard and rarely went anywhere for fun. "Maybe one day when Cousin Edna comes to help Mom you can drive into town and I'll take you out to lunch."

Nancy's green eyes danced with enthusiasm. "I'd like that."

Abby smiled. "I've always wanted a sweet sister like you."

Nancy shook her head. "It's you who's the sweet one. Everyone always says I'm stubborn and bossy."

Before Abby could comment, she heard a loud smack, followed by a groan. Her gaze went to the ball field, and she was shocked to see Lester lying on the ground, with Matthew and several others standing over him. She scrambled to her feet and raced over to the scene.

"Lester, are you all right?"

"Ball. Hit. Stomach," he gasped.

She looked up at Matthew. "Did you see it happen?"

He nodded. "It was my fault. Lester was up to bat and I got a little overanxious when I pitched the ball. Sure didn't mean to take him out."

Lester coughed and struggled to sit up. "I'm okay. Just knocked the wind out of me, is all."

Abby held her hand out to him.

"That's what I get for watching my *aldi* instead of the ball," he said with a red-faced grin.

"That'll teach you not to make eyes at your girlfriend when you're supposed to be playin' a serious game of baseball," Caleb teased.

Jake chuckled. "As if you never made eyes at my sister when you two were courtin'."

"Are you sure you're not hurt?" Abby asked as she and Lester moved to the sidelines and took a seat on the grass.

"The only thing banged up is my pride," he replied with a grunt.

"It wasn't your fault Matthew's aim was off." Abby took a deep breath to settle her nerves. It had frightened her to see him lying on the ground like that. What if he'd been seriously injured? What if. . .

Lester leaned closer, and his warm breath tickled her ear. "Don't look so worried. I'm fine."

"I couldn't stand it if anything ever happened to you."

He touched the side of her face with his thumb. "You worry too much, Abby. I ain't goin' nowhere."

"Except back home. You're still leaving Monday morning, right?"

He nodded. "But it won't be long till your mamm has that boppli; then you'll be comin' home to Ohio." He caressed her chin, and Abby's skin turned to gooseflesh. She could hardly wait until November when she would become Lester's Abby.

❦

"Sure is muggy tonight," Fannie said, squirming restlessly, while she tried to find a comfortable position on the porch swing. At least the swelling in her legs had gone down, and she felt some better. "It wonders me so that anyone would want to play ball in this heat."

Abraham chuckled. "When I was a young man, I could do most anything in the hot weather. Now, by midday I'm feelin' ready for a cold shower and a tall glass of iced tea."

She glanced over at him with sudden concern. "You doin' okay in the fields?"

"Everything's fine."

"Do you ever wish you'd kept running the store?"

He nuzzled her neck. "Only when I'm missin' you."

She giggled, enjoying his attention and feeling like a schoolgirl again. "Need I remind you that I'm not at the quilt shop anymore? So if you really find yourself missin' me, you can always take a break and come up to the house."

Abraham jiggled his bushy eyebrows. "Now there's a pleasant thought, and I just might do it more often." His brows drew together. "'Course once Naomi has her boppli, and Matthew leaves the farm to help at the store, I'll be shorthanded in the fields. Gettin' away for breaks will be harder then."

"I'm sure you can find someone to fill in for Matthew."

"Maybe so, but what if he decides to give up farmin' altogether?"

She squeezed his arm gently. "You'll accept his decision and be glad he's found something he likes to do, same as you've done."

"Jah." Abraham rested his hand on Fannie's stomach. Suddenly, he pulled back like he'd been stung by a bee. *Was in der welt?*

"What in the world, what?"

"Can't ya feel that?"

"Feel what?"

"The boppli kickin'."

Fannie chuckled. "Oh sure. I feel it often these days. It's normal for a baby to kick, ya know."

"That wasn't just any old kick. It felt like a whole baseball team trompin' around in your belly."

She nodded. "I think our little guy likes to kick with his feet on one side of my stomach and punch me with his fists on the other side."

"Hope that don't mean he's gonna be a rambunctious one."

"If he is, we'll handle it, jah?"

"Sure. Always have with my other kinner."

"I know you're countin' on a boy, Abraham, but what if it's a girl?"

He kissed her cheek. "I'll love our child no matter if it's a *bu* or a *maedel*."

"I'm glad to hear that, because we sure can't send it back."

Abraham chortled. "You're such a hoot. I surely do love you, Fannie Mae."

"And I love you."

His face sobered. "For a while I was worried about your health, and the boppli's, too, but I finally committed things to God and decided to put my trust in Him."

She gave his hand a gentle squeeze. "Same here. I've learned that worry never solves anything. It only makes one feel miserable."

Abraham pulled Fannie into his arms. "You're sure smart, ya know that?"

She smiled. "I must be, 'cause I was wise enough to marry you."

❦

Abby had been home from the Beechys' for half an hour, and since she didn't feel ready for bed yet, she took a seat in one of the wicker chairs on the front porch to watch the sun set and enjoy the fireflies as they performed their nightly dance. It was still too warm for sleeping, and she just wanted to sit here and think about Lester. After the game and refreshments, he had borrowed Caleb's buggy and given her a ride home. Tomorrow would be their last day together until she returned to Ohio in early November.

Abby stood. *Maybe I'll take a walk to the barn and see how Callie's new kittens are doing.* She strolled through the yard, and a ray of light greeted her when she opened the barn door. She'd thought everyone in the family had gone to bed, but someone must be inside.

She moved across the straw-covered floor until she came to the source of light. Matthew was inside one of the stalls, grooming his buggy horse. "Sorry to disturb you," she said. "I didn't realize you were out here."

He held up the currycomb. "Thought I'd spend a little extra time on Bonnie tonight. And you're not disturbing me at all."

She smiled. "What made you choose that name for the horse?"

"Actually, it was Jake's idea, and I went along with it so he'd quit buggin' me."

"There's an English woman who comes into my quilt shop back home whose name is Bonnie."

Matthew chuckled. "This horse likes to prance around, and Jake said she looks like one of them Irish dancers he's seen on the neighbor's television set. He thought Bonnie was a good Irish name for her."

Abby rested her hands on the stall door. "I'm surprised your *daed* allows Jake to watch TV. Is he still going through his *rumspringa*?"

"I think my younger brother's been going through his running-around years since he was born." Matthew patted Bonnie's flanks. "One of these days he'll settle down and get baptized into the church. Maybe he'll find a woman desperate enough to marry him, too."

Abby smiled. "How come you're not married yet? And don't tell me it's because you haven't found a woman that desperate."

He snickered. "Haven't found the right one, that's all."

"I knew Lester was the man for me after our first date."

He lifted his head and gave her a curious look. "You could tell so soon?"

"Jah."

While Matthew continued to groom the horse, Abby glanced around the barn. She didn't see any sign of Callie or her kittens. They'd been inside a small wooden box the last time she was here, but now the box was empty. "Do you know what happened to the mama cat and her brood?"

Matthew shrugged. "Beats me. She probably got tired of Mary Ann and Samuel messin' with 'em and carted the kittens off to some other spot."

"That could be." Abby sighed. "That's why I came out here. . .to check on the kittens."

"Didn't figure you'd come out just to chew the fat with me."

She gave a self-conscious giggle. She was glad Matthew was her stepbrother. He was different than Harold, who hardly ever kidded around. Of course, Abby's brother had many other fine qualities.

"Don't believe I've told you this before, but I think it was real nice of you to leave your shop in Berlin and come here to help Fannie. You're a kind and caring woman, just like your mamm."

Abby's throat constricted. "I love Mom very much and would do anything I could to help her."

"Your boyfriend seems like a real nice fellow," he said.

"Jah, Lester has many fine qualities."

"Hope he knows how lucky he is to be gettin' someone as wunderbaar as you."

Abby lowered her lashes as heat flooded her face. "Danki for the kind words, Matthew, but I believe I'm the lucky one."

Chapter 11

On the last day of July, Naomi stepped out of the bathroom at the back of their store. "The boppli's coming, so you'd better find us a ride to the hospital," she whispered to Caleb.

He looked stunned. "You're kidding?"

"I'm not."

"But I thought you said your due date wasn't until August 15."

"Babies don't read calendars, Caleb, and this little one's comin' sooner than expected, so we'd better hurry."

"Have you been having contractions all morning and not said anything until now?"

"Just some aching in my lower back, but now my water's broke, and I'm feeling more pain."

"We'd better notify Abby so she can keep an eye on the store, as well as our sleeping daughter," Caleb said, moving toward the adjoining quilt shop.

"Maybe we should close the store and take Sarah home so your mamm can watch her."

He shook his head. "I'm expecting a supply of kerosene lamps, and if no one's here, the UPS man won't leave the box. Besides, driving Sarah home would take too much time."

Naomi leaned against the edge of the counter, as a painful contraction shot through her middle.

"Tell Abby what's going on, then ask if she's willing to watch Sarah and take her to my daed's after work."

"Okay." Caleb rushed into the other room, and a few moments later he returned with Abby at his side.

"Caleb says you've gone into labor," she said with a look of concern. "Do you want me to call an ambulance?"

"Maybe we should," Caleb agreed. "That would get us to the hospital much quicker."

"And it would cost a lot of money." Naomi shook her head. "Just go to the gift shop down the street and see if Mary Richards is free to drive us."

Caleb's eyebrows drew together. "I don't know, Naomi—"

"I'll be fine. You'll see." She waved her hand. "Now *dummle*—hurry!"

He gave her a quick hug and rushed out the door.

⌒⌒

Abby paced in front of the store window. It had been two hours since Caleb and Naomi had left for the hospital. They'd promised to send word as soon as the baby was born, but that could be hours yet. *If I'm this anxious over Naomi having her baby, I can only imagine how I'll feel when Mom's time comes.*

Abby was glad her mother had agreed to have the baby at the hospital in Lancaster rather than hiring a midwife like some Amish women chose to do. At least they would have plenty of doctors and emergency equipment available should a problem arise.

If I'm not mistaken, Mom had a doctor's

appointment today. Seems she said the doctor planned to do an ultrasound, and I'm anxious to know how that turned out. Abby frowned. *I hope there's not a problem with her pregnancy.*

Abby's thoughts were halted when the front door opened and Matthew walked in. "I heard you were here by yourself and figured you could use some help." He removed his straw hat and hung it on a wall peg by the door.

"News sure travels fast. How'd you know Caleb took Naomi to the hospital?"

"Caleb called his brothers at the buggy shop, and Andy drove over to our place to give us the word."

A muffled cry came from the back of the room. "That must be Sarah. Can you mind the store while I get her up?"

"Sure, no problem."

Abby found Naomi's daughter standing in her playpen, tears streaming down her flushed cheeks, and her golden curls in a tangled mass. She bent over and lifted Sarah into her arms. "Let's change your *windels*, and then you can go see Uncle Matthew."

A short time later, Abby carried the little girl up front and found Matthew sweeping the floor. When he spotted his niece, he set the broom aside and reached for her. "If Naomi has her boppli before the day's out, we can spread the news tomorrow at church," he said, glancing at Abby.

"That would save a lot of time in the telling," she agreed.

Sarah nuzzled Matthew's clean-shaven cheek, and he patted her back in a fatherly fashion.

Such a shame he's not married and raising his own family, Abby thought. *Naomi told me that Matthew's shy around women, but he doesn't seem so whenever he's with me.*

An idea popped into Abby's head. Why not invite her friend Rachel to come for a visit? Rachel had told her many times that she was looking for the right man. Maybe she and Matthew would hit it off. *That's exactly what I'm going to do. I'll write Rachel a letter and invite her to spend some time with me here.*

∽∽∽

"I can't believe we still haven't had any word on Naomi," Fannie said to Abby as they sat at the kitchen table, cutting lettuce and tomatoes for a tossed salad. This was one thing her mamm could do from a sitting position, and since the swelling in her legs had finally gone down, Abby figured it would be all right.

"I thought from the way Naomi talked, the boppli might be born soon after they got to the hospital," Abby said.

"Maybe she wasn't as close as she thought," Nancy put in from her place at the stove.

Mom frowned, and the wrinkles around her eyes seemed more pronounced. "Sure hope when my time comes it'll go quickly."

"Speaking of your time, what'd the doctor say today? Did they do the ultrasound?" Abby questioned.

Mom nodded. "Jah, but I'd rather wait and tell you the results when Abraham and the rest of the family are here."

"Is there something wrong with the boppli?"

Abby couldn't help but feel some concern.

Mom reached over and patted Abby's hand. "Not to worry, dear one."

Abby set her paring knife aside in order to scratch an irritating itch on her wrist. She didn't know why she felt so nervous. Maybe it was because she didn't like to wait for things, especially something as important as the news of her mother's ultrasound. This had been a day of waiting, and she felt rung out.

"Let's get the rest of our supper made," Mom suggested. "As soon as the men come from the fields, I'll tell you about my appointment."

Abby resumed her salad making, cutting a few more tomatoes and tossing them into the bowl. She was glad Mary Ann had volunteered to watch Sarah and had taken her outside to blow bubbles. As jittery as Abby felt right now, she wouldn't have made the best babysitter. She was about to head to the refrigerator for a bottle of salad dressing, when the back door opened and Matthew, Jake, Samuel, and Abraham entered the room. Matthew had gone to the barn after the two of them arrived home from the store, and from the looks of the dirt on the other three men's clothes, she guessed they must have just come in from the fields.

"Any word on Naomi yet?" Abraham asked as he bent to give Abby's mother a kiss on the cheek.

She shook her head. "No, but I have some news of my own to share."

Abraham's eyebrows shot up. "You'd better not have gone into early labor. The boppli's not due for three months yet."

She clucked her tongue. "No need to worry.

I'm not havin' any contractions."

"That's a relief." He dropped into the chair beside her. "So, tell me what's on your mind."

"Would somebody please call Mary Ann? She took Sarah outside awhile ago, and I'd like her to hear my news, too."

"What about Norman?" Matthew asked. "He's already gone home for the day."

"Guess he'll have to wait till tomorrow to hear whatever Fannie has to say," his daed replied, "because I'm not waitin' any longer."

"I'll go get Mary Ann," Samuel offered. He scampered out the door and returned a few minutes later with Mary Ann and Sarah at his side.

"Samuel says you've called a family meeting," Mary Ann said. "Is somethin' wrong?"

Mom wagged her finger. "Not unless you think two bopplin would be wrong." Tears gathered in the corners of her eyes, and she brushed them away.

A muscle in Abraham's jaw quivered, and he blinked a couple of times. "Two bopplin? What two bopplin—Naomi's and ours?"

Mom placed one hand against her stomach and smiled. "I'm talkin' about the two bopplin I'm carryin' right here."

"What?"

"*Zwilling*—twins!"

"How do ya know?"

"That's wunderbaar!"

Everyone spoke at once, until Abraham held up his hands. "Let my fraa tell us the details of this great news." The adoring look he gave his wife put a lump in Abby's throat. *He must feel truly blessed.*

"As some of you already know, the doctor

saw me last week and ordered today's ultrasound," Mom said. "He'd wanted me to have one done a few months ago, but I kept putting it off."

"Why'd he want the test?" Jake asked as he took a seat at the table.

"Because he'd heard two heartbeats." Mom patted her stomach. "Now we know why I've gotten big so quickly."

Abby had to admit that her mamm's stomach had rounded considerably in the last few months, but she figured it was because she carried a big baby.

"So two babies showed up on the ultrasound? Is that what you're sayin', Fannie?" This question came from Matthew, who stood behind Abby's chair.

Mom nodded and swiped at the tears that had splashed onto her cheeks. "It's taken me some time to accept the idea of bein' a mother again, but this news is almost too much to comprehend."

"Thank the Lord for His goodness," Abraham exclaimed. "We're gonna have zwilling!"

A chorus of cheers went up around the room, and no one seemed to hear the pounding on the back door until Abby excused herself to answer it. Caleb's brother Marvin stepped into the room wearing a huge smile on his face. "It's another girl! Naomi's boppli was born an hour ago, and mother and child are doin' fine."

❦

Linda was pleased that Beth's church was within walking distance, because she wasn't about to ask Jim for a ride. He'd been irritable and impatient with her and Jimmy last night. This morning, when she'd awakened him to say they were leaving for church, he'd nearly snapped her head off. She had tried one more time to get him to go with them, but he'd adamantly refused.

Now, as she and Jimmy walked up the steps to the church, she had second thoughts about her decision. *Maybe I should have only agreed to come to church and not Sunday school. It might have been best to work our way into things.*

"There's Allen!" Jimmy shouted, giving Linda's hand a tug. "See, right over there."

Linda turned and saw Beth, Allen, and Beth's other two boys coming up the sidewalk. A feeling of relief washed over her. She found comfort in seeing some familiar faces.

"I'm glad you could make it," Beth said, giving Linda a hug. "My husband wanted to meet your husband, but he came down with the flu last night and couldn't be here this morning."

Linda swallowed past the lump in her throat. "Jim won't be here either. I'm afraid he's not interested in attending church."

"Maybe we can plan a barbecue sometime and get our men together that way," Beth said as they entered the building.

Linda gave a noncommittal shrug. She knew it wasn't likely that Jim would be willing to get together with her new friend's family. She couldn't get him to do much of anything she wanted these days.

"The boys' Sunday school class is downstairs," Beth said. "Allen knows the way, so he, Brent, and Ricky can take Jimmy there while we go to our class."

Linda halted at the top of the steps, clutching

her son's hand. *Am I really ready for this?*

"They'll be fine," Beth whispered, as though sensing Linda's reservations.

Linda didn't admit it to Beth, but she was more nervous about going to the adult Sunday school class than she was about letting Jimmy attend his class without her. He had done well during Bible school and would be going to first grade in the fall, so she was sure he would be okay.

The boys bounded down the stairs, and Linda followed Beth down the hall. *Maybe I should have dropped Jimmy off at church and gone home to be with Jim this morning. We need some time alone, that's for sure.* She thought about her mother's comment when they'd gone to Boise to visit her family the last time. *"I can tell things are strained between you and Jim. Have you thought about seeing a counselor before things get any worse?"*

Linda had made light of it to her mother that day, but the truth was her marriage was in trouble. Later she'd mentioned counseling to Jim, but he'd blown up and said she could have her head shrunk if she wanted to, but he wouldn't be going.

As Linda and Beth entered a large, cheerfully decorated classroom, she forced her thoughts aside and drew in a deep breath to help steady her nerves.

"This is the Young Marrieds' class," Beth said. "For the last few weeks, we've been studying the book of Ruth."

Linda took a seat at the table next to Beth; then Ray and Christine Bentley, a middle-aged couple who seemed quite pleasant, introduced themselves as the teachers.

For the next hour, Linda sat in rapt attention

as she listened to the biblical account of Ruth and Boaz. She was amazed to learn what a caring man Boaz was and couldn't get over how Ruth had willingly gone with her mother-in-law to a strange country. By the time class was over, Linda felt a deep yearning to return to Sunday school next week and to read her Bible at home, which she had discovered yesterday near the back of their bookcase.

When she and Beth reached the sanctuary, they met Jimmy and Allen inside the door. Jimmy's face was flushed and beaded with perspiration.

"If you're running a fever, son, we'll have to go home," Linda said, reaching out to touch his forehead.

"I ain't sick," he insisted with a shake of his head.

She pulled her hand back, relieved to discover that his sweaty forehead was actually cool.

"I think the boys are just overheated from playing," Beth assured her.

Allen nodded. "We always have playtime after the Bible story and snacks."

"Are you ready for church?" Beth asked, turning to Linda. "Pastor Deming's sermon and the music during morning worship are always so uplifting."

Linda nodded, feeling almost hungry for spiritual things. The notion startled her. *If Jim were a better husband, I might not need anything else. But maybe I'll find what I'm looking for here at this church.*

Chapter 12

Abby rubbed her eyes, trying to relieve the gritty, burning sensation. She had worn herself out trying to run the quilt shop and help Mom as much as she could. Since Naomi had given birth to the baby, whom they'd named Susan, Nancy went over to Caleb and Naomi's place to help out whenever Caleb's mother wasn't available.

Cousin Edna dropped by to help Mom as often as she could, and Mary Ann would be around until school started in a few weeks. Even so, Abby felt compelled to pitch in whenever she could. The doctor had cautioned Mom again to stay off her feet as much as possible. But Abby knew how stubborn her mother could be, and she couldn't help but worry about her and the bopplin she carried. Abby continued to have more of those bad dreams and wasn't sleeping well either, which only added to her exhaustion.

"You look tired," Matthew said, stepping into the quilt shop. "Maybe you should close the place up for the rest of the day and go home so you can get some rest."

Abby shook her head. "We're in the middle of tourist season, and there's much to be done."

He tipped his head, and a lock of dark brown hair fell over one eye. "Know what I think, Abby Miller?"

"What's that?"

"You work too hard, worry too much, and concentrate on everyone else's needs but your own."

Abby made no comment as she reached for a bolt of material on the shelf overhead. Matthew didn't understand how important it was for her to keep Mom's shop running smoothly.

"When was the last time you did something fun—just for you?" he questioned.

She whirled around, nearly dropping the cloth, but Matthew caught it before it hit the floor. "There's no time for fun right now. That will come later, after I'm married."

"You really think so?"

"Of course."

His face contorted. "Right. And split pea soup is little brother Samuel's favorite meal, too."

Choosing to ignore his sarcasm, Abby replied, "Once Lester and I are together again, everything will be back to normal."

Matthew cleared his throat. "Know what else I think?"

She shrugged. Why was Matthew going on and on about this? Was he intentionally trying to get under her skin?

"You've been self-sacrificing for so long, I don't believe you know any other way."

Abby opened her mouth to defend herself again, but Matthew cut her right off.

"I've seen how you rush around at home, always worried about your mamm and doin' things that don't really need to be done." He handed her the fabric. "What about you, Abby? Don't your needs count? Shouldn't you be plannin' your wedding instead of workin' so hard to care for your mamm? There are others who can help out, you know."

Abby stood there, too dumbfounded to say a word. What was wrong with her being self-sacrificing? Didn't the Bible teach that she should love others and be helpful? Besides, she owed it to Mom to be there when she needed her.

The bell above the general store door jangled, and Matthew turned toward the door separating the two places of business. "I'd better see who came in, because Caleb's not here at the moment."

As soon as he left the room, Abby sank into a chair in front of one of the quilting frames, tears clogging her throat. Matthew was right about one thing. She did care more about Mom's needs than her own. It was the only way she could keep her promise to Dad. She dabbed at her eyes with the handkerchief tucked in the band of her apron. *Things will go better once Mom's bopplin are born. And soon after that, I'll be on my way home.*

∞

Fannie bunched a small pillow under her head and stretched out on the sofa. It was only one in the afternoon, and she was already exhausted. Right after lunch, she'd realized that she needed a nap but felt too tired to climb the stairs to her bedroom, so she'd decided to rest here awhile.

Her eyes drifted shut, and she was almost asleep when she heard the back door open and close again. She knew it couldn't be Nancy, since she had gone to Naomi's to help out today. Mary Ann was supposed to be downstairs in the cellar washing clothes, so she figured it might be her sneaky husband, who'd come in from the fields to pay her a surprise visit.

Heavy footsteps sounded in the hall, and she turned her head in that direction. "Abraham?"

"No, Fannie, it's me." Matthew stepped into the room and removed his straw hat.

"What are you doing home in the middle of the day? You're not sick, I hope."

He shook his head. "Norman's back kinked up on him yesterday, and he's at the chiropractor's this afternoon, so Papa asked if I could help. Caleb said he could manage at the store without me this afternoon, so here I am."

Matthew's disgruntled look let Fannie know he would rather be anywhere other than on the farm right now. She thought he had seemed much happier since he'd begun working at the general store.

"Sorry your daed hasn't found anyone else to help in the fields yet," she said. "It seems like you're needed in two places at once."

He nodded and plunked down in the easy chair across from her, apparently in no hurry to get outside.

"I'm not the only one who's tryin' to cover all the bases these days," Matthew said, turning his hat over in his hands.

"Are you thinking of Abby?"

"Jah. I saw her this morning, and she looked exhausted."

"Abby always has been a hard worker." Fannie pulled herself to a sitting position. "Is there something more bothering you, Matthew?"

"I'm concerned about her. A couple of times this week I found her nearly asleep at the quilting frame."

Fannie shook her head as she exhaled deeply. "I

didn't realize she was that tired. Whenever I ask how she's doing, she always says she's right as rain. Seems more interested in how I'm doing these days."

"Have you ever thought that your daughter might be too self-sacrificing?"

Matthew's words jolted Fannie to the core. Too self-sacrificing? Was that possible for a Christian?

"Right before I left the store to come here, Abby mentioned that she's been so busy she hasn't written to her future husband for a couple of weeks."

Fannie fiddled with the piping along the edge of the sofa, wondering why Matthew seemed so concerned about Abby's welfare. *He is her stepbrother,* she reminded herself. *Guess that gives him the right to speak on her behalf.*

"I'll have a talk with my daughter," Fannie promised. "If she's so overworked that there's no time for letter writing, then I'd best see if I can find someone else to help at the quilt shop or here at home."

Matthew stood. "I hope you don't think I'm buttin' into business that ain't mine, but I'm worried about Abby."

"I'm glad you told me, because she surely wouldn't have mentioned it."

"Okay then. Guess I'd best be gettin' out to the fields. See you at suppertime, Fannie."

She smiled and lifted her hand. "Have a good day."

∞

Linda relaxed against the seat in the passenger's side of Beth's compact car. The more time she spent with her new friend, the more at ease she felt. And the more times she and Jimmy attended church, the more she desired for Jim to go.

Today she and Beth were on their way to visit the newly remodeled fitness center on the other side of town. When she'd mentioned the place to Jim this morning, he'd said that his shop had done the painting on the building and thought it was a good idea for Linda to go there because she needed some exercise. *Maybe if I firm up my flabby muscles, Jim will be interested in me again.*

"There was a write-up about the fitness center in last night's paper," Beth said, pulling Linda's thoughts aside. "They have new owners now and are offering child care for those who bring their children along when they come to exercise."

Linda glanced over her shoulder at Jimmy in the backseat. "I'm not sure I want to leave my son with strangers."

"You could have left him at my mother's, along with my three boys."

"I—I feel better having him with me." Even though Linda had been trying not to be over-protective, she still wasn't comfortable with the idea of leaving Jimmy with people she didn't know.

Beth pulled into the parking lot and had barely turned off the engine when Jimmy unbuckled his seatbelt and clambered out of the backseat.

"Wait for me," Linda called. "I don't want you running across the parking lot. You might get hit by a car."

Jimmy halted, and Linda grabbed his hand. The three of them headed for the main entrance, and once inside, they located the reception center. Beth stepped confidently up to the desk, but before she could ask any questions, the young auburn-haired woman behind the desk spoke up. "Hi, my name's Ginny Nelson. Welcome to Puyallup's newly remodeled fitness center. Here's some information about our facilities." She grinned and handed Beth a brochure. "Everything's free today, and there's fresh carrot and orange juice at the snack bar. If you have any questions, I'd be happy to answer them."

Linda was tempted to mention that it was her husband who'd done the painting on the building, but she decided to let Beth do the talking.

"I understand you have child care here," Beth said. "It would be easier for my friend to try out some of your equipment if her boy had a safe place to play."

"The children's playroom is just down the hall." Ginny leaned forward, her long hair fanning her face. "Cute boy. How old is he?"

"My son is six," Linda replied.

Ginny squinted her jade green eyes and stared at Jimmy.

"Is—is there something wrong?" A sense of uneasiness crept up Linda's spine, even though she knew it was silly of her to feel so paranoid.

Ginny shook her head. "Nothing's wrong. It's just that—well, I know this will probably sound goofy, but your boy is the spitting image of Samuel Fisher, one of the brothers of an Amish friend of mine back in Pennsylvania. Of course, I haven't seen him for several years now, and he would be much older than this little boy. Your boy is more the age of Naomi's other brother, the baby who was. . ." Her voice trailed and her eyes grew round with wonder. "I mean, he looks the way I would imagine little Zach would look if I saw him now—same hair color and eyes. Even his smile reminds me of the Fisher boys."

Her face flushed. "Oh, never mind me. I am known as a motormouth around here. Talking is by far my favorite exercise." She fidgeted with the phone cord on the reception desk. "Isn't it funny how everybody reminds you of somebody else you know?"

"I guess we all have a double somewhere in the world." Linda offered a weak smile, but she felt uneasy in this gal's presence.

"Yes, I know what you mean. People always mistake me for a Karen or a Gayle," Beth said, nudging Linda's arm.

Linda pointed to the brochure Beth had been given. "Does this include a map of the center?" Linda asked. The fact that the young woman continued to stare at Jimmy made her feel more apprehensive, and she wanted to get away.

"Yeah, sure." Ginny smiled and nodded at Linda.

Beth opened her brochure and studied it. "Look, the map shows the children's center is right here." She pointed to a spot on the paper, but it barely registered with Linda. She grabbed Jimmy's hand and dashed down the hall.

"What's the hurry?" Beth asked when she caught up to Linda and Jimmy.

"I just want to look at the facilities and go home."

"I thought we were going to try out some of the equipment. We can drop Jimmy off, change into our exercise clothes, and see if we can work up a sweat."

Linda shook her head. "I don't feel like exercising. If you want to work up a sweat, go ahead. Jimmy and I can watch from the sidelines."

"You seemed enthused about checking out the fitness center. What's happened to change your mind?"

"I'm just not comfortable leaving Jimmy with strangers," Linda mumbled.

"Is it what that young woman at the reception desk said?"

Linda nodded. "She showed too much interest in Jimmy, and comparing him to an Amish child was so ridiculous."

"I'm sure she was just surprised that he reminded her of someone she used to know."

"But she kept staring at him, and it made me nervous." Linda shuddered. "Just the other day a child was kidnapped in the parking lot at the Tacoma Mall. There are too many nutty people in this world, and parents need to protect their kids."

"I understand. I'm concerned for my boys' welfare, too, but—"

"But you're not unreasonably mistrusting like me? Is that what you're saying?"

Beth blanched as though Linda had thrown cold water in her face. Linda knew her overprotective ways had driven a wedge between her and Jim, and she didn't want anything to spoil her new friendship. She had to set her fears aside and try to relax. The woman at the front desk was probably trying to be friendly so people would sign up for a membership.

"I'm sorry for acting so ridiculous," Linda apologized. "I'll put Jimmy in the children's room, and we can exercise awhile."

"I think it will be fun." Beth offered Linda a reassuring smile. "And I'm sure your little guy will be just fine."

Chapter 13

Abby stood in the middle of her mother's quilt shop, studying it from all angles. Thanks to several Amish and Mennonite ladies in their community, she had a lot more quilts to sell. That was good, since so many tourists flocked to Lancaster County and visited Fannie's Quilt Shop in Paradise. There was only one problem. Abby had run out of room to display all the quilts. "I would hate to start turning quilters away," she mumbled.

"Why would you have to do that?"

Abby spun around at the sound of Matthew's deep, yet mellow voice. "I have no more space to display quilts," she said, motioning to the crowded shelves along the walls and several racks in the middle of the room.

He stepped up beside her. "How did you display things at your shop in Berlin?"

"I had several wooden quilt racks scattered around, and some were draped across a bed we had set up in the middle of the room." Abby sighed. "Of course my shop there is much larger than this one."

"Seems to me what you need are some large hangers you could put on that bare wall with quilts draped over them." Matthew nodded toward the wall facing the adjoining general store.

"The only trouble with that is I have no such hangers."

"I saw some in a quilt shop over in Strasburg a few weeks ago. I like to fiddle with wood when I have the time, and I'm thinkin' I might be able to make you some hangers."

"That would be wunderbaar," she said with a burst of enthusiasm. "I'll pay you for them of course."

He grinned at her, and the dimple in his chin became more pronounced. "How about in exchange for me making the quilt hangers, you take a day off and do something for yourself?"

She frowned. "I can't do that. Mom needs my help here and at home."

"But she's gonna need you a lot more once the twins are born." Matthew leaned on the table closest to him and stared at her. "If you know you'll be workin' harder in a few months, that's all the more reason you should take time to rest or do something fun now."

Abby drew in a deep breath. Matthew was right, as usual, although she hated to admit it. "Okay, I'll take a longer lunch break this afternoon and try to get caught up on my letter writing."

He chuckled while shaking his head. "Abby Miller, you're too much."

She plucked a bolt of material off the table. "I'd best get back to work now, and if I'm not mistaken, you've got some customers in the store needing help, too."

Matthew groaned, but there was a mischievous twinkle in his eyes. "Work, work, work. That's all you ever think about."

She poked him playfully on the arm. "See

you later, big brother."

"Yep." He turned and sauntered out of the room.

⌒

Linda stood at the kitchen window, watching her son play in the backyard. She had given Jimmy a jar of bubbles after they finished eating breakfast, and for the last half hour he'd been keeping himself well entertained.

He's such a sweet, even-tempered boy, she mused. The woman in charge of child care at the fitness center had told Linda that Jimmy was an absolute pleasure to be around. He'd played well with the other children and hadn't given the woman a bit of trouble.

Linda smiled and waved as Jimmy pranced across the lawn in front of the window, wielding his wand and leaving a trail of rainbow-colored bubbles floating behind.

My fears about leaving him with strangers while Beth and I exercised were unfounded, and I'm sure the young woman at the front desk wasn't a threat either.

"What are you staring at?"

Linda whirled around. "Jim! I thought you'd left for work already."

"I did, but I forgot something and had to come back for it."

"What'd you forget?"

"The little book I write my paint jobs in. Can't get any work done without that." Jim stepped up to the window. "I see our boy's getting his exercise for the day."

She nodded. "I got some yesterday, too."

"Oh? What'd you do, jog to the park and back?"

"Beth and I went to that newly remodeled

fitness center you painted. They had an open house and offered free workouts."

Jim grabbed a glass from the cupboard and turned on the faucet at the sink. "You planning to go back?"

"Beth said she'd like to, but the membership fee is pretty expensive. I'm not sure she can afford it."

"Well, we can, so if you want to join, you have my blessings."

Linda shrugged. "I don't know. I'm not sure I'd want to go alone."

He gulped down the water and set the glass in the sink. "Don't get any dumb ideas about me going with you. I don't have the time."

She clenched her teeth. "I know that, Jim. You never have time for anything I want to do."

"That's not true. I took you to the grocery store last night, didn't I?"

"That was for necessities, not for the fun of doing something together."

"You think working out on some stupid rowing machine and getting all sweaty would be fun?"

"It could be, if we did it together."

"And what would we do with Jimmy if we ran off to the health club to get healthy and fit?" he asked in a sarcastic tone. "We have no babysitter, as you may recall, because you don't like to leave Jimmy with strangers."

Linda moved away from the window and dropped into a chair at the table. "Beth was wondering if we could get together with her family for a barbecue sometime soon," she said, hoping the change of subject might relieve some of the tension between them.

"I don't have time to socialize right now. Need to get my outside painting jobs done while we've still got good weather."

"But, I thought—"

"I said no!" Jim stomped across the room and jerked open the refrigerator. "Have we got any beer? I told you to pick up a case last night."

She shook her head. "Sorry, I forgot." *I wish you wouldn't drink, Jim. It only fuels your agitation.*

He slammed the refrigerator door, causing the vase on top to tumble to the floor. It was plastic and didn't shatter, but Linda felt irritated that her husband could lose his temper so easily. Jim hadn't always been this testy, but in the last few years, he often exploded over the littlest thing.

"You could have gone into the store with me instead of waiting in the car," she mumbled.

"Yeah, right, and haul Jimmy in there so he could whine and beg for everything that caught his eye?"

"Jimmy doesn't do that. He's very well behaved. In fact, the lady who watched him at the fitness center commented on what a nice boy he is."

Jim's features softened some as he bent to pick up the vase. "Jimmy's a good kid."

"And cute, too," she added with a smile. "The young woman at the front desk said Jimmy reminded her of a little Amish boy she used to know."

"What?"

"She said Jimmy had the same color hair and eyes as the little boy."

"What else did the woman say?"

"That's about all." Linda's forehead wrinkled.

"I'll have to admit, it did make me kind of nervous the way she kept staring at Jimmy."

Jim's hand shook, and the vase crashed to the floor again.

"Jim, what's wrong? You're trembling like we've just had an earthquake."

"Nothing's wrong. I—I'm tired and need to get to work." He bent to pick up the vase for the second time and placed it back on the refrigerator.

"Are you sure you're okay?"

"I'm fine!"

Her spine went rigid, and she recoiled.

"I think it'd be best if you don't sign up at the fitness center right now."

Jim's wrinkled forehead and eyebrows drawn together let Linda know that he was uptight, but she didn't understand why. "A few minutes ago you said we could afford for me to go there."

"I've changed my mind!"

"You don't have to get so angry."

"I'm not angry." Jim glanced at his watch. "But I am late, so this discussion is over." He turned and rushed out the door.

Linda swallowed around the lump in her throat. Would things ever be right between her and Jim again? Maybe a few minutes in the fresh air with Jimmy would help calm her.

❦

Naomi sat in the rocking chair holding baby Susan. Sarah knelt on the living room floor, playing with the wooden blocks her uncle Matthew had made for her second birthday. A knock sounded at the front door, and rather than disturb the baby, Naomi called, "Come in."

A few seconds later, Abby stepped into the room, carrying a large paper sack.

"It's nice to see you," Naomi said with a smile.

"I thought I'd drop by on my way home from work and see how everyone's doing."

"We're doin' well." Naomi motioned to the sofa. "Have a seat. You look done in."

Abby flopped down and leaned against the throw pillows with a yawn. "It's been a busy day, and I didn't sleep well last night."

"Sorry to hear that. Maybe you should see about hiring a helper at the quilt shop."

"I've thought about it, but sooner or later Mom will take the place back over, and I'm sure I can keep things running smoothly until that time."

Naomi lifted the baby onto her shoulder and patted her gently on the back. "You really think Fannie will be up to running the quilt shop after she gives birth to twins?"

Abby shrugged. "She says she will."

"I thought I'd be going back to help at the store soon after Susan was born, but I've got my hands full right here. If I tried to take my two little ones to work with me every day, I doubt I'd get much done." Naomi sighed. "Caleb would probably still need to hire someone, and the girls and I would just be in the way."

Abby lifted her brows. "Are you saying you're not going back to work at all?"

"I will when the boppli is a little older, but for now Caleb and I have decided that my place is at home."

"Guess that makes sense." Abby reached her hand out to Sarah. "What have you got there, *hatzli*?"

The little sweetheart held up two wooden blocks and grinned. *"Ich schpiele gern."*

"I know you like to play, Sarah." Abby smiled at Naomi. "She's learning to speak so clearly already."

Naomi chuckled. "Jah. Caleb thinks she gets her smarts from him. I don't have the heart to tell him that I started talking clearly before I was two. At least that's what Papa says."

Abby reached into the paper sack she'd brought along. "I made something for the boppli." She removed the baby quilt and handed it to Naomi.

"Oh, it's beautiful, Abby. Danki."

"You're welcome."

Naomi fingered the pink-and-white patchwork quilt done in the Lancaster Rose pattern. Then she draped it across her knees and placed her infant daughter in the center of it.

"I hope you like it."

"It's real nice, Abby, and it will surely be put to good use." Naomi brushed at the tears splattering her cheeks.

"I'm sorry if I made you cry," Abby apologized.

Naomi shook her head. "I love the quilt, and I know Susan will, too, when she's older. Guess I'm just goin' through a bit of postpartum depression right now, and everything makes me feel weepy."

Abby offered Naomi a look of sympathy. "Is there anything I can do to help?"

"Just stop by once in a while for a visit when you have the time."

"I always enjoy being with you, and I'll come

over as often as I can."

Naomi reached for a tissue from the box on the table beside her chair. "I don't know what we'd all do without you, Abby."

Chapter 14

"Oh Matthew, these are perfect," Abby exclaimed.

Matthew beamed as he placed several wooden hangers on the table in Fannie's quilt shop. "Sorry it's taken me so long to get 'em done."

She waved her hand. "It's only been a few weeks since you agreed to make them for me, and I know you've been busy assisting Caleb in the store, not to mention helping out on the farm whenever you can."

"That's true. I'll be glad when things slow down a bit."

"I doubt if they will ever slow down once Mom has the bopplin."

Matthew chuckled. "Things will probably never be the same around our place after those little ones enter the world." His brown eyes seemed darker than usual, and a muscle on the side of his cheek quivered slightly. "I remember when Zach was born and everything seemed to be centered on him. He was such a cute little fellow. Even after all this time, I still find myself missin' him."

Abby could only imagine how painful it must have been for the Fishers to lose their mamm in a terrible accident, and then have their boppli kidnapped just a year later. It had been hard enough

WANDA &. BRUNSTETTER

for her and Mom to deal with things after Dad's heart attack. She winced as a stab of regret sliced through her. "The trials in life are never easy, but God gives us the strength to bear them."

He nodded. "Jah, and as time goes on, the pain lessens."

Feeling the need to change the subject, Abby motioned to the wall across from them. "Would you have time to put some quilts on the hangers you made and get them set in place?"

Matthew's eyes brightened. "For you, sister Abby, I'll make the time."

She smiled. It was nice to have another brother. Especially one who was so willing to help whenever it was needed.

Abby thought about her brother, Harold, and wondered how he and Lena were doing. It had been several weeks since she'd sent them a letter, and nearly that long since she had written to Lester. She'd received a couple of lectures from Mom about working too hard and was asked when the last time was she'd written to her intended. Her mamm had even suggested they might need to hire someone else to help at the quilt shop, but Abby had assured her that she was doing just fine.

"I'm going to try and get a couple of letters written, since there are no customers at the moment. So let me know if you need anything," she called to Matthew.

"Sure will."

Matthew headed to the storage closet to get a ladder, and Abby scurried over to her desk. She found Lester's most recent letter in the drawer and decided to read it again, so she could answer any questions he might have.

> *Dear Abby,*
>
> *The news of your mother carrying twins was sure a surprise. Mom's been talking about all the things she wants to make in duplicate. Guess it won't be long until those bopplin are born.*
>
> *How are things at the quilt shop? Did Matthew ever make the hangers you mentioned in your last letter? If they work out well, maybe he could make some for your quilt shop here.*
>
> *Speaking of your shop, Mom said to tell you that she and my aunt Clara are managing fine. There are still lots of tourists coming in every day, and the quilting ladies have continued to meet at the store once a week.*
>
> *Please write soon. I'm looking forward to hearing from you.*
>
> > *Always yours,*
> > *Lester*

Abby reached for her pen. Lester had probably been watching the mail every day, hoping for a letter. He might think she'd forgotten him by now or didn't care. She'd heard from her friend Rachel last week, too, and that letter would also need to be answered. Rachel had declined Abby's invitation to visit Lancaster County, saying she hadn't been working at the restaurant in Berlin long enough to have vacation time.

If it's meant for Rachel and Matthew to meet, then

WANDA E. BRUNSTETTER

God will work things out, Abby mused. *I've done the inviting. Now the rest is in His hands.*

She lifted her pen to begin Lester's letter, but had only written a few words when Jake rushed into the quilt shop, all red-faced and sweaty. "Fannie's gone into labor! Papa got one of our English neighbors to drive 'em to the hospital in Lancaster, and they left Nancy in charge of things at home."

Abby just sat there, letting Jake's words sink in. *Mom has gone into labor. They are on their way to the hospital. Nancy is at home, overseeing the two younger ones.*

She glanced at the calendar on her desk. Mom wasn't due for another three weeks. The doctor had said that at thirty-seven weeks the babies would be fully developed. Everything should be okay.

Matthew scrambled down the ladder and rushed to Abby's side. "Want me to run over to the gift shop and see if someone can give you a lift to the hospital?"

"What about you? Don't you want to go?"

"I'd like to, but it wouldn't be fair to leave Caleb alone to run the general store and the quilt shop."

"Maybe I can put the CLOSED sign on the quilt shop door, and then he'd only have one store to watch."

"Say, why not let me stay here and help out?" Jake suggested. "We're done in the fields for the day now that Papa's taken off."

Matthew ran a hand over his clean-shaven face. "You wouldn't mind?"

"Not at all."

"All right then." Matthew reached for Abby's hand. "Let's go find us a ride!"

Abby paced the length of the waiting room, anxious to know how things were going in the delivery room. Mom had been taken in shortly before Abby and Matthew arrived at the hospital, and they hadn't heard anything since.

"You're gonna wear a hole in the carpet if you don't sit down," Matthew said.

She turned to face him. "I'm feeling kind of fidgety."

He patted the chair beside him. "You've got every right to be, but you really should try to calm yourself."

With a sigh of resignation, Abby sank into a chair and picked up a magazine, although she didn't know why. All she could think about was Mom. Was she doing okay? Would the babies be born healthy? Would they weigh enough so they could go home when their mamm did? And what were the bopplin—boys or girls? They could have found out the sex of the babies when Mom had the ultrasound done, but she'd been adamant about not wanting to know until the babies were born.

"Everything will be fine—you'll see," Matthew said in a reassuring tone.

Abby smiled, despite the doubts tumbling around in her head. "I hope so."

"God's in control."

"I know."

"And your mamm is in good hands."

Abby set the magazine aside. "You're a special friend, Matthew, and I'm glad you were able to come to the hospital with me."

"That's what a big brother should do," he said with a wink.

When a middle-aged nurse entered the room, Abby jumped to her feet. "Have you any news to give us on Fannie Fisher?"

The nurse nodded. "She just gave birth to a healthy set of twin boys. One weighs six pounds, and the other is six pounds two ounces."

"Two *buwe*?" Abby's heart swelled with joy.

"Wow! Papa and Fannie are doubly blessed," Matthew said. "God took one son and gave my daed two."

Abby wondered if Abraham would see it that way. Had God taken Zach from the Fishers? It seemed more like the sinful nature of the man who had kidnapped him than anything else.

"When can we see my mom and the twins?" Abby asked the nurse.

"As soon as your mother is back in her room and the babies have been cleaned up."

"Are they identical?" Abby questioned.

"It would seem so, but we still have some tests to do."

"I need to notify Harold and Lena right away." Abby started for the door but turned back around. "I'm going down the hall to phone Lester's mom at the quilt shop in Berlin and ask her to get word to Harold and Lena—and of course Lester, too." She grinned at Matthew. "What a joyous day!"

Chapter 15

Naomi halted inside the living room of her father and Fannie's house, awed by the sight that greeted her. She and Caleb had brought the kinner over to visit their twin uncles, who had just come home from the hospital. But now she wondered if they should have waited awhile. Papa and Fannie sat on the sofa together, each holding a baby. Fannie looked tired but happy as she rubbed her chin slowly against one twin's downy dark hair. Papa looked like a kinner with a new toy, rocking the other baby in his arms and crooning softly. It was a blissful scene. One Naomi felt deserved no intrusion.

"Bopplin! Bopplin!" Sarah hollered as she bounded across the room.

Papa lifted the baby to his chest. "Whoa, now! Don't go climbin' up here, little girl."

Caleb, who held baby Susan, reached down with his free hand and grabbed Sarah's arm. "Slow down. You'll get your chance to see the bopplin soon enough."

"Come, let her sit beside me." Fannie patted the cushion next to her.

Naomi joined Sarah on one end of the couch and leaned over to get a better look at the babies. "They're beautiful, and they look exactly alike.

How will you ever tell them apart?"

"They've still got their hospital bracelets on, so that's helping for now," Fannie replied. "We'll figure something else out soon enough, I expect."

"What have you named them?" Caleb asked, taking a seat in the rocking chair across the room and placing baby Susan across his knees.

"This one is Titus," Fannie said, kissing the wee one on top of his head.

"And this here's Timothy." Papa held the baby up for everyone to see. "Did ya ever see any bopplin as cute as these two?"

Caleb cleared his throat. "Jah. Our Susan. She's wunderbaar!"

"Of course she is," Fannie was quick to say. "All babies are special, and ours don't hold no title to bein' cute."

"Sure they do," Papa said with a smirk. He cradled little Timothy in his arms and glanced over at his wife. "Fannie's made me so happy, and our twin buwe are the best."

"Es bescht," Sarah said with a giggle.

"Jah," Papa agreed. "The boys are the best." He stared at Timothy with such a doting expression it made Naomi wonder about a few things. She was pretty sure her daed was only having fun with Sarah, but she couldn't help but feel a bit put out because he showed so little interest in either one of her girls. Not only that, but Papa seemed more enthralled with his twin boys than he ever had with Zach. Maybe it was just the newness of things. A few weeks from now everything would most likely be back to normal, with Papa out in the fields again and Fannie shouldering most of the responsibility of raising their sons.

"Where's the rest of the family?" Caleb asked. "I figured we'd find everyone crowded around the twins."

"Abby's out in the kitchen fixing supper," Fannie said. "Mary Ann and Nancy are helping her."

"Shortly after we got home, I sent Matthew out to the fields to check on Jake, Norman, and Samuel," Papa spoke up. "They've been handling things on their own for the last couple of days, what with me traipsin' back and forth to the hospital."

"Are you managing okay at the store on your own?" Fannie asked, giving Caleb a look of concern.

He nodded. "Matthew's still comin' in, and he's agreed to take care of things in the quilt shop so Abby can stay here to help you."

Fannie sighed. "There's so much to be done, what with me not able to do a lot yet. I wouldn't know what to do without Abby's help, because caring for two bopplin means we'll need every available pair of hands."

"I understand," Naomi said. "I've got my hands full from sunup to sunset trying to keep Sarah out of mischief while I care for little Susan."

"We're thankful for the days when Nancy can help us," Caleb interjected, "but if she's needed here, we can probably call on my mamm."

"I think Abby's got things under control," Papa said. "She's real organized and seems willing to do whatever needs done."

A stab of remorse shot through Naomi. She felt as if Papa's remark had been directed at her. Many times after Mama's death, when Naomi had taken over household chores and helped at the store, Papa had accused her of not doing things right.

I'm just overly sensitive right now, she reminded herself. *Have been ever since Susan was born. I need to keep my eyes on God and quit worrying about what others say and do.*

"Abby's a good daughter," Fannie put in. "She's always had a servant's heart, and she's puttin' her wedding on hold because of me."

"What?" Naomi's eyebrows lifted. "You mean she's not getting married in November?"

"Well, she says—"

"Did I hear someone mention my name?" Abby asked, stepping into the room.

≈

All eyes seemed to be focused on Abby as she took a seat on the arm of the sofa, close to Naomi. "We're having an early supper tonight," she said. "Since Mom just got home from the hospital, I'm sure she's tired and would like to go upstairs as soon as we're done eating." Abby touched Naomi's arm. "You're welcome to stay and eat with us."

"Oh no, we wouldn't think of imposing. We just wanted to drop by and meet the twins, but we'll be on our way in a few minutes," Naomi replied.

"That's right," Caleb agreed. "As soon as I got home from the store, I loaded my brood in the buggy and headed straight here. We were all anxious to see the little miracle bopplin."

Fannie nodded. "That's just what they are, too. After going without more children for so many years, I never expected to give birth at my age, let alone to identical twin boys."

"What were you talking about when I came into the room?" Abby asked.

"I was telling everyone how you're planning to stay awhile longer, and that you've decided to postpone your wedding a few more months," her mother replied.

Abby nodded. "There's no way I could return to Ohio knowing my mamm and little brothers need me. I wrote Lester a letter yesterday, explaining things and saying we can be married sometime in January." She drew in a deep breath and sighed. "I miss Lester of course, but it's nice to be with all of you during this exciting time of so many bopplin being born."

"Isn't your brother's wife due to have a baby soon?" Abraham asked.

"Lena's due date is shortly after Mom's was supposed to be, so she's got another three or four weeks to go."

Mom sighed and reached up to straighten her *kapp*, which was slightly askew. "I wish there was some way I could be there for Lena, but I'll have my hands full right here for some time, I'm afraid."

"Which is exactly why I'm going to stick around until you're feeling stronger and can manage on your own," Abby asserted.

"Such a fine daughter I raised," Mom said with a smile. "I only hope I do half as well with these two boys."

"You're already a good mamm, and you'll do fine by our little fellows." Abraham gave her knee a pat. "The best thing that ever happened to this family was when you came along."

Mom blushed and swatted at his hand. "Oh, go on with ya now. I'm no saint, so don't make me out to be one."

Abraham chortled. "You're the next thing to it, Fannie Mae."

Abby glanced at Naomi and noticed her furrowed brows. Was she hurt by her daed's comments, maybe thinking of her own mamm and wondering if he loved his second wife better than the first?

I must have a talk with Naomi soon, Abby decided. *It wouldn't be good for hard feelings to tear this family apart now that things have been going so well.*

❧

When Abby awoke on Sunday morning, her bed sheets were soaked with perspiration and so was she. She'd had that terrible dream about a fire again, and it had left her feeling physically and emotionally drained. What could it mean, and why had she had it so many times over the past several months?

Her hands trembled as she fumbled to undo the buttons on her nightgown. Would it help to tell someone about the dream? Maybe Mom could soothe her fears, the way she had when Abby was a little girl and had been frightened about something. *Jah, as soon as I get dressed I'll have a talk with Mom.*

A short time later, Abby found her mother in front of the kitchen sink, filling the teakettle with water. "You look tired, daughter. Didn't ya sleep well?"

Abby yawned, stretched, and lifted her choring apron from a wall peg. "I had a nightmare and didn't feel the least bit rested when I woke up."

"I'm sorry to hear that. Maybe it was somethin'

you ate last night that caused the bad dream."

Abby shook her head. "I've been plagued by this same night terror many times, and I don't understand it, Mom."

"How come you've never mentioned it before?"

"I didn't want to bother you, and I figured it would go away."

Her mother pulled out a chair at the table and motioned for Abby to do the same. "Would you like to tell me about it?"

Abby nodded and sank into the chair beside Mom. "In the dream I'm asleep in my bed, but something wakes me up. When I open my eyes, there's smoke and flames, and I can't breathe." She took a quick breath. "I hear a kitten's cry, and I call for someone to help me save it, but nobody ever responds."

Mom's eyebrows furrowed. "Does the same thing happen each time in your dream?"

"Jah, only sometimes I'm covering my head with the quilt on my bed."

"*Hmm. . .*"

"I've read in *The Budget* some articles about fires, and a few months back Lester and I witnessed a fire at the cheese place near my quilt shop." Abby pursed her lips. "Do you think the dream could have been a foreshadowing of what was to come? And if so, then why am I still having the horrible nightmare?"

Mom placed her hand on Abby's arm and gave it a gentle squeeze. "Dreams are often a combination of things we've heard or something we may have read about, but I think it's rare that they'd be a warning of what was going to happen in the future."

Abby groaned. "I wish there were something I could do to keep from having that dream. It's so frightening, and I wake up feeling as if something terrible is about to happen."

"I suggest that you pray about it, Abby." Mom gave her a hug. "Ask God to take away the dream and the fear you feel whenever it happens." She pushed back her chair. "And I'll be praying, too, dear one."

∞

Sitting beside Beth on a pew that was three rows from the back of the sanctuary, Linda marveled at how relaxed she felt on this Sunday morning. Her son and Beth's three boys were in junior church, and she knew Jimmy was happy and comfortable, too.

"My sermon today is entitled 'Life's Disappointments,'" Rev. Deming began as he stepped up to the pulpit. "We all encounter disappointments in life, such as marital discord, trouble with our children, parents, coworkers, neighbors, or friends. People are human, and everyone has certain frailties. People often let us down—even those we are closest to."

Linda thought about Jim and how he seemed to take pleasure in disappointing her. Jimmy wasn't a disappointment though. Adopting him was the best thing they had ever done. She glanced over at Beth and her husband, Eric. *They seem to be so happy. If Jim would just agree to get counseling, we might discover the kind of happiness they obviously share.*

"I'm reading from the book of Psalms, chapter 147, verse 3, New International Version," the reverend continued. " 'He heals the brokenhearted and binds up their wounds.' " He looked out at the congregation. "Are you brokenhearted? Do you have wounds that won't heal? Cast your cares on Jesus and give your troubles to Him."

Tears clouded Linda's vision, and she blinked several times, hoping to ward them off. But it was no use. She felt moisture on her cheeks and reached into her purse for a tissue to wipe the tears away.

Beth's hand closed around Linda's. "Are you okay?"

Linda could only nod in reply. She knew if she uttered one word it would come out in a strangled sob.

As Rev. Deming continued his sermon, Linda felt that every word, every verse of scripture was meant for her. For the first time in her life, she realized how much she really needed God.

"Some of you have had a personal experience with Christ," the pastor said. "For you, it's as simple as recommitting your life to the Lord and letting Him take control of your circumstances." He paused and leaned slightly forward.

Linda's body went rigid, and her stomach churned. *Is he looking at me? Does he know my needs, my pain?*

"Some of you may never have made a commitment to Christ. You may be wondering what it takes to become a believer." Rev. Deming turned in his Bible to another passage. "Romans 3:23 says, 'For all have sinned and fall short of the glory of God.' "

Linda squeezed her eyes shut. She had never consciously admitted it, but she knew she was a sinner. She'd been devious in her relationship with Jim, often scheming to get her way. She had argued, pouted, and martyred herself in the hope of making him give in to her demands. Her thoughts were often negative, and she'd spent hours pondering ways to get even. Sometimes when she and Jim argued, she shouted and called him names.

"Christ died on the cross for you and for me. His shed blood is the atonement for our sins, and the only way we can come to the Father is through His Son, Jesus." The pastor stepped down from the pulpit and stood behind the wooden altar in front of the communion table. "As our organist plays 'Just as I Am,' I would like to invite anyone who wants to be free of their burdens and find forgiveness for their sins to kneel at the altar."

The music began, and the congregation sang softly, "'Just as I am, without one plea, but that Thy blood was shed for me, and that Thou bidd'st me come to Thee, O Lamb of God, I come! I come!'"

"All you need to do is step out of your pew and walk down the aisle," Rev. Deming said in a soft, pleading voice. "Jesus is waiting for you."

Linda heard Beth's harmonious voice beside her, singing, "'Just as I am, and waiting not, to rid my soul of one dark blot, to Thee whose blood can cleanse each spot, O Lamb of God, I come! I come!'"

The words on the hymnal blurred, and Linda's hands shook so badly she was afraid she might drop the book. She couldn't sing. Couldn't think. Couldn't breathe. Her soul ached to kneel at the altar and ask God to forgive her sins. She wanted desperately to let Jesus take control of her life. But could she go forward in front of all these people? What would they think of her? Would they look down their noses or cast judgment?

"Just as I am," the song continued, "tho' tossed about, with many a conflict, many a doubt, fightings and fears within, without, O Lamb of God, I come! I come!"

"Come to Me, Linda. Come to Me just as you are." The voice in Linda's head gave her the confidence she needed. On shaky legs she made her way slowly down the aisle. She'd been living in fear for too long. Her life was full of conflict and doubts. It was time to find rest for her weary soul. It was time to meet Jesus.

Chapter 16

Linda hummed as she stirred a kettle of homemade chicken gravy. The meal she prepared would be a surprise for Jim. She and Jimmy had been home from church about an hour, and Jim was still lounging in bed. She hoped the tantalizing aroma of fried chicken and biscuits would rouse him. She'd thought about sending Jimmy up to get his father but didn't want to chance him snapping at the boy. Besides, Jimmy was playing happily in the backyard, and there was no point in disturbing him.

Linda was anxious to share her altar experience with Jim. Since she had confessed her sins and accepted Christ as her Savior, she felt like a new person.

If only Jim would find the Lord, I'm sure we could get our marriage back on track. Maybe I should speak to Rev. Deming about counseling with us. If we started going to church as a family, I know we'd be happier.

Jim sauntered into the room, halting Linda's thoughts. "What's cookin'? I could smell something all the way upstairs."

She turned from the stove and offered him a smile. "I've made fried chicken, buttermilk biscuits, mashed potatoes, and your favorite gravy."

"What's the occasion? Most Sundays you usually fix something simple and quick."

Linda turned down the stove burner and moved to his side. "I'm celebrating, Jim, and I wanted to fix your favorite meal in honor of the new me."

Jim looked her up and down. "Same hairstyle. Same amount of makeup." He squinted. "Is that a new outfit you're wearing?"

She laughed and smoothed the skirt of her knee-length navy blue dress. "No, it's not new, but I am."

"I hate it when you talk in circles." He pushed past her and headed for the refrigerator. "Is there any beer left?"

Linda slumped and turned back to the stove. Jim didn't even want to know how or why she had changed. She could hear him rummaging around in the refrigerator, and she fought the urge to remind him that he sometimes drank too much and certainly shouldn't be drinking so early in the day.

The refrigerator door slammed shut. "There's no beer," he grumbled. "Guess I'll have to run to the store for more."

She whirled around. "Now?"

Jim dragged his fingers through the back of his thick, dark hair. Hair that she used to enjoy running her own fingers through. "Any objections?" he snarled.

Linda knew they would only argue if she mentioned how uneasy she felt whenever he drank. "Could you wait until after dinner to go to the store?"

He shrugged. "Maybe. How soon will it be ready?"

"Ten minutes."

"Yeah, okay. I'll hang around till after we eat." Jim gave her an odd look. "Say, there *is* something different about you today. Are you sure you didn't change your makeup or buy a new dress?"

She moved to his side and touched his arm, glad when he didn't recoil. "When I said I was new, I meant I've found Christ."

Jim's eyebrows lifted, and his mouth turned up at the corners. "I didn't realize He was missing."

Linda stiffened and fought the urge to say something catty in return. "No, Jim, Christ isn't missing. He's very much alive—right here." She placed her hand against her chest.

He shook his head. "Have you lost it, or what?"

"No, I've found it. I've found the Lord Jesus as my personal Savior."

"What's He saving you from? I didn't know you were lost, Linda."

"I knelt at the altar this morning and asked Jesus to forgive my sins."

He stared at her, and his expression was stony. "Your sins, huh?"

"That's right."

"Have you done something bad, Linda?"

Was he mocking her? Linda closed her eyes, praying for the right words. When she opened them a few seconds later, her courage was renewed. "During church today, the pastor spoke about disappointments in life."

Jim grunted. "He's right about that. There's a ton of 'em!"

"Rev. Deming said we're all faced with disappointments, but God can help us through them if we know Him personally."

He held up his hand. "That's enough, Linda. If I'd wanted a sermon today, I would have gone to church or turned on the TV and listened to one of those boring televangelists."

Tears clouded Linda's vision as her gaze dropped to the floor. *Help me, Lord. Help me make him understand.*

Jim pulled out a chair and took a seat at the table. "Cut out the 'poor little Linda' routine. Your tears and pathetic looks don't work on me anymore."

"I'm not trying to get my way on anything. I just wanted to share my newfound faith, and I'd hoped you might consider going to church with me and Jimmy next week."

Jim's fist came down hard on the table, scattering several napkins to the floor and clattering the silverware Linda had placed on the table earlier. "If you need religion in order to get through the disappointments in life, then go to church all you want. Just don't expect me to follow like an obedient puppy."

With a heavy heart, Linda moved back to the stove. She'd been foolish to believe that because she had changed, Jim might consider her request to attend church.

"Give him time," a voice in her head seemed to say. *"Pray for your husband and set a good example."*

She swallowed around the constriction in her throat. *I'll try, Lord, but I'm going to need Your help.*

⚭

Abby placed a plastic tub filled with warm water on the kitchen table. It was time for the babies' baths. First she would give Titus his bath, and then Mom would dress him while she washed Timothy. While Abby dressed that baby, Mom would feed Titus. The routine seemed easy enough, but both boys were howling in their cradles across the room. Mom had gone upstairs to change clothes, because she'd spilled a glass of goat's milk all over the front of her dress, leaving Abby alone to begin the twins' baths. The only problem was, she couldn't decide which infant to bathe first.

She leaned down and scooped Titus into her arms. At least she thought it was Titus. Abraham had removed their wristbands last night, saying he thought they might become too tight as the babies continued to grow. He'd also said he could tell the boys apart, pointing out the fact that Timothy's right eye was slightly smaller than his left eye, while Titus's looked to be about the same size.

Abby squinted at the twins, still kicking their feet and waving their arms like a windmill. To her, it looked like both boys' eyes were the same size. She picked Titus up, and his crying abated, but as soon as she placed him on the oversized towel she had spread on the table and began to remove his sleepers, the howling began again. To make matters worse, the other twin was still crying, too.

"I hope your mamm comes downstairs soon," Abby crooned. She hurried through the bathing process, anxious to get Titus back in his cradle so she could wash Timothy. She had no sooner carried baby number one across the room than a knock sounded at the back door.

Abby placed Titus in his cradle and hurried to answer the door. When she opened it, she was surprised to see Cousin Edna on the porch, looking thinner than ever. The last thing she'd heard was that Edna had the achy-bones flu and wouldn't be coming over this week. From the looks of the dark circles that rimmed her pale blue eyes, she figured the woman should be home in bed.

Abby glanced over her shoulder at the wailing babies. She knew it would be rude not to invite Edna in, but she didn't want to chance the twins getting sick if Edna was still contagious. "Um. . .we didn't expect you this week."

Edna pushed the door fully open and strolled past Abby. "I'm feeling some better, so I thought I'd come by and see if you needed any help today."

"I think Mom and I can manage on our own all week. Mary Ann's here, too. She's gone out to the chicken coop to check for eggs."

"The bopplin are crying." Edna started across the room. "How come they're howlin' like that? Do they need to be fed or have their windels changed?"

"I just gave Titus a bath, so he has clean diapers," Abby replied.

"Even so, it never hurts to check. I remember when my twins were little. They went through so many diapers every day, and it seemed like all I did was wash baby clothes." Edna moved closer to the twins, but Mom's shrill voice stopped her as she stepped into the room.

"What are you doin' here, Cousin?"

Edna whirled around. "Came over to help. What do ya think?"

Mom clucked her tongue. "I think you look tired and pale, and I'll not have my favorite cousin havin' a relapse on my account." She brushed past

Abby and took hold of Edna's bony arm. "Now you get on back home where you can rest. I insist."

Abby held her breath and waited to see what would happen. To her amazement, Edna nodded and headed for the back door. "You're right, Fannie. I do feel a bit weak and shaky yet. Probably would be best if I waited till next week to offer my assistance."

"Abby and I will manage, but I appreciate your comin' by," Mom said as she followed her cousin outside to the porch.

Abby chuckled softly and moved over to the twins. She was surprised Mom had been able to convince Edna, who clearly had a mind of her own, to go home. She glanced over at the babies and was pleased to see that Titus had settled down and was sucking contentedly on his fist. Timothy, on the other hand, was still howling like there was no tomorrow. "There now, little guy. You'll feel better once we get those dirty windels off and you're all cleaned up." She placed the baby in the center of the quilt, quickly undressed him, and was surprised to see that his diaper was clean and dry. "Guess you're not as messy as your twin brother was this morning."

Abby had just finished bathing and dressing Timothy, when her mother returned to the kitchen. "That cousin of mine is such a character. She kept tellin' one joke after the other, and I finally had to remind her that I was needed inside. Sure hope she doesn't have a relapse by comin' over here today."

Abby placed Timothy in his cradle, noting that Titus was fussing again. "I only hope she didn't expose you or the twins to that flu bug she's had."

"Since I'm nursing, that's supposed to help the babies' immune system. I'm sure they'll be fine." Mom moved to Abby's side. "Did you get them both bathed?"

"Jah. Now I think they'd like to be fed."

Mom bent down and scooped Titus into her arms. "Eww. . .he feels wet. Didn't you say you bathed and changed him already?"

"I did, but—" A light suddenly dawned, and Abby broke into the giggles. "You know what, Mom?"

"What's that?"

"I think I may have bathed Titus twice. The boppli you're holding is probably Timothy, and he's most likely wet through his clothes because he hasn't been bathed or changed at all."

Mom grinned and handed Abby the baby. "Guess you'd better see to that while I feed Titus."

"Good idea," Abby agreed. "And afterwards, I believe we should put on our thinking caps and come up with some way to tell these two apart."

Chapter 17

Jim gripped his paintbrush and swiped it across the wood siding of the house he'd been hired to paint.

"Hey boss, you'd better watch what you're doing," Ed called from several feet away. "You're sloppin' paint all over the place this morning, and we'll end up with a mess to clean up if you're not careful."

"Let me worry about that," Jim snapped.

"Sorry, but you've been so testy lately, and it's beginning to show in your work."

Jim gritted his teeth. "If you had to put up with my wife, you'd be testy, too."

Ed moved closer to Jim. "What's the trouble?"

"Linda flipped out a couple weeks ago and went religious on me. Even suggested the two of us start seeing her preacher for some *Christian* counseling." Jim dipped his brush into the bucket and slapped another round of paint on the siding in front of him.

"Why does she believe you need counseling?"

"Guess she thinks if she gets me into that Bible-thumper's office he'll talk me into going to church with her and Jimmy."

"You got somethin' against church?"

Jim shrugged. "Not church per se, just the

hypocrites who sit in the pews."

Ed flipped the end of his mustache. "Guess there's hypocrites nearly everywhere."

"Are you saying I'm a hypocrite?"

"I'm not saying that at all. I just think it's easier to see other people's faults than we do our own."

Jim let Ed's words roll around in his head as he wondered if his own actions were really so bad. He tried to be honest and aboveboard in his business dealings. He was fair with his crew and paid each one what they were worth. He was a decent husband and father, even if Linda didn't think so. He didn't need church or some holier-than-thou preacher pointing out his sins.

Of course, I have told a lot of lies over the last few years, and if I went to church or started counseling with the preacher, sooner or later he might drag the truth out of me about Jimmy's phony adoption.

Jim grimaced. He knew it had been wrong to kidnap Jimmy, but he'd convinced himself it was an act of love—done in Linda's best interest. And look how she was thanking him for it!

"Going to church would only make things worse," he muttered.

"What's that, boss?"

"Nothing, Ed. I'll be fine once we quit work for the day and I can stop somewhere for a couple of beers."

❧

A knock at the front door drew Abby's attention away from the quilt she was working on. The twins were asleep in their cradles on the other side of the living room, and Mom was upstairs taking a nap. Abby had decided to use this quiet time to get some quilting done.

When Abby opened the door, she was surprised to see nine-year-old Leona Weaver on the front porch. There was something unique about the young girl, and it was more than her luminous green eyes and matching dimples. Leona had a quality about her—sweet, even-tempered, and spiritually mature for one so young. The child probably got it from her father, whom Abraham had said was not only a good friend, but was full of wisdom and godly counsel.

"What brings you over here on this Saturday afternoon?" Abby asked the child. "Do your folks know you're here?"

"Papa's out there, talking with Abraham about doin' some painting on his barn." Leona pointed across the yard.

Abby squinted against the glare of the afternoon sun. Sure enough, there was Jacob Weaver's buggy parked next to the barn.

"I thought I'd have a look at the twins, if ya don't mind," Leona announced.

Abby opened the door fully and bid the girl to enter. "They're asleep in their cradles, but if we're quiet, they'll probably keep on sleeping."

"My little cousin Amos could sleep through most anything when he was a boppli," Leona said.

"Jah, most bopplin do, but for some reason the twins seem to be light sleepers."

Abby led Leona across the living room and stopped in front of the cradles. One twin had kicked his covering off, so she pulled it up under his chin. The days were getting colder now, and it wouldn't do for the babe to take a chill.

"They're so *schee*," Leona murmured.

"They are quite pretty," Abby agreed.

"I can't wait till I'm grown up and can get married and have some bopplin of my own." The child grinned, and her dimples seemed to be winking at Abby.

Abby thought about her upcoming wedding and how she'd felt compelled to postpone it in order to stay in Pennsylvania so she could care for Mom and the twins. Lester hadn't been happy about moving the wedding date to January, but after a few letters of encouragement, he'd finally agreed.

Abby motioned to the sofa. "Would you like to sit and visit until your daed's done talking to Abraham?"

Leona nodded and followed Abby across the room. They sat next to each other on the sofa, and Abby picked up her quilting squares again.

"Titus and Timothy look so much alike," Leona said. "How do you ever tell 'em apart?"

Abby chuckled. "That has been kind of tricky. I thought I had the problem solved when I tied a blue ribbon around Titus's ankle. That worked fine until I bathed him once and forgot to remove the ribbon."

"What happened?"

"The ribbon became soggy and fell off. By the time I got the boppli dried and dressed again, a ruckus broke out in the yard between Samuel's dog and Mary Ann's cat. So I placed Titus back in his cradle and went outside to see about it."

Leona covered her mouth with the palm of her hand and giggled. "Don't tell me—when you came back inside, you thought Titus was Timothy. Am I right?"

Abby nodded. "That's exactly what happened, only this time I figured it out before I gave the same baby a bath."

"You mean that's happened before?"

Abby told Leona the story about her bathing the same baby twice and how this time, she'd discovered Timothy's dirty diaper right away and realized it was he and not Titus. "It's been a job for Mom and me to keep the boys straight, but Abraham thinks we're silly."

Leona's eyebrows lifted. "Why's that?"

"He says Titus has one eye slightly larger than Timothy's, so he always seems to know which twin he's holding." Abby shrugged. "I've never noticed much of a difference in the shape of their eyes, but I wish there were something I could do to identify one from the other without it washing off in the bath water."

Leona smiled. "I know what you could do."

"What's that?"

"Why not take some waterproof paint and make a dot on one twin's toe? Since Papa's a painter, he uses paint to mark lots of things."

Abby reached for the child's hand. "Leona Weaver, you're one smart girl. I wouldn't be surprised if you didn't grow up to be a schoolteacher someday."

Leona's eyes brightened. "You really think so?"

"Might could be. None of us knows what the future holds."

❦

"The weather's been dry, so I think my paint crew can start workin' here sometime next week," Jacob Weaver said as he studied Abraham's barn.

"Sounds good to me," Abraham replied. "It's been too many years since the barn's had a new coat of paint, and you can see how it's peelin' and chippin' all over the place. I should have had you do it much sooner, but I kept puttin' it off."

Jacob stroked his long, full beard, which was beginning to show a few signs of gray. "What color are you thinkin'? Want it to be white again?"

Abraham nodded.

"White it is then." Jacob lowered himself to a bale of straw sitting in front of the barn. "Mind if I sit a spell? We haven't had ourselves a little chat in some time."

"You're right about that," Abraham agreed, and he also took a seat. "Between me and the older boys tryin' to get the harvest done, and you and your son havin' so many paint jobs, we rarely see each other except on preaching Sundays."

"I imagine you're kept busy with those zwilling of yours, too," Jacob commented.

Abraham grinned. Just thinking about his identical twin boys brought a smile to his face. "The truth is, Abby and Fannie do most of the work. I mostly get to hold and cuddle my sons, but that's fine by me."

"Sure is a miracle the way God gave you those boys."

"Jah. It's like He took one son and gave me two."

Jacob frowned, and his bushy eyebrows drew together. "I wouldn't say God took Zach away, my friend. It's more likely He allowed free will to be done."

"That's what I meant to say." Abraham decided it was time for a change of subject. Otherwise, Jacob would end up giving him a full-fledged sermon. "When you first showed up, I saw your daughter go into the house. I'll bet she wanted to see Titus and Timothy."

"Leona loves bopplin and is real good with 'em. She'll make a fine mamm someday, I expect."

"She sure has a good-natured disposition. Kind of reminds me of Abby, who's always so agreeable."

Jacob gave his earlobe a couple of pulls. "I've never told ya this before, but I used to hope my Leona and your Zach would end up marrying each other some day."

Abraham stiffened. Jacob's comment was a painful reminder that he had not only been cheated out of seeing his son grow up, but would never know if Zach got married or to whom.

"Even if my boy hadn't been snatched away, it ain't likely our two would have ever gotten married," he mumbled.

"Why not?"

"Leona's almost three years older than Zach."

"Humph! Who worries about a little thing like that?" Jacob stood and arched his back. "I hear tell our bishop's five years younger than his second wife."

"Really? Didn't know that." Abraham shrugged as he also stood.

Jacob yawned. "Guess I should round up my daughter and get on home. I've got some paintin' of my own that the wife's been after me to do for some time."

Abraham chortled. "Isn't that the way? Seems like the last thing on our list of things to get done is usually at the top of the list our wives are keepin'."

"That's how it goes once a body's been married awhile." Jacob patted Abraham on the back. "Before I go, mind if I take a look at those growin' boys of yours?"

Abraham clasped his friend's arm as they began walking toward the house. "Don't mind at all. Fact is, I'd be pleased to show 'em to you."

Jacob halted, and Abraham almost ran into him. "Oh, I nearly forgot. I stopped by the general store yesterday afternoon and spoke with Caleb."

"How are things going there? Are he and Matthew managing okay?"

Jacob's expression turned serious, and for a moment Abraham was afraid he was about to receive news that his old business was failing.

"Caleb's concerned for Naomi and asked me to pray about things."

"What's wrong with Naomi? Is she sick?"

Jacob shook his head. "She's not sick, just seems kind of depressed." He paused and slid his tongue across his top teeth. "I hesitate to say anything, but I think you have the right to know."

"Know what? If there's somethin' you're not tellin' me, then please do so."

"Well, Caleb thinks Naomi's hurt because you show the zwilling so much attention."

Abraham's mouth fell open. "What? They're my twin boys. Why wouldn't I give 'em lots of attention?"

Jacob cleared his throat a couple of times. "It's fine to love on your little ones, Abraham, but Naomi's concerned you may have forgotten about Zach and believes the twins have replaced him in your heart."

Abraham clapped his hands together. "That's

lecherich! I'll never forget Zach."

"It may seem ridiculous to you, but Naomi's hurtin' just the same. I think she feels you haven't shown her daughters much attention either."

Abraham felt a sense of irritation well up in his soul, but as he mulled things over, he realized he might have been remiss in showing enough love to his granddaughters. He supposed he could have said or done a few things to make Naomi think he cared more about Titus and Timothy than he did Zach, too.

"I'll drop by Naomi's place soon," he promised. "There were enough hard feelings between us after Zach was kidnapped, and I don't want anything gettin' in the way of our relationship now."

Chapter 18

Naomi had just started supper when she heard a knock on the back door. She glanced at the wall clock above the refrigerator. Caleb wasn't due home from the store for another hour. Besides, he wouldn't be knocking on his own door.

She turned down the burner on the propane stove and went to the door. When she opened it, she was surprised to see her father standing on the porch.

"Papa, what are you doing here? Is everything all right at home?"

"Everything's fine. I dropped by so we could talk." He glanced over her shoulder. "Is this a good time?"

She nodded and stepped aside. "I'm just heating some bean soup, but it can warm on the stove while we visit. The kinner aren't up from their naps yet, so if you'd like to go into the living room, we can visit there."

Papa removed his straw hat and hung it on a wooden peg by the door. "Why don't we sit at the kitchen table? That way you can keep an eye on your soup."

"Okay." Naomi pulled out a chair, and her father did the same. "What'd you want to talk about?"

He cleared his throat a couple of times and gave his beard a quick tug. "I. . .uh. . .it's come to my attention that you think I've forgotten about Zach."

Naomi stared at her hands, folded in her lap. "Who told you that?"

"It don't matter who told. The question is, do you believe it?"

Naomi lifted her gaze. "I have noticed the way you dote on the twins, and you hardly ever speak of Zach these days."

Papa fiddled with the stack of paper napkins nestled in the wicker basket on the table. Finally, he leaned forward and leveled her with a most serious look. "Zach's gone, Naomi. Unless God performs a miracle, he ain't comin' back."

"I know that, and I was dealing with things fairly well until the twins were born. That's when I began to wonder—"

He held up his hand. "Zach's not here, but the zwilling are. Don't ya think I should be giving them my love and attention instead of pining for the child I lost and can't bring home?"

Tears clouded Naomi's vision, and the lump in her throat prevented her from answering his question.

"I still love Zach, and I always will," he went on to say. "I pray for him often, too."

"So do I." Naomi almost choked on her words, and she swallowed hard. "I miss my little brother. There are times when I still feel guilty for leaving him on that picnic table five years ago."

Papa shook his head. "The past is in the past; it can't be changed. What counts is what we do with the days God gives us now."

"I know that, but—"

"God's blessed you with two little girls, so rather than dwellin' on the things you wish could be changed, why not focus on Sarah and Susan? They need you, and so do my twin boys."

Naomi grabbed a napkin and blew her nose. "Why would Titus and Timothy need me when they have you and Fannie?"

"You're their big sister, and your kinner are their nieces." Papa paused and gave his beard a couple more quick pulls. "Each member of our family is important, and we need each other. Don't you agree?"

She nodded.

"At times it may seem like I'm favoring my twin sons, but they're still little and need all the love and attention Fannie and I can give 'em right now." He smiled. "Just as your kinner need you and Caleb to shower them with love."

Naomi drew in a deep breath and released it quickly. "What about you, Papa? Is there enough love in your heart to show my girls a little attention once in a while?"

"Of course there is." Papa pushed back his chair, and it scraped across the hardwood floors. "If you'd like, I'll go upstairs right now and see which one of them is howlin' like a stuck pig."

Naomi jumped up. One of the girls was crying? She'd been so engrossed in their conversation she hadn't even heard it.

"Please let me go," Papa said, starting for the door that led to the stairs. "Why don't you check on that good-smelling soup, and I'll find out which girl needs tendin' to?"

"Danki, Papa." Naomi turned toward the stove, her heart filled with gratitude that she and her daed had been able to talk things through. She knew he was right about Zach, and with God's help Naomi would try to pray more, love more, and live each day to the fullest. She must leave Zach in God's hands and move on with her life.

∞

Abby turned down the burner under the pot of savory stew that was simmering on the stove. Then she opened the oven and slipped in a baking dish filled with biscuits. Supper was nearly ready, Mom would be up from her nap soon, and when Abraham returned from Naomi's and the men came in from the fields, they could eat.

She glanced at the windowsill, where the letter lay that she'd received from Lester today. Mom had received a letter from Harold, too. He wanted to let them know that three days ago Lena had given birth to a healthy baby boy they'd named Ira. Abby wished she could be there to help her sister-in-law, but she was needed here. Lena did have her own mamm living nearby, and that made her feel some better.

Abby turned her attention back to Lester's letter. She'd been too busy to read it until now. She opened it and took a seat in the rocking chair near the stove so she could keep an eye on things.

Dear Abby,
*   I'd thought about making another trip to Lancaster County to see you, but things have gotten real busy at the blacksmith shop,*

and it would be hard to get away at this time.

I wish you could come home right now, but I know that's not possible, since you've got your hands full caring for the bopplin, and helping your mamm with the things she needs to have done. Even though January is only two months away, it seems like a long ways off to me. I'm trying to be patient though.

Say hello to the family there, and please write soon. Your letters don't come as often as I'd like them to.

Always yours,
Lester

"I wish I had time to answer his letter right now. But I'd no sooner get it started and it would be time to serve supper." Abby yawned, and her jaw popped. She'd been so busy since she came to help Mom that she barely had any time to herself. There were days when she wished she could be alone to write letters, read a book, work leisurely on a quilt, or take a walk to the creek. She missed spending time with Lester and longed to go for buggy rides, picnics, or simply walk by his side. *Lester might not realize it, but I'm as anxious as he is to marry and begin our family. Being around Naomi's little girls and my new twin brothers has made me yearn even more to be a wife and a mother.*

Abby glanced at the calendar tacked on the wall next to the refrigerator. If things had worked out differently, she and Lester would be getting married in a few weeks. Now they had two more months to wait, and that was only if Mom could manage on her own by then.

Abby's mother was slowly getting her strength back, but she still needed one or two naps every day. Mary Ann helped out when she wasn't in school, and Nancy alternated between their home and Naomi's. Then, there was dear Cousin Edna, who'd been more than willing to help at first, but she'd been fighting a cold after her bout with the flu, so she'd been unavailable to come over for the last several weeks.

Abby grimaced as she thought about the prospect of having to postpone her wedding a second time. How would Lester take the news if she decided to stay even longer? Would he be angry and break their engagement? She prayed he would understand. After all, he'd put off setting a date for their wedding for a couple of years due to his daed's passing and him trying to get the blacksmith shop running smoothly on his own. It wasn't until he'd hired an employee and gotten him trained to do things the way he and his daed had done that Lester felt ready to make the commitment to marriage.

"Guess I'd best not borrow trouble," Abby said, tucking Lester's letter inside the mending basket at her feet. "I'll have to pray harder and trust that Mom's strength will fully return before January."

A shrill cry followed by one equally high pitched alerted Abby that the twins were awake and needed her attention. She pushed herself out of the rocker and started across the room. *My own needs must be set aside. All that's important right now is caring for Mom and those baby brothers of mine.*

Linda hung up the phone, then quickly dialed Jim's cell number. "Guess what?" she said when he answered on the second ring.

"Beats me."

"I just got off the phone with my mother. She and Dad are coming for a few days' visit, and they'll be staying through Thanksgiving."

"That's nice."

Linda moved to the living room with the cordless phone so she could check on Jimmy, who'd gone there a short time ago to watch Saturday afternoon cartoons.

"Is that all you wanted?" Jim asked in an impatient tone. "I'm really busy."

She grimaced. Why did he always seem so irritated with her? In the early years of their marriage, he'd never minded when she called him on the phone.

"I won't keep you long," Linda said, clicking off the TV and heading back to the kitchen. Jimmy had fallen asleep on the couch. "I was wondering if you might be able to take some time off while Mom and Dad are here. Maybe we could make a trip to the ocean. It's usually nice there in late fall."

"Get real, Linda," Jim snapped. "I've got a ton of work lined up clear into January. The only time I'll be taking off that week will be on Thanksgiving Day."

Tears stung the back of Linda's eyes, but she willed herself not to cry. Jim hated it when she gave in to her emotions—as he'd so often said. "It was only a thought," she mumbled. "I'll let you go so you can get back to whatever you were doing."

"I'm painting, Linda. That's what I do for a living."

She flinched, feeling as if he'd thrown cold water in her face. It seemed that no matter how hard she tried to be sweet and set the example of a Christian wife, Jim responded negatively. She and Beth had recently begun attending a women's Bible study on Wednesday mornings. The fellowship and lesson helped some, but Linda felt she needed something more, something that would teach her how to respond to Jim's nasty attitude and eventually lead him to Christ.

Maybe I'll speak to Rev. Deming after church tomorrow. He might have the answers I need.

Chapter 19

"Mom! Dad! I didn't expect to see you until later in the day." Linda grabbed her parents in a hug, as the three of them stood in the hallway outside her living room.

"We left Boise yesterday afternoon and drove as far as Yakima," her father said, running his fingers through the back of his thinning brown hair. "Then we got a hotel for the night and left early this morning to come here."

"I'm glad you're early." Linda smiled, feeling happier than she had in a while. She missed her family and wished they lived closer. "Have you had breakfast yet?"

"Just one of those continental things the hotel provided," her mother replied. "But if you haven't eaten, I'm sure we could eat again."

"Since it's Saturday, Jimmy and I slept in this morning, so I haven't fixed anything yet. Jim left for work before we were up. He probably grabbed a doughnut and cup of coffee somewhere on the road."

Dressed in his pajamas, Jimmy padded out of the living room, where he'd been watching TV. "Grandpa! Grandma!"

Linda's father bent down and scooped Jimmy into his arms. "Look at you! I think you've grown at least a foot since we were here in the summer."

Jimmy giggled and nuzzled his grandfather's cheek. "I only grew a few inches. My daddy said so."

Dad set Jimmy on the floor again. "Say, how come Jim's working on a Saturday? Doesn't that man ever stay home?"

Linda sighed. "He's trying to get a group of condos painted before Thanksgiving, so he and his crew have been working a lot of overtime."

Mom slipped an arm around Linda's shoulder. "Why don't we let Grandpa and Jimmy carry our bags upstairs while the two of us go to the kitchen to see about fixing breakfast?"

"That's a good idea." Linda looked down at Jimmy, who was already racing for the front door. "Get your jacket, and don't try to carry anything too heavy."

Her father frowned. "You're just like your mother, Linda. You worry too much. I won't let the boy do anything I wouldn't have done at his age."

Mom's gaze went to the ceiling. "That's what she's afraid of, Thomas."

Linda led the way to the kitchen. She would have to trust her father not to let Jimmy carry anything heavier than he could handle. "How's my big sister and her family?" she asked. "Are they still going to visit Dean's parents for Thanksgiving?"

Mom nodded. "Cheryl and the children have all had colds, but I'm sure they'll be well enough to drive up to Lewiston to share dinner with her husband's family."

"It would have been nice if they could have come here," Linda said wistfully. "Jimmy hasn't seen his cousins since his birthday in April, and I know he would have enjoyed playing with Cameron and Pam." She smiled. "Of course, I realize they have to spend some holidays with the Pattersons."

"That's true," her mother agreed. "So how are you doing, dear? The last time we were here you looked kind of down, but this morning you seem happier and more at peace."

Linda pulled out a chair and motioned her mother to take a seat at the table. "I am feeling peaceful about my spiritual life, and it's all because of Christ."

Her mother squinted her pale blue eyes. "What do you mean?"

"Jimmy and I have been going to church, and awhile back I accepted Christ as my personal Savior." Linda took a seat on the other side of the table. "I wrote you about it, don't you remember?"

Her mother shrugged and started folding napkins into perfect triangles. "You may have mentioned something about it, but I figured it was only a passing fancy."

Linda released a sigh. "It's not a passing fancy, Mom. I've made a decision to follow the Lord, and—"

"What were you planning to have for breakfast, dear? Shouldn't we get it started?"

Linda pushed her chair back and stood. "I guess we can talk and prepare the meal at the same time." She went to the refrigerator and took out ham and a carton of eggs. "Do you want your eggs scrambled, poached, fried, or boiled?"

"Scrambled is fine. Would you like me to make some toast?"

"Sure. There's a loaf of bread in the refrigerator. Do you remember where the toaster is?"

"I'll find it."

Linda placed the ham and eggs on the cupboard and decided to broach the subject of her newfound faith again. "There's going to be a Thanksgiving service at my church on Thursday morning. I was hoping we could go."

Her mother whirled around. "All of us?"

She nodded. "First there will be a program about the pilgrims and how they came to America to find religious and political freedom. That will be followed by some singing, and then Rev. Deming will deliver a short message."

"What about dinner?"

"I can put the turkey in the oven before we leave. I'm sure we'll be home in plenty of time to get everything ready so we can eat by one thirty or two."

"If your father is willing to go, I will be as well." Mom reached up to fluff one side of her blond hair, which she wore in a short bob. "I really should see about getting my hair done if I'm going to church, and maybe I should buy a new dress, too."

Mom and Cheryl are just alike. All they ever think about is how they look and how much money they can spend on new clothes. Linda cracked an egg into the bowl she'd placed on the counter. "There's no reason for a trip to the beauty shop or a new dress, Mom. I'm sure whatever you brought to wear on Thanksgiving Day will be fine."

"But it might be fun to go on a shopping spree, don't you think? How does tomorrow afternoon sound, dear?"

Linda nodded. "Sure, Mom, that would be fine." Maybe she would have the opportunity to talk about Christ later on.

❧

"It's been almost two months since the twins were born, and I'm sure I can handle things on my own now," Fannie told Abby as the two of them began lunch preparations for themselves and the crew of men who were painting Abraham's barn. "I think it's time for you to return to Ohio."

Abby shut the refrigerator door and turned to face her mother. "Not before Thanksgiving, Mom. You'll need help with the dinner, and I've been looking forward to spending the holiday with my family here."

Fannie took a large, enamel kettle from the bottom drawer of the stove and placed it on the cupboard. "Wouldn't you like to be with Lester for Thanksgiving?"

Abby handed her mother the container of chicken noodle soup they had made last night. "Of course I would, but Lester and I will be together at Christmas. Soon January will be here and then we'll be getting married. After that we can spend every holiday with each other—some here and some in Ohio."

Fannie nodded. As much as she wanted to have her daughter with them for Thanksgiving, she felt bad for Lester. He'd been without Abby for several months and had to postpone his wedding. She was glad he and Abby would finally be together for Christmas.

"If you're feeling up to being on your own for a few hours, I thought I'd go into Paradise after we serve lunch to Jacob Weaver's painting crew. I'd like to see how things are going at the quilt shop," Abby said.

"That's a fine idea. You work too hard around here, and it will give you a chance to see which of the quilts you might want to take home to Berlin."

"I'm not sure I should take any of the quilts back with me," Abby said as she began setting the table.

"Why not?" Fannie poured the soup into the kettle. "You've made a couple of nice ones since you've been here, and I would think you'd want to try and sell them in your own shop."

Abby grabbed a handful of napkins and placed them beside each plate. "I'm sure Deborah has plenty of quilts we can sell, but if it would make you feel better, I'll take a look at them when I go there after lunch."

Fannie smiled and turned down the stove burner. The soup was already beginning to simmer, and the pleasant aroma of chicken broth tickled her nose and made her stomach rumble.

"I'm going to miss you," Abby said, coming to stand beside her mother.

"I'll miss you, too. Fact is, I'm sure the whole family will."

"Everyone's been so kind and helpful. I can't get over the way Matthew has been willing to help at the quilt shop now that Naomi's working at the store again." Abby moved back to the table. "He's been like a big brother to me, and it means a lot."

Fannie sighed. "Matthew's a fine man. I wish he'd find a nice wife and settle down."

"I invited my friend Rachel to come here for a visit, but she hasn't been able to get away," Abby said. "I'd planned to introduce her to Matthew and hoped they might hit it off."

"Maybe when we come to Ohio in January for your wedding, they'll have a chance to meet."

Abby moved to the cupboard and took a loaf of bread from the breadbox. "You don't think Matthew's afraid of getting married, do you?"

Fannie chuckled. "I doubt that. He probably hasn't found the right woman yet."

Abby nodded. "Guess I'll have to pray that the Lord sends my stepbrother just the woman he needs."

❧

When Abby arrived at the general store later that afternoon, she found it full of customers. Caleb was waiting on an Amish man buying a new shovel, and Naomi was kneeling in front of a shelf, restocking it with rubber stamps.

"Looks like business is booming," Abby whispered as she wandered over to Naomi. "I'll bet Caleb's glad you're back at work again."

Naomi nodded. "Jah, things have been busy today, both here at the store and in your mamm's quilt shop. I'm glad Matthew is able to help out."

Abby glanced around. "Where are your girls? Did you leave them at home with Caleb's mamm?"

"They're in the back room, sound asleep."

"I wonder if Mom will be able to work in her quilt shop soon and bring the twins along," Abby said. "She suggested I return to Ohio, saying she could manage on her own, but I think she only meant at home."

Naomi nodded toward the adjoining room. "Matthew's got things well under control in the quilt shop. Now that I'm not needing Nancy's help so much at home, maybe she can help him there."

"That makes sense. If Nancy were to come to the store every day, she could help Matthew and would be available to watch your kinner whenever it's needed."

"That's what I thought." Naomi smiled. "Are you here for anything in particular today?"

"Just came by to see how things are going, and Mom suggested I look over some of the quilts I've made and decide if I want to take any home with me next week."

"I can't believe you're actually leaving." Naomi stood and gave Abby a hug. "I'm going to miss you, sister."

Abby refused to give in to her threatening tears. She would be going home to Lester soon, and that was something to be happy about.

"I'll miss everyone," Abby said. "But it won't be long before you'll be coming to Ohio for my wedding."

"Jah. January's not far off, and we're looking forward to the big day."

"Guess I'd best go see about those quilts." A few seconds later, Abby entered the shop and was surprised to see that Matthew had hung several more of his quilt hangers on the wall opposite the door. A few English women were shopping in the store, and since Matthew was busy waiting on a customer, she decided not to bother him.

Matthew must have seen her come into the room, for he gave her a friendly wave. Abby smiled and headed over to the box where she'd put some of the quilts she had made. She was about to open it when Naomi called out to her.

"Abby, Caleb just answered the phone, and it's

someone from Ohio. They asked if you were here and said they needed to talk to you."

Anxious to speak with anyone from home, Abby hurried from the room. She slipped behind the counter and took the phone from Caleb. "Hello. This is Abby Miller."

Her forehead wrinkled as she tried to make sense out of the jumbled words on the other end of the line. "Deborah, is that you? I can barely hear what you're saying. Can you speak a little louder, please? What was that?"

There was a long pause, and Deborah's high-pitched voice came on the line again.

Abby's mind reeled as she tried to digest everything that was being said. She wished Deborah would slow down. She wished. . .

"A fire! At the quilt shop? Wh–what did you say?" Abby gripped the edge of the counter as the room began to spin.

Chapter 20

A bby, Abby. Wake up!"
        "Is she okay?"
"She hit her head."

"It's bleeding."

"Better get a clean towel."

"Maybe we should call 911. She might have a concussion."

"Let's wait a few minutes and see if she comes around."

Somewhere in the distance, Abby heard muffled voices. Where was she? Why did it seem so dark? She tried to open her eyes, but her head hurt too much. She tried to think, tried to focus. Had she fallen into a deep, dark pit, or was this another one of her horrible nightmares?

Something cold touched her forehead, and a stinging sensation followed. Abby flinched.

"Abby, please say something."

She recognized Matthew's voice and struggled to open her eyes.

"She's coming around."

Someone's cool hand touched the side of her face. She blinked and tried to sit up, but a heavy weight seemed to be pressing her down.

"Wh—what happened?" she murmured, as the faces of Naomi, Caleb, and Matthew came into view.

"You were talking on the phone one minute, and then you fainted." Naomi held a small wet towel against Abby's forehead.

Matthew clasped her hand. "You must have hit your head on the edge of the counter when you went down."

Abby's mind whirled as she forced herself to remember the conversation she'd had with Lester's mamm.

"The phone. Where's Deborah? I—I need to speak with her." Tears blurred Abby's vision, and she attempted once more to sit up.

Caleb knelt beside her, placing a gentle hand against her shoulder. "When you passed out, the phone went dead. Was it Lester's mamm you were speaking to?"

Abby nodded, and the room tipped precariously. She swallowed the bitter acid taste in her mouth. *No, no, it can't be. I had to be dreaming. That's all it was—that frightening nightmare I've had about fire and smoke and a kitten being trapped with me.*

Abby trembled and squeezed Matthew's hand. "It—it wasn't a kitten that was trapped; it was Lester."

"What are you talking about?" Naomi gave Abby's arm a gentle shake. "Please, tell us what Deborah said."

Abby turned her head away. "Fire. The quilt shop."

"Did your shop in Berlin catch on fire? Is that what Deborah told you?" Caleb asked. Obvious concern creased his brow as he leaned closer to Abby.

She nodded and drew in a quivering breath

as her stomach churned.

"What happened? Was anyone hurt?" Naomi questioned.

Abby rolled her head from side to side, while the realization of what Deborah had said became clearer. She gazed at the gas lamp that hung overhead and wished she were dreaming. "He's gone."

Matthew leaned closer. "Who's gone?"

"My Lester. He's dead." Abby choked on a sob and fell into Matthew's arms.

∞

Fannie paced the living room floor, anxious for some word on Abby. Matthew had brought her home from the quilt shop half an hour ago, and they'd called Dr. Frazier, who lived nearby. He'd been kind enough to make a house call and was upstairs with Abby right now.

"Fannie, won't you please sit down?" Abraham said, taking hold of her arm. "I'm sure we'll hear something soon."

She turned and looked up at him, tears flooding her eyes. "I can't believe this has happened. Why would God allow it, Abraham?"

He pulled her gently to the couch, and they both took a seat. "Many times I've asked God that same question. First, when Sarah died, again after Zach was kidnapped, and once more when Naomi ran away." Abraham took hold of Fannie's hand and massaged her fingers. "My friend Jacob has reminded me many times that God's ways are not our ways. He allows certain things to happen that often become a testing of our faith."

"But Abby deserves to be happy," Fannie wailed. "She was planning to return to Ohio right after

Thanksgiving, and she and Lester were going to be married in January." She dabbed at the moisture on her cheeks. "I should never have let my daughter stay here so long."

"Fannie, you can't blame yourself for this."

"Abraham's right," Matthew spoke up. He'd been sitting in the rocking chair across the room ever since Abby had been taken upstairs. "It was an accident, plain and simple."

"If I had insisted that Abby return to Ohio sooner, the fire might not have happened and Lester would still be alive." Fannie's chin trembled. "My dear girl should be returning to Ohio to marry Lester, not bury him."

Abraham squeezed her hand. "Please, don't talk that way. It ain't your fault. Abby came here to help because she wanted to. I know she would never cast the blame for this terrible loss at your feet."

Fannie sat there, too numb, too full of remorse to comment.

"I still don't understand how the quilt shop caught fire or why Lester was in there and couldn't get out," Matthew said.

"We won't have the answers until we speak with Deborah Mast. Even then, I'm not sure she will have all the details," Abraham replied.

Fannie stood. "Dr. Frazier's been with Abby long enough. She needs me."

"Give them a few more minutes." Abraham reached out to her, but she bolted from the room.

Just as Fannie reached Abby's door, the doctor stepped into the hall. "There's a small cut on her forehead, but no concussion from what my examination showed. I think with a few days' rest she'll be fine."

"Fine? How can my daughter be fine? She's just received news that the man she was planning to marry has been killed in a fire that destroyed her quilt shop."

Dr. Frazier shook his head. "I was talking about her physical condition, Fannie. Abby's in shock right now."

"I need to see her." Fannie pushed past the doctor, rushed over to Abby, and took a seat on the edge of her bed.

Abby lay quietly, her eyes shut and a small bandage taped to her forehead. Her cheeks were chalky white and stained with tears. It nearly broke Fannie's heart to see her sweet daughter that way.

Fannie took Abby's hand and squeezed it gently. "My dear girl, I'm so sorry this happened. If there were a way I could shoulder your pain, I surely would."

Abby's eyes opened, and Fannie studied her through the dim circle of light cast by the oil lamp at her bed. She not only looked pale, but her brown eyes appeared faded, as though her tears had washed some of the color away. There was no question about it—Fannie knew her daughter's heart was broken and bleeding.

"He's gone, Mom. Lester is gone." A strangled sob escaped Abby's lips, and she moaned.

Fannie nodded and swallowed around the lump in her throat. "I know, dear one." A deafening silence hung in the air, separating them like a closed window. *If only I knew what I could say to comfort my girl. If I could just take this dreadful pain away.*

"Why? Why'd this happen now, when I was ready to go home? What was Lester doing at my quilt shop, and how did it catch on fire?"

Fannie shook her head. "Caleb and Naomi are making phone calls to Ohio. After they've spoken with Deborah, we'll know more details."

Abby struggled to sit up. "I need to go home. Need to be there for Deborah, to attend Lester's funeral, and see about the quilt shop."

Fannie wrapped her arms around Abby and held her tight. "We can talk about all that later. You don't have to think about any of this right now."

Abby released a shuddering sigh. "It's—it's my fault Lester is dead."

"No, no. You mustn't say that."

"It's true. I know now what those dreams I've been having meant."

"You do?"

Abby nodded. "Don't you see, Mom? The kitten in my dream represented Lester, and I was supposed to save him."

"Oh Abby, I don't think—"

"The dreams were a warning of what was to come. I should have returned to Ohio sooner. I might not have been able to keep the fire from happening, but I could have prevented Lester from going in after my quilts."

"You can't know that," Fannie argued. "Once a man determines that he's going to do something, there's little a woman can say that will change his mind."

Abby shook her head. "He listened to me when the cheese place caught on fire. He'd wanted to go inside the building to see if his friend Joe was all right, but he didn't because I asked him not to."

Unsure of what to do or say to ease her daughter's pain, Fannie held Abby, and they wept together.

⚬⚬⚬

Naomi sat on the wooden stool behind the counter in their store, waiting for Caleb to get off the phone. He had called his cousin Henry, who ran a buggy shop outside of Berlin, asking for the phone number of Lester's blacksmith shop. Now he was talking with one of Lester's employees, trying to get some details about the fire and Lester's death.

Oh Lord, Naomi prayed, *please help Abby during this difficult time. She's so sweet and kind, always caring for others while she sets her own needs aside. Show me how I might help her.*

Caleb hung up the phone and groaned.

"What is it, Caleb? What did you find out?"

"The cause of the fire is still unclear, but there was a witness who overheard Lester say he was going inside to save Abby's quilts." Caleb shook his head, and his eyes darkened. "The first time he went into the burning shop, he was able to bring out a couple of quilts. But when he went in the second time, he didn't make it out again. By the time the firemen were able to get inside the store, Lester was dead."

Naomi covered her mouth with the back of her hand as mist welled in her eyes. She dropped her hands to her lap and looked at her husband. "How will Abby get through this, Caleb? What can we do to help her?"

Caleb squeezed her shoulder. " 'I will instruct thee and teach thee in the way which thou shalt go:

I will guide thee with mine eye,' saith the Lord."

She nodded, remembering the words of Psalm 32:8 that their bishop had quoted in church a week ago. Oh, how they required God's instruction—this needy family, who'd already been through so much pain.

Chapter 21

Abby sat on a wooden bench, waiting for the early Monday morning bus to depart. Abraham had hired an English driver to take her to the station in Lancaster. Mom had wanted to send Nancy along on the trip, but Abby insisted she would be fine and preferred to go alone. She had told her mamm that going back to Ohio was something she must do on her own, and she'd meant it.

She clutched the straps of her black purse and drew in a deep breath as she struggled for control. She felt all stirred up. Her insides burned like hot coals. *I can do this. Deborah needs me. Lord, give me the strength.*

When the bus pulled into the station a few minutes later, Abby climbed aboard. She looked for a seat at the back of the bus, hoping she wouldn't have to sit next to anyone. She didn't want to make polite conversation. She didn't want to think or even feel. Sleep. That's what she needed right now.

Abby leaned her head back and squeezed her eyes shut against the tears that were so determined to fall. Controlled by an irrational need to hear Lester's voice, she allowed her thoughts to carry her away.

A vision of Lester inside his blacksmith shop

popped into her mind. She could smell the pungent aroma of hot metal being forged and feel the heat of glowing embers beneath the anvil. His green shirt and tan suspenders accentuated the crimson flush on his face. Lester smiled in that easygoing way of his; then he reached out his hand. The memory was painful, yet strangely soothing.

Suddenly, Abby saw herself inside her bedroom, with fire and billowy smoke threatening to choke her to death. Lester was by her side, grabbing the quilt off her bed. Their fingers intertwined as they pulled on the doorknob, but it didn't budge. Abby and her betrothed were trapped in the inferno and would perish together.

Abby's eyes snapped open, and her trembling fingers trailed along the narrow ties of her black bonnet. Had she fallen asleep and been dreaming again? She sat for a few minutes in the company of her bitter regrets, then decided she must forcibly rearrange her thoughts. She stared out the window, attempting to focus her attention on the passing scenery, but it was no use. All she could think about was Lester, and how he wouldn't be waiting for her when she arrived in Ohio. He'd given his life trying to save her quilts, and she should have been there to stop him.

Abby gripped the edge of her seat as tears blinded her vision. *Oh Lester, how can I go on living without you? I'll never forgive myself for causing your death.*

❧

Jim entered the kitchen, switched on the overhead light, and glanced at the clock. It was four in the morning, and he didn't have to get up for work until six, yet he hadn't been able to sleep. He'd gone to bed late last night, tossed and turned for hours, then finally gotten up.

"Why did I let Linda talk me into attending church with her folks on Thanksgiving morning?" he groused as he ambled over to the refrigerator. He pulled out a container of apple juice, grabbed a glass from the cupboard, and filled it to the brim. *If I go to church on Thanksgiving, will Linda keep nagging me to attend services with her and Jimmy on Sunday mornings?*

He gulped the juice down, placed the empty glass in the sink, and snapped off the light. *Might as well see if I can sleep a few more hours. Maybe I'll just crash on the couch.*

Jim headed for the living room and tripped over a pair of Jimmy's sneakers on the way. He cursed and gave one shoe a swift kick. It flew into the room and hit the coffee table with a thud.

He dropped to the couch but jumped up when something sharp jabbed his hip. He groaned when he realized it was a toy truck. "If I've told that kid once, I've told him a hundred times, not to leave his things lying around." Jim grabbed the truck, pitched it across the room, and flopped down with his head on a throw pillow.

He lay there with his eyes closed, hoping sleep would come quickly. A few seconds later, Jim heard a click, and he bolted upright. A ray of light coming from the hallway streamed into the room. Who would be milling around this early in the morning?

Jim heard the sound of running water coming from the kitchen, so he decided to investigate. He found Linda's father, clad in a pair of navy blue flannel pajamas, standing at the sink.

Thomas whirled around. "Jim! You scared the daylights out of me. What are you doing up at this hour?"

"I could ask you the same question."

"Woke up to use the restroom and decided I was thirsty."

"Same here. I mean, about the thirsty part," Jim said with a snicker. "I bedded down on the couch, hoping I could get a little more sleep before it was time to get ready for work."

Thomas raised his dark, bushy eyebrows. "Are you and Linda getting along okay?"

"Sure. Why do you ask?"

"Just seems as if there's some tension between the two of you. And then with you sleeping on the couch I figured there might be some serious problems."

Jim grunted and flopped into a chair at the table. "She didn't kick me out of our room, if that's what you're getting at, Tom."

Linda's father shook his head and took the seat opposite Jim. "That's not what I meant to imply." He grinned. "And thanks for not calling me Thomas. I've hated that name since I was a boy, but it's what most people call me, and it's kind of late in the game to start using a nickname."

Jim fingered the edge of the blue vinyl table-cloth. "It's never too late for anything."

Tom cleared his throat. "About you and Linda. . ."

"Yeah?"

"Are you having some problems?"

Jim compressed his lips. Just how much should he tell Linda's dad? Would he be in for a lecture if he voiced his complaints? It was only natural that a father would defend his daughter, and it wasn't likely that his father-in-law would take Jim's side.

"Whatever you tell me won't go any further than these kitchen walls," Tom said with a nod.

Jim drew in a deep breath and decided to plunge ahead. "To tell you the truth, things haven't been good between Linda and me for some time."

"I see."

"Linda has always been somewhat needy, and after we got Jimmy, she became overprotective and whiny, always wanting her own way." Jim grimaced. "This doesn't feel right, me talking about my wife to her father."

Tom shook his head. "That's okay. I'm not so naive as to think my daughter has no faults."

"I appreciate your understanding."

"How is Linda acting now?"

"She's done an about-face." Jim popped a couple of his knuckles. "Awhile back, she began going to church with some religious friend of hers. Ever since then she's been syrupy sweet and way too compliant. It makes me wonder if she has some ulterior motive."

"Such as?"

He shrugged. "Maybe getting me to go to church with her and Jimmy. Maybe adopting another child."

"But you're going to church on Thanksgiving, right?"

"Yeah, against my better judgment."

"And you don't want more children?"

Jim blew out his breath. How could he explain things without Tom asking a bunch of questions he wasn't prepared to answer? "I think Jimmy's enough for us. And since Linda and I don't see eye-to-eye on many things that pertain to raising the boy, I can't feel good about bringing another kid into our home."

Tom nodded. "I think I understand. Claire tended to be overprotective with both our daughters when they were growing up, but Cheryl has always had an independent spirit and has pretty much done as she pleased since she's been out on her own. Linda, on the other hand, was afraid of everything when she was a child, and she's never had much confidence, not even as a young adult."

"Yeah, I know. She has improved in that area some, but we still have a lot of problems."

"Have you considered seeing a counselor?"

Jim clenched his teeth. Not the counselor thing again. He shook his head. "Don't need a counselor. Things will be fine. You don't need to worry." He pushed away from the table. "I think I'll go upstairs and get ready for work."

"So soon? It's only five o'clock."

"Might as well get an early start. Since I'll be losing a whole day on Thursday, I need to get as much done these next few days as I can."

"Linda thinks you work too hard, and I'm inclined to agree with her."

Jim frowned. "How else can I provide a decent living for us if I don't put in long hours? Can't pay the bills and buy the things Linda might want if I sit around the house all day."

"That's true, but—"

"Gotta run, Tom. I'll see you after work this evening." Jim rushed out of the room before Linda's father could say anything more.

∞

Fannie sat at the kitchen table, watching a wisp of steam as it curled and lifted from her cup of tea, then vanished into the air. Abby had only been gone a few hours, and already she missed her. Would her daughter be all right on her own? Could she handle the pressure of going back to Ohio and facing the remains of her shop, knowing Lester had been killed trying to rescue her quilts? The thought sent a shiver tingling down Fannie's spine. So many hopes for the future had been dashed in a single moment. If only there was some way to change the past.

"Are you okay, Mama Fannie?"

Startled by the sound of Nancy's voice, Fannie whirled around. The young girl stood off to one side, and Fannie realized Nancy must have slipped into the room while she was deep in thought. "I was just havin' a cup of tea," she mumbled.

"Mind if I join you? The twins are down for a nap, and I could use a little break."

Fannie nodded at the pot sitting in the center of the table. "It's probably empty. I've already had three cups."

Nancy reached for the teapot and carried it over to the stove. "I'll add some hot water and another tea bag. Would ya like some zucchini bread to go with it?"

Fannie shrugged. "I'm not so hungry right now."

A few minutes later, Nancy joined her at the table. She poured them each a cup of tea and passed the plate of zucchini bread to Fannie. "You need to keep up your strength."

Fannie glanced at the clock on the wall across from her. "Wonder how Abby's doing. Sure hope she'll be able to sleep on the bus. She's had a rough couple of days, and I hated to see her leave for Ohio so soon."

"She did have a pretty nasty bump on the head."

"I wasn't talking about that. I was referring to the trauma of Lester dying."

Nancy nodded. "I can't imagine how she must feel, losin' her entire quilt shop and the man she was plannin' to marry."

"It's always hard to lose a loved one, but having them die in a tragic accident is ever so sad." Fannie took a sip of tea and hoped it would push down the lump that seemed to be stuck in her throat.

"I remember how we all felt when our mamm was hit by a car," Nancy said. "It was like a part of us died that day."

Before Fannie could comment, Nancy reached across the table and patted her hand. "'Course, havin' you as our new mamm has helped to heal that pain."

Fannie's eyes filled with tears. "Bein' married to your daed and helpin' him raise his brood has filled a void in my life, too."

Nancy leaned her elbows on the table. "You think Abby will ever find love again?"

"It's too soon to be thinking of such things. Abby needs time to grieve and put her memories to rest before she can consider love or marriage again."

"She sure is brave, going back to Ohio by herself."

Fannie nodded. "Brave and determined to do what's right by Lester's mamm."

"Abby's a real special woman, ain't it so?"

"Jah, but I wish she would learn to care for her own needs."

"Doesn't the Bible teach that we should love others and do to them as we would have done to us?"

"It does, but it also teaches that we need to love ourselves."

"Where's it say that?"

"In the New Testament Gospels, Jesus tells us that the second greatest commandment is to love thy neighbor as thyself." Fannie smiled. "How can we love others if we don't love ourselves and take care of our own needs?"

Nancy took a sip of her tea. "And you don't think Abby does that?"

"Most of the time she's worried about everyone else and tries to meet their needs instead of her own. Many times, my daughter has done without or given up her plans for me. She did that when she came to help during my pregnancy." Fannie shook her head. "To tell you the truth, Abby's been overly self-sacrificing ever since her daed died of a heart attack when she was sixteen."

"When she stayed on after the twins were born, it made sense, but then after you seemed strong enough, I figured she would go right back to Ohio," Nancy said.

"Exactly. Now I'm wishin' I had insisted she go sooner. If she had, Lester might still be alive."

Nancy's dark eyes showed obvious concern.

"You can't blame yourself for that, Mama Fannie. Abby came here of her own free will, and she stayed because she wanted to. I'm sure she doesn't blame you for what happened to the quilt shop or to Lester."

"That's what Abraham says." Fannie sighed. "About all we can do now is pray for Abby. Pray that in the days ahead she will find comfort from us, as well as the Lord."

Chapter 22

Abby's heart shook like a trapped animal as she stood on the sidewalk, holding Deborah's hand, in front of the remains of her quilt shop. A pile of ashes and charred timber was all that remained. It had been burned beyond repair. *If only there was a way to turn back the hands of time. If I just hadn't gone to Pennsylvania to help Mom. If only I had returned to Ohio a few days sooner. If I had understood the meaning of my dream, this would not have happened.*

Abby's chest heaved, and her throat burned, but she wouldn't give in to the tears stinging the back of her eyes. She needed to be strong for Lester's mamm. She needed some answers.

"Did the firemen say why the store caught fire?" she asked Deborah.

Deborah's shoulders lifted, and she drew in a shuddering breath. "I. . .I believe it's my fault, Abby. I think I'm the cause of my son's death."

"Wh—what are you saying?" Abby couldn't imagine that Lester's mamm could be responsible for this tragic accident.

Deborah sank to a nearby bench, and Abby did the same. "A cat got into the shop the afternoon before the fire and hid. I tried to find him but finally gave up." She sniffed and dabbed at the tears trickling down her cheeks. "I completely forgot about the cat when I closed up the shop and went home. I thought about it after I made it to the house, but I figured I'd just find him and shoo him away in the morning."

"I don't understand," Abby said. "What would the cat have to do with the fire?"

"The fire chief said they found the remains of a kerosene lamp overturned." Deborah gulped on a sob. "I. . .I think I may have forgotten to turn it off, and the cat—"

"Knocked it over," Abby said, finishing Deborah's sentence.

"Jah. Then the following morning, Lester came through Berlin before any of the other stores had opened. He said they had a lot of work to do at the blacksmith shop and he wanted to get an early start. He must have passed by your store on the way and caught sight of the fire. Instead of waiting for help to arrive, he went inside with the hope of saving some of your quilts."

"How do you know this?" Abby asked with a catch in her voice.

"Some carpenters who'd come to work on the cheese shop down the street saw it all. They'd already called the fire department, and one man said he had cautioned Lester about going inside." Deborah drew in a quick, shaky breath. "I was told that the first time Lester entered the store, he came out with four quilts. But then, foolishly, he went back for more. That was when the roof caved in, and he was knocked unconscious. By the time the firemen arrived, my son was dead."

The haunting memories of Abby's dream crept

into her mind and tightened its grip. It wasn't just an ugly dream as Mom had suggested. It really had been a warning, and maybe the cat in the dream represented the one that had gotten into her quilt shop.

"I'm ever so sorry, Abby," Deborah wailed. "Sorry for the loss of your shop, and sorry for the loss of my boy, who would have been your husband soon if this hadn't happened."

The silence between them was thick and draped around Abby like the heavy shawl she wore. She sat awhile, picking at the cuticle on her index finger until it bled. Her life had been cut back like a pruned vine, but she didn't hold Deborah responsible for the accident. Many times at the end of the day, she had been distracted or overly tired. She could have easily left one of the gas lamps burning, the way Deborah thought she had done. Abby could see herself doing the very same thing with the cat. No, she couldn't allow Lester's mamm to carry the blame for this. It was Abby's fault the shop was now a pile of rubble. She was to blame for Lester's horrible death. It had been her decision to go to Pennsylvania. It was she who'd decided to stay so long. And she had not heeded the warning of her recurring dream.

She reached for Deborah's hand. "You're not to blame. If I had returned to Ohio sooner, Lester would still be alive." The words stung, but she had to say them. "If I had been here, he wouldn't have gone inside."

"You can't know that."

Abby nodded. "Jah, I'm certain of it."

Deborah's dark eyes shimmered with tears. "No

matter who's to blame for this tragedy, I know my son loved you, Abby. He loved you enough to risk his life to try and save some of your quilts."

Abby sniffed back tears that threatened to spill over. "I know."

"The four quilts Lester managed to save are at my house. Maybe you'd like to get them after Lester's funeral service."

Deborah's last statement was nearly Abby's undoing. She didn't think she could ever look at another quilt without feeling guilty and remembering her loss. Yet she knew she couldn't leave the quilts with Deborah. Maybe she would have them shipped to Mom's house. When and if she felt ready, she might decide to sell them.

❧

"I wish I could have gone with Abby to Ohio," Naomi told Caleb as they opened the store for business. "She's going to need someone to help her get through Lester's funeral."

"Lester's mamm is there, and so are Abby's brother and sister-in-law," Caleb reminded her.

"I know, but I wish I could be there for her."

"You can be, when she returns to Pennsylvania."

"Do you think Abby might decide to stay in Ohio? It is her home, you know."

Caleb turned on the gas lamp hanging above the counter. "What's left for her there? The quilt shop's gone, and Lester is dead. I'm sure she'll want to get away from all those unpleasant memories."

"You're probably right." Naomi opened a sack of toys for Sarah and went to put baby Susan in the crib at the back of the room. When she returned, she found Caleb struggling to open a carton of books. She was tempted to offer her help, but then she reminded herself how important it was for him to be independent. Caleb had given up a lot when he'd sold his buggy shop and purchased the store. He'd done it so they could be married and he would have a way to support them. Most things in the store he could do fairly well, but the forefinger and middle finger on Caleb's left hand had been badly crushed when Mose Kauffman's buggy gave way. Since that time, Caleb had limited use of his hand.

Naomi was relieved when Caleb found a utility knife and finally accomplished his task. She knew he wouldn't have liked it if she'd stepped in to help.

Naomi headed to the quilt shop, where Matthew was opening for business. He looked sad, probably feeling Abby's pain and wishing he could do something to ease it for her.

"Anything I can do to help you here?" she called to her brother.

Matthew turned from his job of lighting the gas lamps. "Unless we get a lot of customers, I think I can manage on my own today."

"With Thanksgiving only a few days away, I doubt we'll get too many customers in the store or the quilt shop."

"You're probably right. Most women are at home getting ready for the holiday." Matthew's eyes darkened, and he released a groan. "Sure won't be much of a Thanksgiving for Abby this year. Do you think she'll spend it in Berlin or come back here to be with our family?"

Naomi shrugged. "I'm guessing she'll want to stay in Ohio a few days after the funeral. Abby's worried about Lester's mamm, and I'm sure she'll offer Deborah as much support as she needs."

Matthew's gaze went to the ceiling. "Abby thinks too much of others and not enough about herself. She should have gone back to Berlin several weeks ago, like Fannie wanted her to."

"Abby's a caring woman, and she was only doing what she felt was best for her mamm and little brothers. You can't fault her for that, Matthew."

"Don't fault her. I was just voicing my thoughts, that's all."

Naomi knew it was best to drop the subject. Truth be told, she had a hunch Matthew cared a great deal more for Abby than he let on. It made her wonder if somewhere down the line, after Abby had time to heal, there might be a chance for her and Matthew to become a courting couple.

Better not mention that, Naomi decided. *It's too soon after Lester's death to even be thinking such things.* She turned toward the door. "If you need me for anything, be sure and let me know."

∽

Linda rolled out of bed, fumbling around for her robe. She thought she'd heard Jimmy calling, and when she tried to rouse Jim she discovered his side of the bed was empty.

She snapped on the light to check the alarm clock and realized it was only six in the morning. Had Jim left for work already, or had he slept on the couch again? He'd been doing that a lot lately. But surely he wouldn't do it with her parents here.

Since her conversion, Linda had made every effort to restore peace to their household, but Jim seemed to be growing more distant as the weeks went by, and she didn't know what to do. She knew he was angry because she had convinced him to attend church on Thursday morning.

"I'll go this once," Jim had muttered when they got ready for bed last night. "But don't think I'm going to make a habit of it."

I need to pray, set a good example, and leave this situation in God's hands. Linda opened the door and headed down the hall to Jimmy's bedroom. A quick peek let her know he was still sleep. Probably just dreaming. She shut the door again and returned to her room.

Wide awake and not wanting to go back to sleep, she took her Bible from the dresser and curled up on the bed to read a few chapters. The first passage she chose was 1 Peter 3:1–2. " 'Wives, in the same way submit yourselves to your own husbands so that, if any of them do not believe the word, they may be won over without words by the behavior of their wives, when they see the purity and reverence of your lives.' "

Linda closed her eyes. "Lord, I'm trying to be that submissive wife, but it gets harder all the time. If Jim would only show some response, it would give me a ray of hope. I want him to know You personally, and I know that without You in the center of our lives, our marriage will never be what it should."

A knock on the bedroom door caused Linda to jump. "Jim?"

"No, honey, it's me."

"Come in, Dad," she called.

The door opened, and Linda's father poked his head inside. "You alone?"

She nodded.

"I thought I heard you talking to someone."

"I. . .I was praying."

Her father frowned. "At six in the morning?"

"There's no special time to pray, Dad." Linda smiled. "Did you need something?"

He shook his head. "I was heading downstairs to get a glass of water and heard Jimmy crying, so I thought I'd better let you know."

She jumped off the bed. "Is he okay?"

"Don't know. Figured I'd let you handle things."

Linda started for the door. "I checked on him a few minutes ago, and he was sound asleep."

"He's probably having a bad dream."

"I'm sure that's all it is, but I'd better make certain he's not sick."

"I'm going downstairs to start a pot of coffee," her father said. "Call if you need me. I think Jim's already gone to work."

"I figured as much," Linda said as she slipped past him.

When Linda entered Jimmy's room, she found him awake and crying. "Honey, what's wrong?" She brushed Jimmy's hair aside and felt his forehead. No fever. That was good.

"I've got a stomachache. Can I stay home from school? I wanna be here with Grandma and Grandpa all day."

Linda kissed his soft cheek. "Thursday is Thanksgiving, and there's no school for the rest of this week, remember?"

Jimmy's eyes brightened, and he bounded off the bed. "Yippee! Me and Grandpa can go to the park. Maybe Allen will be there, too."

She smiled at her son's exuberance. Not more

WANDA E. BRUNSTETTER

than a minute ago, he'd complained of a stomachache, and now he was bouncing all over the place,
excited about going to the park. *At least one of my
men is happy about my folks being here. Jim's been so
aloof since Mother and Daddy came, it's downright
embarrassing.*

She reached for Jimmy's hand. "Let's go downstairs and see about making some blueberry pancakes."

"Can we do the kind with faces?"

She released his hand and ruffled his hair.
"Sure, sweetie. If that's what you want."

Jimmy scampered out of the room, and Linda
followed, thanking the Lord for the joy this little
boy had brought into her life.

∽

Huddled beside the other mourners who stood
near Lester's plain, wooden casket, Abby struggled to keep her emotions in check. Her chest
burned and her nose ran, but she held her breath
until the urge to cry diminished. When someone
took her hand, she felt the warmth and comfort
flow all the way to her bones.

"I'm sorry for your loss," her friend Rachel
whispered. "If there's anything I can do, please let
me know."

"Danki. I'll be fine." Except for the tears
Abby had shed in her mother's arms the day she'd
received the news of Lester's death, she had not
truly wept. She glanced over at Deborah, sobbing
uncontrollably and leaning on her daughter
Emma's shoulder. Emma had come from Indiana
for her brother's funeral, and Lester's other two
sisters, Bernice and Hattie, who lived in Florida,
were there, too. Deborah had told Abby earlier that

day that she would be moving to Indiana soon to live with Emma. Abby figured it was just as well, since there was nothing left for Deborah here, now that her only son was gone.

Abby had been tempted to stay in Berlin in order to see to Deborah's needs, but she knew it would be too painful for her or Lester's mamm if either of them stayed. She had promised to spend Thanksgiving with Harold and Lena, but as soon as she fulfilled that commitment, she would be on a bus bound for Pennsylvania.

Chapter 23

Abraham entered the living room and went to the woodstove to add another log. It had been a fairly pleasant day, with most of their family gathered around the table sharing a delicious Thanksgiving meal. With the help of Naomi, Nancy, and Mary Ann, Fannie had put on a happy face, cooking the dinner and then serving it as though everything was normal.

But Abraham knew his wife was in pain. He was sure Fannie missed Abby and wished her daughter could have been with them. Fannie was a good mamm, and if she could shield Abby from the trials of life, she would. But that wasn't possible. Fannie needed to rely on God and leave things in His hands the same way Abraham had done countless times.

He opened the woodstove door, tossed the log inside, and then moved across the room to check on the bopplin—first his youngest granddaughter, asleep in her portable crib, then his twin sons, lying in their cradles. "So young and innocent," he murmured. "I pray none of you will ever know the heartaches I have had to endure. I pray each of you will grow up healthy, happy, and relying on God to meet all of your needs."

Abraham's thoughts went to Abby. She had

phoned Naomi at the store yesterday and said she planned to catch a bus to Pennsylvania late this evening. She would arrive in Lancaster early tomorrow morning, and Abraham had arranged for one of their English drivers to pick her up.

Some people never find the joy I know, Lord, he silently prayed. *Some lose a loved one and spend the rest of their lives grieving. I pray it won't be so with Abby.*

Abraham meandered back to the woodstove, where it was warm and comforting. *Lord, please be with Fannie's daughter. Give her a safe trip to Pennsylvania, and grant her healing, peace, and comfort in the days ahead.*

Fannie stepped into the room just then and joined him in front of the stove. "Would you care for a piece of apple crumb pie and a cup of coffee?" she asked, slipping her arm around his waist.

He shook his head. "I'm still full from that big dinner we had. Sure was a good meal, and I thank you for it."

She smiled, although he could tell it was forced. "Everyone ate plenty of ham and turkey, not to mention all the trimmings that went with it."

He thumped his stomach a couple of times. "That's for certain sure."

Fannie glanced across the room. "I see the boys and little Susan are still sleeping. Guess that means they'll be wide awake half the night again."

"I hope not. You and Naomi both need your sleep."

"That is so true." She lowered herself into the rocker. "Mary Ann took Sarah upstairs to play with her doll, the menfolk went out to the barn to look at Jake's new horse, and Naomi and Nancy are doing the dishes. I was planning to help, but they said I'd done enough and insisted I come out here to rest awhile."

Abraham took a seat on the sofa across from her. "Guess I raised some smart girls."

She nodded. "Jah. They take after their daed."

"Your daughter's smart like her mamm, too."

Fannie smiled, but even from where Abraham sat, he could see the tears in her eyes. "I'm glad Abby's comin' back to Pennsylvania. There are too many memories for her in Berlin. It will be easier for her to heal if she's not living close to the heartbreaking reminder that Lester's dead and her store is gone." She sniffed and reached for a tissue. "I wish I could take away her pain, Abraham. If I could fix this hurt the way I used to fix her scraped knees and bruised elbows, I surely would."

"Just be there for her," Abraham said. "Love Abby, pray for her, and let the Lord do His work in her life. It's the only way."

She nodded. "I know."

∞

Jim shifted uncomfortably on the pew near the back of the church. Not only were the pews too hard and the music too loud, but the pastor's sermon was boring. So far all the man had talked about was how people should be thankful and give praise to God for the blessings He had given them.

Any blessings I've got came about because of my own doing, he thought ruefully. *I work hard, and everything we have is due to the long hours I put in. I've never understood why some people think they need God in order to feel good about their successes.*

"So on this Thanksgiving Day," the pastor said, breaking into Jim's thoughts, "I want to remind you to give thanks for your family."

Jim glanced down the pew. Linda sat on his right, with Jimmy squeezed in between them, and Linda's parents were on the other side of her. *We look like a model family, all decked out in our best clothes. But are any of us really happy?* He studied his son, nestled against his arm. *Jimmy seems happy most of the time. As happy as any kid could be, I suppose.*

Jim gave his shirt collar a couple of tugs and loosened the knot in his tie. *I've got everything a man could want—a beautiful wife. . .a successful business. . . and a son who practically idolizes me. Then why do I feel as if something is missing?*

His gaze came to rest on the crude wooden cross nailed to the wall behind the pulpit.

"Jimmy's not yours. You stole him."

As Jim stared at the cross, he wondered if he might be losing his mind.

"You need to confess. The truth will set you free."

Jim reached into his jacket pocket and pulled out a hankie to wipe the sweat dripping from his forehead. *Now I'm hearing voices? If this is what happens when you attend church, I don't want any part of it.*

He forced his gaze away from the cross and focused on his hands clenched in his lap. *Guess I didn't get my nails clean enough when I showered this morning. I've still got paint under some of them.* He turned his wedding ring over. No paint there, but then he didn't wear it whenever he painted. The only time Jim put the band of gold on his finger was when they went out, and then it was only to please Linda. *I've spent a good deal of our marriage trying to please that woman, and look where it's gotten me—a seat on a hard pew in a church that's seen better days.*

He glanced around the room. The off-white walls looked like a blind man had painted them. There were roller marks in numerous places and several runs here and there. Sloppy work, that's what it was.

Jim jerked when Jimmy's elbow connected with his ribs. "Daddy, you're supposed to stand up."

"Huh?"

"Church is over. It's time to pray."

Heat flooded Jim's face as he stood. *Free at last. Now to go home and carve that fifteen-pound bird. A few helpings of turkey and some mashed potatoes, and I'll be good as new.*

∞

"I wish you didn't have to leave so soon. You barely touched your Thanksgiving dinner, and now you're heading home when you could have waited until morning."

The chilly November wind whipped at Abby's black woolen shawl, and she gave her brother a hug. "There's nothing here for me anymore. I have no reason to stay."

"You've got Lena, me, and your new nephew, Ira," Harold reminded. "You could stay and be part of our family."

Abby shook her head and blinked against the burning behind her eyes. She wouldn't give in to the threatening tears. Not here in front of Harold. One life had been taken, and another had recently entered the world. It was the way of things, and she must learn to deal with it.

"Well, if you're set on leaving, tell Mom and all of Abraham's family that we send our love," Harold said, hugging Abby one last time.

"I'll do that." Abby offered him her bravest smile and stepped onto the bus. She found an empty seat near the back, and a few minutes later, the bus pulled out of Dover.

Abby leaned back and closed her eyes, but uninvited visions flashed through her mind—the charred remains of the quilt shop—Lester's gloomy funeral service—the dinner afterward at Deborah's house—Thanksgiving with Harold and Lena. Abby didn't know how she had gotten through any of it without falling apart, but she'd managed to put on a courageous front and remain strong for Deborah's sake. It was the least she could do to make up for the poor woman's loss.

Abby felt as if a black cloud had settled over her heart, and she knew it wasn't good to hold her grief inside. But she was afraid if she gave in to the emotions swirling through her body, she might never stop crying. Her shoulders ached from the pressure and stress of holding everything in these last few days, and the emptiness in her heart threatened to envelop her.

She gripped the armrest on her seat, forcing her gaze to the scenery whizzing past her window. *I can get through this if I don't take time to think. When I get back to Mom's place, I'll keep busy helping her the way I did after Dad died. Surely in time, the pain will get better.*

Chapter 24

"Come sit with me awhile, Abby," Fannie said, patting the sofa cushion beside her. "We can have a cup of tea and look at the schee snow out the living room window."

Abby swished her dust mop back and forth across the hardwood floor like there was no tomorrow. "I don't have time to watch the pretty snow, Mom. I've got bread rising in the kitchen, clothes needing to be washed, more cleaning to do, and babies to bathe when they wake up from their morning naps." Her eyes looked hollow and tired, like she hadn't slept in many days, and Fannie felt concerned.

"We've got all day to finish our chores, daughter," she said softly. "And you don't have to do everything yourself."

"Jah, well, the work won't get done if we sit around watchin' the snow fall, now will it?" Abby said sharply, holding her body rigid.

The air between them felt thick, and Fannie's muscles coiled tight. It wasn't like her sweet girl to be so rude. Abby was usually soft-spoken and kind, no matter what the circumstances. "Are you feelin' all right this morning?"

"I'm fine." Abby squinted and massaged her temples, like she might have a headache. "If you need to relax, then please do, Mom."

"It's you who needs to relax. Ever since you returned from Ohio three months ago, all you've done is work."

Abby held the dust mop in midair. "The floor's dirty from the kinner tracking in mud and snow; there's always lots to be done."

"That's true, but you don't have to do it alone."

"You still tire easily, and it's my responsibility to help."

"Why do you feel it's necessary to care for me, Abby?"

Abby blinked. "Because—because Dad asked me to before he died."

Fannie's eyebrows lifted. "What?"

"He asked me to see that your needs were met if he didn't make it, and I'm keeping to that promise."

Tears clouded Fannie's vision, while guilt gnawed at her stomach. She should have had this discussion with Abby sooner. "Oh Abby, I'm sure your daed didn't mean for you to work yourself to death in an effort to meet my needs. He would have wanted you to build a life of your own and take care of your needs, too."

Abby sniffed. "It's too late for that, Mom. I gave up bein' with Lester to come here, and now he's gone." She quickly ran the dust mop across the floor near the woodstove. The hiss and crackle of the logs burning should have offered comfort, but they seemed only to fuel her frustration.

Fannie reached for her cup, sitting on the coffee table in front of her. Should she say what else was on her mind, or would it be best to let it go? "I'm thinkin' your needing to work has more to do with you tryin' to forget the past than it does with keeping your promise to your daed," she blurted.

Abby compressed her lips and kept right on sweeping.

Fannie sent up a quick prayer, determined to try one more time. "I was wondering if you'd be willing to work at the quilt shop on Monday of next week. Naomi's made a doctor's appointment for the boppli that day."

Abby's eyebrows drew together, and the floor creaked under her feet. "Is Susan sick?"

"It's just for a checkup, and I suppose it might include a shot or two if the doctor says it's time."

Abby moved to the other side of the room, swishing the dust mop along the baseboard near the wall.

"Would you be willing to manage the quilt shop for Naomi that day?" Fannie persisted.

"I can't, Mom. You know I can't."

"It's hard for Naomi to haul both girls into town and try to watch them, plus help Caleb in the store, and wait on customers in the quilt shop, too."

"I'm sorry about that." Abby pushed the mop under Abraham's favorite rocker, and then did the same to the chair beside it. "Can't Matthew be there on Monday?"

"He's got a dental appointment that day. Besides, now that he's planning to open a wood-working shop—"

"I didn't realize he was."

Fannie nodded. "He's been talking about it for some time. Haven't you heard him mention it?"

Abby shrugged. "I thought he enjoyed working at the quilt shop."

"He's only been filling in, and I doubt he'd be happy doing that for the rest of his life."

"What about Nancy? Can't she work there on Monday?"

"Nancy started working as a maad for Anna Beechy last week. Have you forgotten?"

"Maybe you should close the shop until you're ready to work full time again," Abby said, making no comment on Nancy's new job.

"That might not be for a while, if ever." Fannie took a sip of tea, savoring the pleasant mint flavor and hoping it would help her relax. She wasn't getting anywhere with her daughter and didn't know if anything she could say would get through to her. "The twins are a handful, and I'm not sure how well it would work for me to take 'em to the quilt shop every day."

"Naomi does it."

"I know, but her girls are further apart in age than my two little fellows."

"I can watch Timothy and Titus while you go to the quilt shop."

Fannie shook her head. "You're at home too much as it is. Wouldn't you enjoy workin' among the quilts again?"

Abby's winced as though she'd pricked her finger with a needle. "I can't."

"Why?"

"You know why, Mom. If Lester hadn't tried to rescue my quilts, he wouldn't have been killed." Abby sucked in a deep breath and moaned. "I doubt I'll ever have the desire to make another quilt, much less run a quilt shop."

"Don't you think it's time to begin moving on

with your life, Abby?"

"I am moving on."

"No, you're not. You stay cooped up here most of the time, minding the twins and working until you're ready to drop."

Abby headed for the door, holding the dust mop in front of her, and stepped outside.

A blast of cold air whipped through the open doorway, and Fannie shivered. She glanced out the window and saw Abby on the porch, shaking the mop so hard she feared the head might fly right off. *Lord, please intervene on my daughter's behalf. I fear if she doesn't soon deal with her pain she'll likely cave in.*

Abby reentered the living room a few minutes later, leaned the mop in one corner, and grabbed the dust rag from the table where she'd placed it earlier. She swished it across the front windowsills and worked her way around the room, dusting every nook and cranny.

"Naomi told me that Gladys Yutzy and Rhoda Lapp were by the quilt shop the other day," Fannie commented. "They both asked about you."

No response.

"I think they'd like to get together and do some quilting."

Still nothing.

"Rhoda thinks it would be fun to make a friendship quilt."

"They can do that without me."

"Gladys mentioned a quilt auction that's to be held in Kentucky this spring. They're looking for Amish quilts from all over the country, so I thought maybe we could send a few from my shop."

"Whatever you want to do, Mom. It doesn't concern me."

Fannie set her cup on the coffee table and stood. "Oh Abby, if you'd only get back into the routine of things maybe you would—"

"I won't work at the quilt shop, and nothing is going to change my mind!" Abby whirled around and fled the room.

Fannie flopped onto the couch with a groan. "Oh Lord, what's it gonna take to reach her?"

❦

"Why do you have to leave for work so early this morning?" Linda asked Jim as he turned off the alarm clock and crawled out of bed.

"I've got an early job, and I told you that last night. Just go on back to sleep."

"I'm already awake, so I may as well get up with you," she murmured, although it was tempting to stay under the warmth of their cozy Amish quilt.

"I can make my own lunch. There's no reason for you to get up," he insisted.

"And let you leave the house with nothing but a thermos full of black coffee and a couple of doughnuts?" Linda pushed the covers aside and reached for her fuzzy yellow robe, lying on the chair near her dressing table.

"Yeah, okay, whatever."

While Jim headed for the bathroom, Linda put on her slippers and padded down the hall. She stopped long enough to peek into Jimmy's room and was relieved to see that he was still asleep.

A short time later, she and Jim were in the kitchen. He stood in front of the coffeepot while she worked at the counter making a ham-and-cheese sandwich. "Would you like me to fix some scrambled eggs?" she asked. "I can put some of this ham in with them."

"Nope."

"A bowl of oatmeal?"

"I'm not hungry."

"Well, how about—"

"I said no!"

Linda recoiled, feeling like she had been slapped. "You don't have to be so mean."

"I get tired of you hounding me about things," he muttered.

"I don't do it on purpose." She turned her attention back to the sandwich, hoping he wouldn't see the tears clouding her vision.

"You push too hard and try to smother me the way you do Jimmy," he grumbled.

Linda grabbed a knife and slathered some mayonnaise on the bread, willing herself to keep quiet. Since she'd become a Christian, she had tried harder to please Jim, but she often fell short. It seemed nothing she did or said was good enough. Jim had become critical, finding fault with even the smallest things.

"I think if you found something constructive to do, we'd all be happier," Jim said with a grunt.

She whirled around to face him. "What is it you think I should be doing?"

He eyed her critically. "You've gained a few pounds since Christmas. It might not be a bad idea if you started exercising so you can shed some of it."

Linda's hands went immediately to her hips. Had she put on weight? Maybe a little. "I could enroll in the fitness center you painted. If you've changed your mind about me going there, that is."

Jim's face turned red, and his forehead wrinkled. "Forget I said anything. The fitness center's a bad idea."

"Maybe I could buy an exercise tape and get together with Beth to work out."

"You already spend too much time with that religious fanatic!" He stomped across the room, jerked open the refrigerator door, and grabbed a carton of milk. Then he turned, marched over to the cupboard, and reached around her to retrieve a glass.

"I'm sorry you don't approve of my new friend," Linda said, her defenses rising further. "If you weren't so unwilling to get together with Beth and her husband and weren't too stubborn to attend church regularly, you might realize there are more important things in life than painting twelve hours a day or hanging out with the guys at the pool hall when you aren't working!" Linda's hands shook, and she berated herself for losing her temper. This was no way to set a Christian example for Jim.

He slammed the glass down hard on the counter, and she was surprised it didn't shatter. "Don't start with me this morning, Linda. I'm not in the mood!"

She moved slowly toward him, praying they might be able to resolve this before he left for work and hoping their shouting hadn't roused Jimmy. "Let's not argue, Jim. I love you, and—"

"Then get off my back!"

A knot formed in Linda's throat as her eyes flooded with tears. What had happened to their storybook romance? Had they both changed so much over the last few years that everything they said to each other turned into a disagreement?

She slunk back to the cupboard to put Jim's sandwich in some plastic wrap as a feeling of despair weighed her down. Right after she got Jimmy off to school, she planned to give Rev. Deming a call. She'd put it off long enough.

∞

Abby leaned over the crib and pinned Timothy's diaper in place. Titus would be next, and then she planned to take the boys downstairs to the parlor, where Mom was working on a new Sunday dress.

Titus began to cry, thrashing his arms and legs. In the process, he bopped his brother on the nose, and Timothy started to howl.

"Hush now; I'll be done in a minute." Abby's patience was beginning to wane. She loved her little brothers, but there were times when they got on her nerves. Of course she'd never let Mom know that.

Abby finished diapering the other twin and reached into the crib. Timothy had settled down, so she figured he could wait a few minutes while she carried Titus downstairs. She had no more than picked the boy up, when Timothy let loose with an ear-piercing wail. "I can't carry you both at the same time," she said, remembering when they were newborns and she'd been able to manage two at once. But the boys had been growing quicker than summer grass and were turning into a couple of chunks.

Timothy let out another yelp, and Abby felt as if she could scream. She hurried out of the room and down the hall.

Downstairs, as she put Titus in the playpen, she could still hear Timothy's desperate cries.

"I'd better get that little fellow," Mom said, looking up from her sewing project at the treadle sewing machine.

Abby shook her head. "I'll do it." She rushed up the stairs and stopped at the top long enough to catch her breath. A pulsating throb in her right temple let her know a headache was forthcoming, and a wave of heaviness settled on her shoulders. *Keep going. Keep working. Don't stop. Don't take time to think.*

The baby's cries seemed to bounce off the walls and echo into the hallway. Abby lifted her shoulders and sucked in a deep breath. "I'm coming, Timothy!"

Chapter 25

I'm glad we decided to visit my daed and the family today," Naomi said to Caleb as they loaded the girls into their sleigh. "We haven't spent much time together since Christmas."

Caleb nodded. "Jah, and since this is an off-Sunday and there's no preaching, it's the perfect time to get in a good visit." He reached over and took her hand. "Besides, a sleigh ride in the snow is pretty romantic, don't ya think?"

She chuckled. "It used to be, when we were courting."

"Still can be," he said with a wink. "We've just got ourselves a couple of chaperones now."

"I hope Abby's willing to sit awhile and visit with us," Naomi said, changing the subject. "The last time I dropped by, she kept running all over the place, fiddling with this, fixing that, and fussing over the twins. If she doesn't slow down, I fear she'll end up sick in bed."

"Each person deals with their grief in a different way," Caleb said, picking up the reins. "Giddyap there, boy!"

"You think that's why Abby works so hard and won't go to any social functions?"

"Yep. Most likely she's still pinin' for Lester."

"But it's been three months since he died, and

she never talks about her pain."

Caleb shrugged. "Remember what I was goin' through when I crushed my hand under Mose Kauffman's rig and knew I could never work on buggies again?"

"Jah. You refused to see me or even talk about what had happened."

"I thought if I didn't discuss it, I wouldn't have to deal with the agony. But after your daed set me straight on a few things, I finally came to realize that life goes on, despite the trials that come our way. It's what we do about our situation that makes the difference." Caleb gave Naomi a lopsided grin. "I'm glad I listened to Abraham and bought his store. Otherwise we might not have gotten married or become the parents of such *siess* little girls."

Naomi glanced at the baby in her arms and then looked over her shoulder at their other daughter. "Jah, Sarah and Susan are both mighty sweet. Two more precious girls cannot be found in all of Lancaster County."

"My advice is for you to continue being Abby's friend, pray for her, and encourage her to get back to quiltin' again."

"You're right, that is what she needs," Naomi agreed. "Fannie confided in me the other day that Abby won't work on quilts and has tried to take over the care of Timothy and Titus so much so that Fannie feels as if she's not able to raise her own boys."

"Can't say as I blame her for feelin' frustrated. I wouldn't want someone else takin' over the care of our kinner, would you?"

Naomi shook her head. "Not unless I was sick or injured and couldn't do it. But Fannie's been feeling fine for some time, so there's no logical reason for Abby to take over the way she has."

"No reason except she's drivin' herself to keep from dealin' with her pain."

"I asked Fannie to speak with Abby about filling in for me tomorrow while I take Susan to her doctor's appointment."

"You think she'll do it?"

Naomi shrugged. "Guess I won't know till we get to their place and I've had a chance to speak with her."

⚬⚬⚬

Abby glanced out the kitchen window and saw the Hoffmeirs' sleigh pull into their yard. The realization that she would never experience the joy of bundling up in the snow with her husband and children hit her like a vicious punch to the stomach. When her quilt shop went up in flames, so did her hopes and dreams. When Lester was killed, so was her chance to marry and raise a family.

"Naomi's here!" Mary Ann hollered from across the room. "Now I get to play with my nieces."

Abby was tempted to hurry upstairs to her room so she wouldn't have to socialize, but that would be rude. Instead, she scooted over to the stove and flicked the propane switch on. She would heat water for tea and serve it to their guests, along with the apple crumb pie she'd made yesterday.

A short time later, the adults gathered around the table, and Nancy, Mary Ann, and Samuel went to the living room to entertain the little ones.

"Umm. . .this is sure good pie," Matthew said,

smiling at Abby.

"Danki."

Naomi nodded. "Apple crumb pie and hot cinnamon tea hits the spot on a cold, snowy day."

Abraham chuckled and thumped his stomach. "I can eat pie most any time of the year. Or any time of the day or night for that matter."

Abby's mamm reached over and jabbed him in the ribs. "I knew you would say something like that, Husband."

He tickled her under the chin. "You know me so well."

Tears pricked Abby's eyes, and she blinked to keep them from spilling over. All this happy talk was one more reminder of her great loss.

"My favorite pie is cherry," Jake said, swiping a napkin across his chin.

"Mine's peach, although I don't get it as often as I'd like." Caleb gave Naomi a sidelong glance, but she ignored him.

Mom pushed away from the table. "I think I hear my boys crying."

Abby jumped up, nearly knocking over her chair in the process. "I'll see to them. You stay and visit with your company."

"But they might need to be fed," her mother said firmly. "Besides, our company came to see you, too." She hurried out of the room before Abby had a chance to argue the point.

Feeling like a caged animal, Abby grabbed her shawl off a wall peg and made a beeline for the back door.

"Where ya goin'?" Abraham called after her.

"Just need a bit of fresh air."

Outside, Abby stepped carefully over the ridges of frozen snow as she made her way to the barn. The ground was slippery beneath her feet, and she knew she mustn't run. A few minutes later, she opened the barn door and stepped inside, relieved to discover a lantern had been lit and a fire blazed in the woodstove. She took a seat on a bale of straw and leaned her head against the wall. *Everyone must think I'm terrible, but I couldn't stay in there a minute longer.*

A fluffy, gray-and-white cat rubbed against Abby's legs and purred. When she was a young girl, she'd enjoyed playing with the kittens in their barn and found comfort in holding one close and letting it lick her nose with its sandpapery tongue. Not anymore. Abby felt irritation as soon as the cat showed up.

She stood and moved closer to the stove. *What's wrong with me? Why can't I enjoy any of the things that used to bring me pleasure?*

The door squeaked, and Abby turned to see who had entered the barn. It was Naomi.

"I came to see if you're all right," Naomi said, crossing the room.

"I'm fine."

"Would you mind if I stay awhile so we can talk?"

Abby shrugged. "I'm not good company today."

"That's okay; you don't have to be." Naomi motioned to the bale of straw. "Let's have a seat, shall we?"

Abby didn't want to hurt her stepsister's feelings, so she lowered herself to one of the bales.

"Did Fannie ask you about filling in for me

at the store tomorrow?"

"Jah, but I can't do it. Sorry."

"How come?"

"There's too much to do here, and it wouldn't be right to leave Mom with all the work."

"I'm sure she could manage for one day."

Abby just sat there, hoping Naomi would change the subject.

"Your mamm's concerned about you. We all are."

"No need to worry about me," Abby mumbled.

"I'm not trying to tell you what to do, but I think it might help if you talk about the accident and the pain of losing Lester."

Abby clenched her fingers until they dug into the palms of her hands. Didn't Naomi realize that talking about the fire wouldn't make her feel better? It wouldn't bring Lester back either.

Naomi reached over and took Abby's hand. "Keeping things bottled up isn't a good thing. Your pain will never leave until you've come to grips with it."

Abby's face grew hot, and she looked away. "That's easy for you to say. The man you love isn't dead."

Naomi didn't reply. She merely sat quietly, and Abby did the same. The only sounds were the gentle nicker of the buggy horses and the crackling wood from the nearby stove.

Finally, Naomi spoke again. "You're right, Abby. I don't understand what it's like to lose the man I love, but I do know the pain of losin' my little brother."

Abby grimaced. She hadn't meant for Naomi to think about her past. "I—I know it must have been hard for you when Zach was kidnapped."

"Jah, it was hard on the whole family. I blamed myself for a time, but I sought forgiveness and finally came to realize that I couldn't undo the things I had done."

"There's no point in talking about this," Abby mumbled.

"I think there is. I believe that in time—"

"Have you lost all hope of Zach ever coming home?" Abby interrupted.

"I still pray for my little brother, but I know, short of a miracle, it's not likely we'll ever see Zach again."

"But there's still some hope, right?"

"There's always hope. Fact is, the Bible teaches that *mir lewe uff hoffning*—we live on hope."

Abby knew what the Bible taught, but it didn't apply to her situation. "If Zach is still alive, then there might be hope of him coming home some day. Lester's dead though, so there's no chance for him to return."

∞

Fannie had no more than finished diapering the twins when she heard a horse and buggy roll into the yard, making crunching noises against the hard-packed snow. She went to the bedroom window and peeked out. There was Edna, stepping down from her buggy.

Fannie hurried from the room and leaned over the banister. "Come on up!" she hollered as Edna stepped into the hallway. "I'm about to nurse the twins, but we can visit while I feed them."

"Be right there!" Edna called in response.

Fannie slipped back to the boys' room and

seated herself in the rocking chair with Timothy in her arms. Titus seemed content to suck his thumb for the moment, but Timothy had been fussing ever since she'd come upstairs.

Soon Edna entered the room, her cheeks rosy and her eyes aglow. "Wie geht's?" she said, flopping to the end of Fannie's bed.

"I'm fine, and you?"

Edna rubbed her hands briskly over her arms. "At the moment, I'm cold, but other than that, I'm right as rain." She giggled. "Make that right as snow."

Fannie smiled.

"How are our growin' boys?" Edna asked. "Are they sittin' up by themselves yet?"

"No, but I expect it won't be long in comin'."

"How's Abby these days? And where is she? I didn't see her downstairs with the others."

"She must have gone outside. She was pretty worked up earlier." Fannie shook her head. "I'm really worried about her, Edna. All my daughter does is work, and she won't consider making quilts or helpin' out at the shop. Not even part time."

Edna clucked her tongue. "It's never easy to lose a loved one, but when you're Abby's age and on the brink of marriage, I think it hurts even more."

"She blames herself for the fire, you know."

Edna's dark eyebrows rose. "How so? She wasn't there. She didn't knock over that kerosene lantern."

"You and I know it wasn't her fault, but my daughter thinks otherwise."

Fannie finished nursing Timothy; then after he had burped, she put him back in the crib. Now it was Titus's turn to be fed. "Abby believes if she'd gone back to Ohio sooner the accident wouldn't have happened. Also, she told me that she'd had a recurring dream about a fire, and she thinks it was some kind of warning—one she should have heeded."

"But if it was Lester's time to go, nothing Abby said or did could have prevented the fire or him gettin' killed."

Fannie shook her head. "I know some believe that's the way things are, but I've never been so sure about it."

Edna shrugged and moved over to the crib, reaching through the slats and tickling Timothy's bare toes. Apparently she didn't want to debate the issue.

"To tell you the truth," Fannie went on to say, "I'm beginning to wonder if Abby will ever get over Lester's death and become part of our world again."

"She's not pinin' away in her room or givin' in to fits of tears, is she?"

"No, but she keeps everything bottled up and works from sunup to sunset." Fannie sighed. "Won't even talk to her own mamm about things."

Edna walked away from the crib, and Timothy howled. She scooted back across the room and picked him up. Taking a seat on the bed, she rocked the baby in her arms.

"Say, I have an idea," she said in an excited tone.

"What's that?"

"I'm wonderin' if it might help Abby if she went away for a while."

Fannie blinked. "Away? Where would she go?"

"Give me a minute, now. I'm thinkin' on that."

Fannie hated the idea of Abby going anywhere, but she'd be willing to send her to the moon if it would help with the depression.

"Hmm. . ."

"What?"

"My late husband's sister is a widow who lives in a small Amish community in northern Montana."

"And?"

"Elizabeth's been through a lot, losin' both her husband and son in the same accident."

"How'd she deal with it?"

"Better than you can imagine."

"Do you think she might be able to help my daughter?"

Edna shrugged. "It's worth a try, don't ya think?"

"Maybe so, but how are we going to convince Abby to go to Montana to visit a woman she's never met?"

Edna's smile stretched ear-to-ear. "Just leave that up to me."

Chapter 26

Linda fidgeted with the straps on her purse as she sat across the desk from Rev. Deming, waiting for him to get off the phone. *Should I have come here this morning? Will the pastor be able to help me?* She gripped the armrest of the chair. *If Jim finds out, he'll be furious.*

Rev. Deming hung up the phone a few minutes later. "That was my wife calling from the church's daycare center. They're shorthanded today and she can't get away, so I'll ask my secretary to join us, if you don't mind."

"Your. . .your secretary?" What was the man planning to do, ask Mrs. Gray to take notes during their counseling session?

He nodded. "My wife usually sits in whenever I counsel with women."

"Can't we leave the door open or something?" Linda leaned forward, her shoulders stiffening. "I wouldn't feel comfortable discussing my problems with anyone but you or Mrs. Deming."

The pastor sat silently for several seconds. Finally, he nodded and reached for his Bible. "The door stays open. How can I help you, Linda?"

She drew in a deep breath. "My. . .my husband needs the Lord but he refuses to come to church."

"I believe he was here for our Thanksgiving

service and the children's Christmas program."

"Yes, but he only came out of obligation, and it was obvious that he was miserable."

"Perhaps in time he will feel more comfortable about attending on a regular basis."

She shook her head. "Unless things get better at home, I doubt he'll ever agree to come to church with me and Jimmy on Sunday mornings."

Pastor Deming placed his hands on top of the Bible and leaned slightly forward. "Would you care to explain?"

"Jim and I were high school sweethearts, and during the first few years of our marriage we got along well."

"And now?"

"Ever since we adopted our son, things haven't been right between us. Jim works long hours and is rarely at home. When he is there, he's edgy and often says harsh things to me. We hardly ever do anything just for fun, and whenever I've suggested we go back East to visit his folks, he flatly refuses." Linda paused and licked her lips. "At first I thought it was my fault that our marriage was falling apart, because I tend to be overprotective of Jimmy. But then, after I became a Christian, I made more of an effort to please my husband and not be so overbearing where our son is concerned."

"How does Jim respond to that?"

"It's made no dent in his moods. If anything, I think he's become more impatient with me. There are times when he seems so agitated, and I'm afraid he might—" Tears clouded Linda's vision, and she sniffed, hoping to keep them from spilling over.

Pastor Deming opened a drawer in his desk

and pulled out a box of tissues. "Take your time, Linda. I know this is hard."

"Thanks." She wiped her eyes and blew her nose. "I have no proof, but I've got a terrible feeling that Jim might be hiding something from me."

"Do you think he could be involved with another woman?"

Linda trembled. "Oh, I hope not. But I suppose—" Her voice faltered. What if Jim was having an affair? How would she cope if he wanted a divorce? She had no job, no way of supporting herself and Jimmy. And what if he tried to get custody of their son? "Do you think I should hire a detective?"

The pastor ran his fingers through the back of his thick gray hair. "That's your decision of course, but if your husband found out he was being followed, it could make things worse."

"You're probably right. Besides, how would I pay for a detective without Jim knowing?"

"I'd like to give you a list of scriptures to read," the pastor said. A few minutes later he handed her a slip of paper. "I would also suggest you keep praying and try to set your husband a good example." His eyebrows drew together. "Do you think Jim might be willing to come in for counseling, either by himself or with you as a couple?"

She shook her head. "I've suggested that, but he flatly refuses."

Rev. Deming offered to pray with Linda before she left, and she nodded in agreement. At this point, only God could save her marriage.

∞

Abby stood at the kitchen sink, peeling potatoes for supper. She had struggled with guilt ever since she'd turned down Naomi's request to fill in for her at the quilt shop. But there was no way she could go to the shop without falling apart.

She cut up the potatoes and dropped them into the pot of stew, then glanced out the kitchen window when she heard a horse and buggy pull into the yard. It was Cousin Edna, and she was heading for the house. Abby hurried to open the back door.

Edna stamped the snow off her boots before entering the kitchen. "Whew! Sure is a blustery day! I wish spring would hurry and get here."

"I'm surprised you would make the trip from Strasburg in this kind of weather," Abby commented.

Edna hung her heavy black shawl and matching bonnet on a wall peg, then went to warm herself in front of the woodstove. "I don't enjoy drivin' the buggy in the snow, but I needed to speak with you today."

"I thought it was Mom you came to see."

"Nope." Edna glanced around. "Where is Fannie, anyway?"

"Upstairs feeding the twins."

"And the menfolk?"

"They're out in the barn." Abby thought her mother's cousin was acting kind of strange, but then Edna always had been a little different than most. "Would you like a cup of hot apple cider or some mint tea?"

"Jah, that sounds good."

"Which one do you want?" Abby asked, feeling a bit impatient. She had things to do and didn't have time for a visit with her mamm's happy-go-lucky cousin.

Edna shrugged and pulled out a chair at the

kitchen table. "It doesn't matter. Just as long as it's hot. Need somethin' to warm my insides, don't ya know?"

Abby served them each a cup of tea and took a seat across from the woman. "Would you care for something to eat? I believe there's still half a shoofly pie left over from this morning."

Edna patted her stomach. "I'd better pass on the pie. Think I gained a couple of pounds over the holidays."

Abby studied the woman's slender figure. Even if she had gained a few pounds, it wouldn't be a bad thing. From all that Mom had said, Edna had never dealt with a weight problem. Not the way Mom struggled with it, that was for certain sure.

"So, what'd you want to talk to me about?" Abby asked.

Edna took a sip of tea and smacked her lips. "Umm. . .this surely hits the spot."

An uncomfortable silence passed between them, and Abby glanced at the door leading to the hall-way. She wished Mom would come downstairs and rescue her. If Edna didn't say what was on her mind pretty soon, Abby might leave the table and cut more vegetables for the stew simmering on the stove.

"I've been in touch with my sister-in-law who lives near Rexford, Montana," Edna announced. "She's wantin' me to come there for a visit, but it would mean I'd have to travel by train."

Abby had no idea what this had to do with her, but she waited to hear what else Edna had to say.

"I've never been on a train before, and to tell ya the truth, I hate the idea of travelin' alone." Edna paused and took another swallow of tea. "So, I was wonderin' if you'd be willing to accompany me."

Abby squinted. "You want me to make a trip to Montana?"

"Jah."

"But that's clear across the country."

"It's not so far by train."

"I can't leave Mom and the kinner. Surely there must be someone else you can ask."

Edna shook her head. "Can't ask my daughter. She's got three little ones to care for. Gerald, my son, has his dairy farm to run."

"What about Gerald's wife? Couldn't she go with you?"

"Mattie helps Gerald with the cows. Besides, she's got four kinner still living at home."

Abby's head began to throb, and she massaged the bridge of her nose, hoping to ward off the headache she felt was coming.

"It would mean a lot to me if you'd agree to be my traveling companion," Edna persisted. "To tell you the truth, I think it might do you some good, too."

Abby's hand trembled as she reached for her cup. She gulped some tea and scalded her lips. "Ouch!"

"You okay?"

"Just drank it too quickly."

"Want me to get you a glass of cold water?"

"No, no. I'm fine." Abby grimaced. *Liar. You're not fine. Your hands are shaking, and your cheeks feel hot as the stove.* The thought of leaving this safe haven made her stomach feel like it was tied up in knots.

Edna sat staring at Abby. For the life of her,

Abby couldn't imagine what her mother's cousin was thinking.

"If your mamm says she can get along without you, would ya be willing to go?"

Abby opened her mouth to decline, but before she got a word out, Mom stepped into the room.

"What's all this about me gettin' along without Abby?"

Abby breathed a sigh of relief. Mom would set Edna straight on things.

"My sister-in-law, who lives in Montana, has invited me to come there for a visit," Edna said, motioning Mom to join them at the table. "I've invited Abby to go along, since I'm nervous about ridin' the train by myself."

Mom helped herself to a cup of tea and took a seat at the table. "I think the idea of you going to Montana is a fine one, daughter."

"What?" Abby could hardly believe her mother would say such a thing. Didn't Mom realize how hard it would be to get along without her help?

"Nancy and Mary Ann are capable of helping in your absence, and I think the trip would do you a world of good." Mom gave Edna a quick wink. "Besides, I'd never sleep nights if I thought my favorite cousin was travelin' all that way by herself."

Abby squirmed in her chair, feeling like a helpless bug trapped in a spider's web. *Tricked might be a better word for it,* she thought ruefully. *I wouldn't be surprised if Mom and Cousin Edna didn't cook this whole thing up in order to get me away from here.* She took another sip of tea, this time being careful not to burn her lips. It wasn't good for a body to get so worked up, and she knew she probably wasn't thinking clearly. Truth was, she hadn't had many clear thoughts since Lester died.

"How about it, Abby?" Edna persisted. "Will you go with me to Montana?"

Abby glanced at Mom, then over at her cousin. Both women wore expectant looks, and Abby figured if she didn't say yes, she would be forced to sit here all day and listen to their arguments. She sighed and set her cup on the table. "Jah, okay. I'll go."

Chapter 27

Y ou're lookin' mighty glum, Matthew," Naomi said to her brother as he entered the store. "Did you have trouble with the roads this cold Friday morning, or did you get up on the wrong side of the bed?"

Matthew brushed the snow off his heavy woolen jacket and hung it on the closest wall peg. "Neither one."

"Then why the long face?"

He shrugged and removed his black felt hat, hanging it over the top of his jacket.

Naomi skirted around the counter and stepped up beside him. "Come now, brother. I know something is bothering you, and I won't stop asking till you tell me what it is."

Matthew grunted and leaned against the front of the counter. "It's Abby. She's gone."

"Gone?"

He nodded.

"What do you mean? Where'd she go? Not back to Ohio, I hope."

"No, she left for Montana. Caught an early morning train with Fannie's cousin, Edna."

Naomi's mouth fell open. "This is the first I've heard of it. Why would they go to Montana?"

"Yeah, why would they?" Caleb asked as he

strolled across the room with Sarah toddling beside him and Susan snuggled in his arms.

"Guess Edna has a sister-in-law who lives near Rexford, and she's decided to go visit her," Matthew replied.

"In the dead of winter?" Caleb's eyes were wide. "Jah."

"But why'd Abby go with her?" Naomi questioned. "Ever since Lester died, she hasn't wanted to do much of anything except hang around my daed's place and help Fannie."

Matthew reached up to scratch the side of his head. "From what I gathered, Edna's afraid to ride the train alone. She practically begged Abby to go along."

Naomi smiled. "I believe Edna and Fannie might have cooked this up in order to get Abby off someplace where she could rest and allow her broken heart to mend."

"Makes sense to me," Caleb put in. He handed the baby to Naomi. "I think she's wet."

Naomi squinted at him. "Would it kill you to change a windel once in a while?"

"It might." He wrinkled his nose. "Especially if it was a dirty one."

She groaned. "You're such a *hatzkauer*."

"I ain't no coward."

"Prove it."

"All right, I will." Caleb took the baby from her. "Is it all right if I leave Sarah here with you?" he asked with a grin.

"Jah, sure. She can play with her doll while Matthew and I finish our discussion."

Caleb headed for the back room, while Naomi

found Sarah's faceless doll and got her settled on the braided throw rug behind the counter. Then she called to Matthew, who had headed in the direction of the quilt shop. "Where are you going?"

"I'm workin' here today."

Naomi followed him into the next room and waited until he had all the gas lamps lit. "Are you planning to tell me why you're so upset about Abby going to Montana?"

He shrugged his broad shoulders. "Just don't think it's a good idea. What if she likes it there and decides to stay?"

"Ah, so that's the problem. I've been suspicious for some time that you cared for her."

Matthew moved to the window and lifted the dark shade. "Of course I care. She's part of our family."

Naomi studied her handsome brother.

"Why are you starin' at me like that?" he asked, moving to the wooden counter in the center of the room.

"You're in love with Abby, aren't you?"

Matthew's ears turned red, and the color quickly spread to his face. "Wouldn't do me no good if I was."

"Why do you say that?"

"She's in love with Lester."

Naomi shook her head. "Lester's dead."

"Don't ya think I know that?" Deep creases formed above Matthew's brows. "Abby doesn't see me as anything more than a big brother. So even if her pain should heal, I doubt she could fall in love with me."

Naomi's heart went out to Matthew. She knew

well the frustration of being in love with someone and thinking things would never work out. Yet God had worked a miracle in her life where Caleb was concerned, and He could do it for Matthew and Abby, too.

Naomi touched her brother's arm. "My advice is to pray about a relationship with Abby and keep being her friend."

He grabbed a stack of invoices from under the counter. "No problem there."

∞

Abby leaned her head against the back of the seat, a sense of relief washing over her. Edna had finally drifted off to sleep, after spending the last several hours talking nonstop and telling one joke after another. All Abby wanted to do was watch the passing scenery and be left alone with her private thoughts. Her mind spun with the details of Lester's death and fueled her anxiety. Snippets of her last letter from him rolled around in her mind. He'd been anxious for her to return home—anxious for their wedding.

Clickety-clack, clickety-clack, the train rumbled over the tracks, taking them farther and farther away from all that was familiar to her. What would Montana be like? How long would Elizabeth expect them to stay? Would there be something for Abby to do there so she wouldn't have to think about Lester or the quilt shop in Ohio that no longer existed? She swallowed around the perpetual lump in her throat and closed her eyes. *I mustn't allow myself to think about Lester or what might have been. Maybe a nap would be good for me, too. When I wake up, I hope my headache is gone.*

Abby had just nodded off when someone bumped her shoulder. She opened her eyes and turned her head toward the aisle. A tall, dark-haired man, wearing blue jeans, a fancy red-and-white western shirt, and a black cowboy hat, smiled down at her. "Excuse me, ma'am," he said in a slow, lazy drawl. "I was tryin' to get something outta the overhead luggage rack, and I sure didn't mean to wake ya."

"I—I wasn't sleeping," she stammered.

He nodded toward Edna, who leaned against the window with her mouth slightly open. "Guess I didn't wake your mama either."

"Oh, she's not my mamm. Edna's my mother's cousin."

He grinned. "Where ya headed?"

"Rexford, Montana."

"What's up there?"

"Edna and I are goin' to visit a relative of hers."

"Amish, like you?"

Abby nodded.

"Didn't realize there were any Amish out West."

"There aren't that many, but—" Abby stopped in mid-sentence. She didn't care for the way the cowboy was looking at her, with his dark eyes narrowed and his lips curled in a crooked smile. It made her feel like a feeble mouse about to be pounced on by a hungry cat. Truth was, she felt as out of place talking to this friendly cowboy as a prune in a basket of apples.

As the train rounded a curve, it rocked from side to side, and Abby gripped her armrest. "Maybe you should take a seat so you don't topple over," she told the man.

"Aw, I'm a professional bull rider; I've been up against worse than this." He winked at her.

Abby squirmed in her seat, feeling more uncomfortable by the minute. She was tempted to wake Edna.

"Well, guess I'd best be gettin' back to my seat. Nice jawin' with ya, ma'am." The man tipped his hat and shuffled across the aisle.

Abby gave a brief nod as she breathed a sigh of relief.

∽

Abraham entered the kitchen and found his wife sitting at the table, sobbing. He hurried across the room and touched her shoulder. "Fannie, what's wrong? Arc ya sick? Has somethin' happened to one of the twins?"

She looked up at him, her cheeks flushed like ripe cherries. "The boys are fine, and I'm not sick."

Abraham pulled out a chair and sat beside her. "What is it then?"

Fannie sniffed. "I'm missin' Abby and wondering if we did the right thing by sending her away."

"We? Who's *we*, Fannie?"

"Me and Edna."

He tugged on his beard. "You and Edna set up this whole Montana trip to get Abby out of town?"

She lifted her shoulders in a quick shrug. "We thought it would be good for her to get away. To tell you the truth, I'd begun to resent the way she took over the bopplin's care and so many of my chores around the house."

Abraham let his wife's words sink in before he said anything. He'd known she was worried about

Abby's depression, but he had no idea she'd felt so frustrated over her daughter's help.

"Don't get me wrong," Fannie said, as though she could read his mind. "I'm not sayin' I didn't appreciate all the things Abby did around here. She was a big help, especially when the twins were first born."

Abraham took her hand and gave it a gentle squeeze. "You don't have to explain. I know you love Abby. It just never occurred to me that you might be feelin' resentful about not bein' in charge of your house anymore. You should have said something. I could have spoken to Abby about it."

She shook her head. "That would have only made things worse, Abraham. Abby's still going through troubled waters and needs to be handled with tender loving care."

"I expect you're right about that."

"When I shared my concerns with Edna, she came up with the idea of taking Abby with her to Montana. She said her sister-in-law has been through the fire herself, so she's hoping Elizabeth might be able to help Abby through this difficult time." Fannie groaned. "I sure have failed in that regard."

"Don't be so hard on yourself, my love. You've done your best by Abby."

"You think so?"

Abraham nodded. "But Edna might be right about Abby needin' some time away." He gave his beard another good tug. "Got any idea how long they'll be gone?"

Fannie offered him a sheepish grin. "Edna plans to come back in a few weeks, but she's not told my daughter that. She hopes to fix it so Abby will stay on through the rest of winter and into the spring awhile."

He frowned. "How come so long?"

"In June there's to be a big auction in the Rexford Amish community, and one of the main things they auction off is quilts. So Edna figures—"

"But Abby's been sayin' she wants nothing to do with quilts," Abraham interrupted.

She sighed. "I know, but if she's ever to move on with her life, then she's got to work through her grief. I'm hoping someday she'll enjoy quilting again, too."

"What if that doesn't happen?"

"Then I'll keep praying for her." Fannie's voice broke. "Oh Abraham, I can't bear the thought of my daughter spending the rest of her life in such grief."

Abraham's mind drifted back in time. Back to when his first wife had been killed, and then on to when his baby boy was kidnapped. If he hadn't finally let go of his pain, he wondered where he might be today. Certainly not sitting here with his sweet Fannie Mae. He'd probably still be a cranky old storekeeper who felt sorry for himself and yelled at his kinner when he should have been loving them.

He leaned over and kissed Fannie's cheek. "We need to put Abby's future in our heavenly Father's hands."

Fannie smiled through her tears. "How'd ya get to be so smart, Husband?"

He chucked her under the chin. "Guess bein' around you so much has caused some of your wisdom to rub off on me."

She swatted him playfully on the arm. "Go on with ya now."

A piercing wail drifted down the stairs, and Abraham tipped his head. "Sounds like the boys are awake."

"I'd best go see to them." Fannie started to stand, but Abraham beat her to it. "Let me get 'em while you fix yourself a cup of tea."

She lifted her shoulders in an exaggerated shrug. "What are you tryin' to do, Abraham, take over where Abby left off?"

He winced as though she'd wounded him, but then followed it with a quick wink. "You're right, Fannie Mae. Far be it from me to take over your chores."

She gave him a quick hug, then rushed out of the room. Abraham decided he would head back to the barn, because that's where he did his best praying.

Chapter 28

Linda tried to relax, curling her legs underneath her and pushing against the sofa cushions. It was Saturday, and she was alone. Jimmy had gone over to Allen's to spend the day, and as usual, Jim was working. She'd decided this was a good time to reread the verses of scripture Rev. Deming had given her earlier in the week.

Linda opened her Bible and turned to 2 Timothy 1:7: "'For the spirit God gave us does not make us timid, but gives us power, love, and self-discipline,'" she read aloud.

The reverend must have realized that I'm full of fears. Fear that Jim will leave me. Fear that I won't be able to love him as I should. Fear that he will never find the Lord as his personal Savior.

Linda turned to the next verse of scripture, Galatians 5:22: "'But the fruit of the Spirit is love, joy, peace, forbearance, kindness, goodness, faithfulness, gentleness and self-control. Against such things there is no law.'" She squeezed her eyes shut. *Lord, I need the fruits of the Spirit—especially peace and patience. In my frustration over our relationship, I've often become impatient and said things to Jim out of anger. Help me become the kind of wife he needs, and help him see You living in me.*

The telephone rang, and Linda jumped. She

hurried across the room and grabbed the receiver, hoping it might be Jim. "Hello, Scott residence."

"Linda, this is Marian. Is my son at home? I need to speak with him."

Linda frowned. Couldn't Jim's mother have asked how she and Jimmy were doing before demanding to speak with her son? "Jim's working today, Marian. May I take a message?"

"I have something important to tell him, and I'd rather he hear it from me."

"I suppose you could call his cell phone. Do you have that number?"

"I thought Jim had given it to me, but I can't seem to find it."

Linda gave her mother-in-law the phone number slowly, then repeated it.

"All right, thanks. Be sure to give Jimmy a hug from his grandma and grandpa Scott."

"Yes, I will. Good-bye, Marian."

Linda hung up the phone, wondering what Jim's mother wanted to tell him that she couldn't have said to her. She hoped it wasn't bad news, but if it was anything serious, she felt sure Jim would call and let her know.

∽

"Fannie is really missing Abby," Naomi told Caleb as the two of them set out some new rubber stamps in the store. "I hope she and Edna won't be gone too long."

Caleb grunted. "I would think Fannie might be glad to have her house back. Abby pretty much took over after the twins were born."

Naomi nodded. "That's true, but she was only trying to help. After Lester died, the poor thing needed something to keep herself busy."

"Let's hope that when Abby returns to Pennsylvania she'll feel better about things and will be willing to work at the quilt shop again," Caleb said. "We can't keep buying quilts from the Amish and Mennonite ladies in our community to sell in the shop and expect Matthew to work there. He's trying to get his woodworking shop going, you know."

"I've not heard him complain."

"Men don't complain, Naomi."

She slapped him playfully on the arm. "Is that so?"

"Hey, quit that!"

She snickered. "See, you're complaining now."

He chuckled and pushed the last box of stamps over to her. "Here you go. I'd better go see who just came into the store."

"Okay, you wait on the customer, and when I get done with these stamps, I'll go to the back room and check on our sleeping girls."

Caleb gave her a peck on the cheek and headed up front.

As Naomi set the last of the stamps in place, she thought about Ginny Meyers and how she used to come into the store to buy rubber stamps for her scrapbooking projects. It had been some time since Naomi had heard anything from Ginny, and she wondered how her old friend was doing. Ginny had only come home once since she'd headed west with Naomi, and that was just for a short visit with her folks one Christmas. To Naomi's knowledge, Ginny's family had never even met Ginny's husband.

How sad, she thought, *that some families rarely*

see each other and live so far away. If I had stayed out West, I would have surely missed my family.

"Got any new stamps?"

Naomi jumped at the sound of a woman's voice. She turned her head while rising to her feet. "Ginny?"

"Yep, it's me."

"Ach, I was just thinkin' about you." Naomi gave her friend a hug. "How are you? What brings you to town? How long are you here for?"

Ginny laughed. "Slow down, Naomi. I'm only good for one question at a time."

"Jah, okay. I'm just so surprised to see you. Did your folks know you were coming?"

"No. Today's Mom's fiftieth birthday, so Chad and I flew in for the surprise party my brother and his wife are putting on." Ginny smiled. "I decided to stop by and see you first. Thought maybe there might be something in your store I could buy for Mom."

Naomi nodded toward the adjoining room. "How about a nice quilt from my stepmother's quilt shop?"

Ginny shook her head. "That won't work. Mom already has an Amish quilt."

"Maybe a wall hanging or pillow then?"

"She might like a couple of throw pillows."

"Follow me, and I'll see what's available."

A few seconds later, they were inside the quilt shop. Ginny wandered around the room, commenting on how beautiful the quilted pieces were, as Naomi pointed out various pillows she thought Ginny's mother might like.

"You mentioned your stepmother's shop in

one of your letters, but I had no idea it was so big," Ginny commented.

"Papa added onto the store shortly after he and Fannie were married."

"So where is Fannie? Doesn't she work here?"

"She does all her quilting at home these days because she's got her hands full takin' care of the babies."

Ginny ran her fingers over a beige-and-green pillow with the Lone Star pattern. "Ah yes, that's right. Your dad and Fannie have twins—isn't that what you told me in one of the letters?"

"Jah. Timothy and Titus, and they're identical." Naomi grinned. "Took us the longest time to tell 'em apart, but we finally figured out who was who."

"So now you have two little brothers."

"And two little girls of my own." Naomi nodded toward the back room. "They're both down for naps at the moment."

Ginny's auburn eyebrows drew together. "I remember when Zach used to sleep in that room."

Naomi stared at the floor as memories cascaded over her like water from a broken dam. Even though it had been almost six years, she could still picture her baby brother's sweet face. He was such an agreeable child, always giggling and making everyone laugh.

"Sorry if I upset you by bringing up Zach." Ginny touched Naomi's shoulder. "I don't imagine you've heard anything more since his disappearance?"

Naomi shook her head. "Not since we saw that ad in *The Budget* letting us know he was all right. I doubt we'll ever see my little bother again, but I still pray for him and trust that whoever took Zach is taking good care of him."

"I think about the little guy sometimes, too."

"You do?"

Ginny nodded. "One day a couple of women came into the fitness center, and one of them had a little boy who made me think of Samuel when he was that age. I'm guessing he's exactly how Zach would look about now."

"In what way?"

Ginny shrugged. "He had Samuel and Zach's same dark chocolate eyes and golden brown hair. And the boy was about the age Zach would be these days, too."

"Did you happen to look behind his right ear?" Naomi didn't know why she was asking such a silly question. The idea that the boy Ginny saw could be Zach was ridiculous, despite his familial resemblance to her brothers.

"I never got close enough to see behind the kid's ear. Why do you ask?"

Naomi shook her head. "Never mind. It was only a silly notion that popped into my head."

"As I recall, you always were one for silly ideas." Ginny picked up the Lone Star pillow. "I think I'll take this one, and maybe I'll get a wall hanging for Mom, too."

"Jah, okay." Naomi led Ginny to the wall hangings on the other side of the room. She was glad to see her old friend again but wished the subject of Zach had never come up. He was gone, and no amount of wishful thinking could bring him back.

As the train pulled into Whitefish, Montana, Abby breathed a sigh of relief. It had been a long, two-day journey, and she was exhausted not only from the trip, but from being forced to make conversation with Edna. The only time the woman didn't talk was when she was asleep.

Abby knew her mother's cousin was trying to be friendly, but Edna's silly jokes and idle chatter grated on Abby's nerves. Another thing that had set her nerves on edge was the cowboy sitting a few seats away. She'd caught him staring at her on several occasions, and a couple of times he'd tried to make conversation. Edna said the man was probably lonely or curious about their Plain clothes, but the way his dark eyes bore into Abby made her feel uneasy.

She shivered thinking about all the questions the cowboy, who'd said his name was Bill Collins, had asked her. She'd not given him any more information than her name, where she was from, and where she and Edna were going. Truth was, he seemed more interested in talking about himself, and he'd told her that he'd been traveling to various rodeos across the United States ever since he had graduated from high school. Bill said he was going to Whitefish to visit a relative and then would be boarding the train again to go to McCall, Idaho, where his folks lived. Unlike most Englishers, the cowboy admitted that he hated to fly and preferred to travel by bus or train.

Abby couldn't imagine traveling all over the country, much less living the life of a rodeo cowboy. Until her trip to Pennsylvania, she'd never been out of the state of Ohio. This trip to Montana seemed like a real adventure. One she'd rather not be a part of.

When the train came to a stop, Abby slipped out of her seat and reached overhead to open the luggage compartment where their carry-on items were stowed.

"Let me help you with those," the cowboy offered as he stepped up beside her.

"I. . .I can manage." Abby quickly pulled Edna's black satchel out and handed it to her.

"Danki," Edna said as she scooted over to the seat Abby had previously occupied.

Abby reached for her own carry on and noticed that the strap was wrapped around someone else's piece of luggage, which was near the back of the compartment and out of her reach. She struggled with it a few seconds, until she felt someone touch her shoulder. When she turned around, she realized the cowboy still stood there wearing a silly-looking grin on his face.

"I'm taller than you and can reach that better," he drawled. "Besides, it's my bag your strap's stuck on, so it's my duty to free it for you."

"I'm sure I can get it," she argued.

"Let the nice man help," Edna said. "Our driver's probably waitin' inside the station, and we don't want to keep him any longer than necessary."

With a shrug, Abby stepped aside. She knew Edna was anxious to see her sister-in-law. Truth be told, she, too, would be glad once they were headed for Rexford and the Amish community they would be visiting. At least there she wouldn't feel so out of place and she wouldn't have to deal with any overfriendly cowboys.

A few seconds later, the man handed Abby her satchel and retrieved his as well.

"Danki—I mean, thank you." She stepped farther into the aisle so Edna could join her.

Bill nodded. "Glad to be of service, ma'am. Will ya be needin' help with your other bags?"

Edna opened her mouth as if to say something, but Abby cut her off. "No thanks. I'm sure our driver will help us gather the ones we checked through."

"All right then. You ladies have a nice drive to Rexford." Bill tipped his hat and gave Abby a quick wink. "It's been nice meetin' ya."

"And you as well," Edna said.

Abby merely nodded and hurried to exit the train. The sooner she got away from Cowboy Bill, the better she would feel.

Chapter 29

Abby couldn't get over all the trees that scattered the hills and bordered Lake Koocanusa in the Kootenai National Forest of northern Montana. Tim Hayes, their middle-aged driver who was an English neighbor of Elizabeth's, had informed his passengers that there were a variety of trees in the area—noble fir, stately pine, tamarack, and cedar. Homes made of logs dotted the land, and Tim was quick to point out that the local Amish men had made some of them. "In fact," he said, as they drove past the general store, run by an Amish family, "building log homes is how a few of the Amish men support themselves. Others make log-type furniture, which is a good business."

"I hear that the yearly Amish auction also brings money into the community," Edna commented.

He nodded. "That's true. The auction's held in June, and more than a thousand people come to West Kootenai to buy and sell that day."

Edna glanced at Abby as they sat in the backseat of Tim's minivan and smiled. "Your mamm might be interested in sendin' some of her quilts to be auctioned off, don't ya think?"

Abby's gave a quick shrug. She had come here with the hope of getting away from quilts and didn't want to think about them, much less talk about the ones in her mother's shop.

"This is Elizabeth King's place," Tim said, as he pulled onto a graveled driveway and stopped in front of a small log home set well off the main road. "She'd have ridden with me to Whitefish, but I had a few stops to make along the way, and I guess Elizabeth thought she could use that time getting ready for her two houseguests instead of waiting on me." He chuckled and massaged the top of his balding head. "She's quite an independent woman, living here by herself and doing some teaching at the Amish one-room schoolhouse in the past."

Abby looked over at Edna. "I thought you'd mentioned that your sister-in-law is married and has a little boy."

Edna's pale eyebrows drew together. "Jah, but Dan and their son Abe were killed a few years ago. Don't you remember, as we traveled here I told you the story of how the car they were riding in slid on a patch of ice and was hit by a truck."

Abby's brain felt dull and fuzzy. Truth be told, she remembered very little of what Edna had said to her on the train.

"Oh, there's Elizabeth now," Edna said excitedly. She opened the van door and hopped out.

Abby watched out the side window as Edna ran up the path and was greeted with a hug by a tall, dark-haired woman who looked to be in her late thirties.

"I'll get your luggage," Tim said, looking over his shoulder.

Abby nodded and drew in a deep breath. Whether she liked it or not, it was time to meet Elizabeth King.

∽

"Slow down, Mom. I can't understand what you're saying." Jim shifted his cell phone from one ear to the other as he moved away from two of his painters who worked in the hallway of a new apartment complex on the east side of Puyallup.

"I said your father hasn't been feeling well, but he refuses to see the doctor." She sniffed. "Will you talk to him, Jim? He'd be more apt to listen to you than he would me."

"Sure, Mom. I'll give him a call when I get home from work this evening."

"I wish you and the family could come here for a visit. You and Dad used to be so close, and I'm sure if he saw you he wouldn't say no to your suggestion that he see the doctor."

Jim grimaced. He cared about his dad and would do his best to talk him into going in for a physical, but he'd have to do it by phone. Besides, knowing Mom, she was probably making more of this than there really was. In all likelihood, Dad only had a touch of the flu. Give the man a few more days, and he'd probably be good as new.

"Look, Mom," Jim said patiently, "I can tell that you're worried, but it's impossible for me to get away right now. I promise I'll call Dad as soon as I get home."

"If you're short on money, I'd be happy to pay for your plane ticket," she offered.

He cringed. Didn't his mother realize he was making a good living at his profession? Did she think he was too poor to buy a plane ticket and that was the reason he hadn't been back to Ohio since they'd gotten Jimmy? *If Mom only had an inkling of the real reason I've stayed away from home. What would she think if she knew her son was a kidnapper who'd taken an Amish baby from Pennsylvania?* Jim knew he was probably being paranoid by refusing to visit his folks. After all, Millersburg, Ohio, was several hours from Lancaster, Pennsylvania. Still, Amish people lived there, and one of them might know Jimmy's birth family. If someone saw Jimmy and recognized him. . .

"Jim? Did you hear what I said? I'd be happy to—"

"I can afford the ticket, Mom. I'm busy right now with a couple of big paint jobs, and since Dad's not critically ill, I see no reason to make the trip. Maybe this summer we can come for a visit," Jim lied. *Tell her what she wants to hear and she'll get off my back. That usually works with Linda.*

"Your father could be dead by then." There was a brief pause. "Oh, I wish we had stayed in Boise and not moved to Ohio. He surely could have found a job as a high school principal in Idaho as easily as here."

He lifted his gaze to the ceiling. A ceiling that still needed to be painted.

"Jim, are you there?"

He blew out his breath. "Yes, Mom, I'm still here."

"I guess if you're not willing to talk to your dad in person, I'll have to be satisfied with a phone call." There was another pause. "Please don't tell him I called about this."

"I won't even mention that we talked."

"Thanks, son."

"Let me know what the doctor says."

"I will. Good-bye, Jim."

"Bye, Mom."

Jim clicked the phone off and slipped it inside the leather case he wore on his belt. He was sure there was nothing to worry about, but he would feel better once he talked to Dad.

⟳

Linda paced the living room floor as she waited for Jim. His foreman had called around six o'clock, saying Jim wouldn't be coming home for dinner and that he wasn't sure when they would be done for the day. It irritated Linda that her husband couldn't have told her himself. Avoidance seemed to be the way he dealt with things these days.

She glanced at the grandfather clock on the opposite wall. It was almost nine, and she'd put Jimmy to bed half an hour ago. "This is ridiculous," she fumed. "It's bad enough that Jim has worked every Saturday for the past two months, but lately he's been working so many long hours, he has no time to spend with Jimmy." A lump lodged in her throat, and she blinked against the smarting tears that threatened to spill over.

Linda sank to the couch and picked up her Bible from the coffee table. She turned to another passage her pastor had recently given her—this one in Lamentations—and read it aloud. " 'The Lord is good to those whose hope is in him, to the one who seeks him.' Lamentations 3:25." She closed her eyes. *At least I know I'll always have You, Jesus. If only Jim would see his need, too.*

When a car door slammed shut, her eyes snapped open. A few minutes later Jim appeared, dressed in his white painter's overalls and wearing a matching hat. "Sorry I'm late, but we ran into a problem with the paint we were using."

She left the couch and rushed to his side. "Did your mother get hold of you? I gave her your cell phone number when she called here earlier today."

Jim nodded and ran his fingers along the white speckles of paint dotting his chin.

"What did she say?"

He tipped his head and stared at her in a peculiar way. "Didn't Mom tell you what she wanted?"

"No. She asked to speak with you, but her voice sounded strained. I got the impression it was something important."

Jim flopped into the closest chair and sighed.

"I hope you don't have any fresh paint on those overalls," Linda said, stepping forward. "I wouldn't want—"

"It's dried paint, Linda, so don't worry."

She recoiled, feeling that familiar hurt whenever he snapped at her. "Sorry."

"Do you always have to look for something to complain about?"

"I wasn't."

He pulled the hat off his head, flopping it over one knee. "Do you want to hear what Mom said or not?"

"Of course I do."

"Then have a seat."

Linda returned to her spot on the couch and waited for Jim to continue.

"Mom said Dad hasn't been feeling well, and she wanted me to talk him into seeing the doctor. Since I knew I'd be working late, I gave Dad a jingle during my dinner break."

"What did he say?"

"Not much. He made light of the whole thing and guessed that Mom had put me up to calling."

Linda felt immediate concern. If Bob was anything like most men, his making light of it meant he was sicker than he was admitting. "I hope it's nothing serious."

"Guess we won't know until he sees the doctor."

"Do you think we should go to Ohio, Jim? I mean, just in case—"

He shook his head. "I can't get away from either of the jobs I'm on right now. I'm sure Dad will be fine."

"But how can you be certain of that when he hasn't been to the doctor yet?"

"Trust me. I know my dad. If he says he's feeling better, he probably is." He stood and started for the door leading to the hallway.

"Where are you going?"

"Upstairs to bed. I'm exhausted."

Linda watched Jim's retreating form, wishing he would stay awhile and visit with her. In the days before her conversion, she would have probably whined and begged. But now as a Christian wife trying to win her husband to the Lord, she knew the best thing to do was keep silent. She hurried to turn off the living room lights and follow him upstairs. Since tomorrow was Sunday, maybe they could spend some time together as a family after she and Jimmy got home from church.

∞

Abby stood at the window in the small loft above Elizabeth's living room. This would be her sleeping quarters for the next few weeks, until she and Edna headed back to Pennsylvania. It was a pleasant room, just high enough for her to stand without bumping her head. Against one wall was a single bed made of knotty pine. A matching dresser sat against the other wall, and a wooden rocking chair was positioned near the window. The moon shone bright and clear tonight, casting rays of golden light against the snowy yard below. She was keenly aware of how quiet and isolated it was here in the mountains. *It's almost eerie,* she thought. *I wonder how many wild animals are out there lurking about?*

Abby shivered and rubbed her hands against the sleeves of her long flannel nightgown. She needed to focus on something else, or she would be awake all night, thinking some strange creature would sneak into the house and attack her while she slept.

Her thoughts went to Edna and Elizabeth, who had stayed up until after eleven, chattering and getting caught up on one another's lives. Not wishing to appear impolite, Abby had joined the conversation by providing a listening ear and answering any questions that had been asked of her. Elizabeth seemed like a nice enough woman, and she was much younger than Abby had expected. She also seemed to be full of energy and exuberated over life with the kind of joy Abby had once known.

She leaned against the windowsill and sighed. *If Elizabeth lost her son and husband, how can she be so cheerful and positive?* She turned from the window and flopped onto the bed. *Maybe it's an act, to make people think she's doing okay, the way*

I've done with Mom and Abraham's family. Maybe deep down inside, Elizabeth is hurting as much as I am and doesn't want anyone to know it.

Abby closed her eyes, hoping sleep would come quickly. She had given up saying her nighttime prayers. Truth was, since Lester died she'd only pretended to pray before and after meals, as well as during church. There wasn't much point in praying when God didn't answer her prayers. She'd prayed for Lester and asked the Lord to keep him safe and bless their upcoming marriage. And what good had that done?

Grief rose in her throat like bile, and scalding tears seeped under Abby's lashes, rolling onto her cheeks. She leaned over the bed and reached into her small satchel, pulling out a handkerchief—the same one Mary Ann had made her several months ago—the one with the initials *A.M.* embroidered in one corner.

Abby dabbed at her eyes and blew her nose. *Oh, why couldn't it have been me who was killed in that fire instead of Lester?*

∽

Linda had just drifted off to sleep when she was awakened by the sound of deep moaning. She turned her head and saw Jim writhing about and punching his pillow. She was tempted to wake him but thought better of it, remembering how irritable he got if his sleep was disturbed.

"No, baby. Put the Amish quilt back," he mumbled. "No. I said, no."

Amish quilt? Baby? What was Jim talking about? Linda knew he must be dreaming, and since they had an Amish covering on their bed, the fact that he'd mentioned a quilt did make sense. But she couldn't figure out what would cause him to dream about a baby. Had he recently been watching a rerun of *Witness* on TV? No, there were no babies in the movie that she recalled. Maybe Jim's dream was a combination of things locked away in his subconscious. The Amish quilt, which Linda had wanted a long time. The baby they had adopted when they'd gone to the East Coast and toured Amish country. That's all it was. . .just a silly dream full of blended things that had occurred in the past.

Linda was relieved when Jim's moaning subsided and turned to soft snores. Maybe now she could get some sleep. In the morning, if she didn't forget, she would ask if Jim remembered the dream.

Chapter 30

Abby proceeded down the lane on foot, heading to the general store and mindful of the snow that still lay in patches. She couldn't believe she had been in Montana two weeks already. She was beginning to like it here. The trees seemed greener, the air fresher, and other than Cousin Edna, no one knew her situation.

Although Abby still felt empty, at least she didn't have the pressure of trying to measure up to what others expected of her. She'd always been a hard worker, but truthfully, she was getting tired of doing chores all the time in order to keep from thinking about Lester and what her quilt shop had done to him. All she wanted to do was rest and saturate her mind with the things of nature, the way she could do here in the Kootenai National Forest, where it was ever so peaceful and quiet.

When Abby reached the mailbox at the end of the driveway, she slipped her hand into her jacket pocket and retrieved the letter she'd written to her mother last night. She knew Mom was worried about her; she could read it between the lines of the letter she'd received last week. Mom probably hoped Abby wouldn't be gone too long, but Cousin Edna seemed in no hurry to leave, and that was fine with Abby.

When Abby opened the mailbox, she was disappointed to see that the mail had already come. If she put the letter to Mom inside now, it wouldn't go out until tomorrow. Still, it was better than taking it back to Elizabeth's house and trudging down here again in the morning. So, she placed the envelope inside the metal box and lifted the red flag.

Thumbing through the stack of mail that had been delivered, she noticed a letter for Edna bearing her daughter Gretchen's return address. *Should I take the mail up to the house now or continue on to the store?* Abby decided on the latter, figuring the letter for Edna was probably nothing important and that she could wait another hour or so to read it. She dropped all the mail into her black canvas satchel and kept walking.

A short time later, Abby stepped inside the general store, feeling a rush of warm air that quickly dispelled the chill she had encountered on her trek over here.

"Can I help ya with somethin'?" the young Amish girl behind the counter asked.

Abby rubbed her hands briskly together and shook her head. "I just need a couple of items, but I think I can find them."

"All right then. Let me know if you need help findin' anything."

"Jah, I will." Abby proceeded to the back of the store, where the notions were kept. She was almost out of writing paper and planned to buy a new tablet and maybe some colored pencils for drawing. Elizabeth had asked her to pick up two spools of white thread as well.

When that was done, Abby decided to climb the stairs and see what might be up there for sale. She'd been in the store a couple of times since her arrival but had never thought to look in the loft above.

At the top of the landing she spotted a couple of men's black felt hats lying on a chest of drawers that was also for sale. Several other pieces of Amish-made furniture filled a large area—two rocking chairs, a small table, and a couple of straight-backed chairs. To the left, four quilts hung on a makeshift clothesline.

The sight of them almost brought Abby to the floor in a pool of tears, but she gritted her teeth and looked away. She knew it was silly to feel so anxious whenever she looked at a quilt, but she couldn't seem to help herself. Quilts were part of the Amish life. They were warm and cozy, and she had covered up with one nearly every night since she was a child.

Guess it's not the quilt itself that bothers me so much, but the sight of one hanging in a store reminds me of my own quilt shop and the grief it caused the day it burned to the ground.

Abby moved slowly around the small upstairs and finally headed back down, deciding there was nothing she needed.

Up front near the counter stood a refrigerated dairy case where Abby found a brick of Swiss cheese, her favorite kind. She was surprised to see that it had been made by one of the cheese places near her hometown in Berlin. Abby missed Ohio, especially the times spent with Lester during their courting days.

For a moment her sorrow dissipated, as she allowed memories of Lester to bathe her in warm thoughts. They had gone to the cheese store down the street from her quilt shop on several occasions, sampling the various cheeses, laughing, and talking with others they knew. Seeing the cheese now was a painful reminder that Lester was gone, yet in some ways it was comforting to find something so familiar.

Abby drew in a deep breath. *At one time I thought Lester and I would be together as husband and wife for many years and that our love could withstand anything, even time spent apart. But now he's gone, and others expect me to move on.* She blinked against the tears clinging to her lashes. Despite her resolve to push thoughts of Lester aside, Abby often dreamed of him. Not the nightmare with fire and smoke, but dreams of happier days, when they'd been courting. *Help me, Lord. Help me let go of Lester if I need to, and show me if there's any meaning in life.*

With a determination not to give in to her tears, Abby turned and set her purchases on the counter.

"Will you be needin' anything else?" the young woman asked, as she rang up the items.

Abby shook her head. "That'll be all. Danki."

The girl opened her mouth, like she might be about to say something, but the telephone rang and she reached for it.

Abby counted out the money for her purchases and left it on the counter, not wanting to interrupt the phone conversation.

∽

Fannie didn't know what had possessed her to load both boys into the buggy and drive over to Caleb and Naomi's store. She could have left them at home with Nancy, who wasn't working at Anna Beechy's today, but decided the fresh air would do them some good. Besides, she needed a few things from the store, and she didn't want to wait until Abraham was free to take her.

Just a short way from the house, Titus started to holler, and then Timothy joined in. Fannie figured they probably wanted her attention and felt frustrated because they were confined in the buggy.

"Calm down!" Fannie clutched the reins and tried to keep her focus on the road. The last thing she needed was to get in an accident while trying to settle her fussy sons.

The boys howled all the way to Paradise, and it wasn't until Fannie took Titus out of the buggy that he finally stopped crying. She was relieved when Caleb, who'd been sweeping the store's front porch, spotted her and came to offer his assistance.

"Danki," she said as Caleb reached into the buggy and scooped Timothy into his arms. "These two are sure gettin' to be a handful."

Caleb nuzzled the top of Timothy's downy dark head. "I hope Naomi and I are blessed with a couple of boys some day." He gave Fannie a sheepish grin. "Not that I'm unhappy with Sarah and Susan, you understand."

Fannie chuckled. "Jah, I know. Most men want at least one son to carry on their name."

He nodded and lifted his left hand. "With this bein' practically useless, it'd be nice to have a boy's strong arm when there's heavy stuff to be done at the store."

Fannie followed Caleb into the building, wondering if he ever regretted his decision to buy Abraham's store and sell his buggy shop to his two younger brothers. Of course he'd done it because of his love for Naomi.

So many sacrifices some folks make in order to care for their loved ones, she thought. *Look at what Abby sacrificed on my behalf. And what's she got to show for it but a lot of heartaches and regrets?*

"It's nice to see you," Naomi said, stepping out from behind the counter and giving Fannie a hug. "Have you come alone, or is one of the girls with you today?"

"It's just me and the twins."

Naomi touched Titus's rosy cheek. "Looks like he's been crying. Is everything all right?"

Fannie motioned with her head toward Timothy, still held in Caleb's arms. "They carried on somethin' awful the whole way here. Guess they wanted my full attention and were determined I should know about it."

Naomi groaned. "I can relate to that. Bringing our girls to the store every day can present some problems whenever one of them acts up."

"Where should I put this little fellow?" Caleb asked, stepping between Naomi and Fannie. "I'd hold him all day, but I've got some boxes on the back porch that need to be brought inside."

Fannie glanced around. "Matthew's not working here today?"

"Nope. Said he had some things to do in his woodworking shop at home."

"I didn't see him at all this morning. He never even showed up for breakfast."

"Maybe he had errands to run," Naomi put in.

"That could be." Fannie motioned to the back room. "Are the girls down for their naps right now?"

Naomi shook her head. "Susan's in her playpen, but she's not sleeping. Sarah's on a throw rug by the bookcase with some of her favorite children's books. I'll get Susan out of her playpen and set her next to her big sister, and then you can put the twins in the playpen while you shop. Would that work?"

Fannie smiled. "Sounds fine to me."

A few minutes later, the twins played happily in the playpen, while little Susan sat on the floor beside Sarah. Fannie smiled at the older girl pretending to read to her eight-month-old sister. Even though the girls weren't Fannie's grandchildren by blood, she'd become quite fond of them.

She thought about Harold and Lena and the baby boy they now had, wishing they lived closer and wondering when they might come to Pennsylvania for a visit. It wasn't easy making a trip by bus or train when you had a baby or two to care for.

"You think you might want to run the quilt shop again?" Naomi asked, driving Fannie's thoughts to the back of her mind.

"I'd like to, but with the boys keeping me so busy, I believe it's best that I do my quilting at home and leave the store to someone more capable."

"Wish I could do more," Naomi said, leaning her elbows on the counter. "But I've got my hands full helping Caleb in the store, and about all I can do for the quilt shop is ring up folks' purchases and answer a few questions."

Fannie nodded. "I understand, and I don't expect you to do any more than you're already doing. Things will just have to stay as they are until Abby returns and we see how she feels."

"Have you heard anything from her lately?" Naomi asked.

"Got a letter from her last week. She seems to like it in Montana, and I believe the change is good for her."

Naomi's next words were cut off by an ear-splitting crash.

"Heavens! What was that?"

Both women headed to the back of the store and reached the girls just as both Sarah and Susan started to howl.

"Der bichler!" Sarah sobbed, pointing to the stack of books strewn on the floor.

"Susan must have pulled one out, and then they all tumbled down," Naomi shouted over the noise of her daughters' weeping.

Titus and Timothy began to holler, and Fannie clicked her tongue. "See why I can't come back to work?" She headed for the storage room. "I'm comin', boys. Jah, your mamm's right here."

∾

Linda sat at the kitchen table with a cup of hot apple cider in one hand and her open Bible before her. She'd seen Jimmy off to school a few minutes ago, and Jim had left for work before she'd gotten out of bed. He'd been leaving early almost every morning and coming home late. It was hard to have any family time with him gone so much.

Linda hadn't even been able to ask about the dream he'd had a few weeks ago, when he'd mumbled something about a baby and an Amish quilt. She'd forgotten all about it until now.

"I'm supposed to focus on God's Word, not worry about some silly dream," she muttered. "It probably didn't mean anything other than Jim had eaten too much junk food before going to bed. Unless he has the dream again and talks in his sleep, I won't bother to ask him about it."

The phone rang, and Linda placed a bookmark inside the Bible to indicate the spot in 1 Corinthians where she wanted to begin reading. She hurried across the room and picked up the receiver. "Hello, Scott residence."

"It's Marian, Linda. Is Jim there?" Jim's mother's voice sounded even more strained than the last time she had called, and Linda felt immediate concern.

"No, he's not. He left for work early this morning. Can I take a message?"

There was a brief pause. "I guess I'd better try his cell phone then."

Linda glanced at the kitchen counter where Jim had left his phone. This was the second time in the past week he'd forgotten to take it with him. She wondered if he'd become forgetful because he wasn't getting enough sleep.

"Sorry, Marian, but Jim forgot to take his phone this morning. Would you like him to call you when he gets home?"

"I've got bad news, and it can't wait until then." Marian's voice caught on a sob.

"What is it? What's wrong?"

"Bob's in the hospital and may be faced with

open-heart surgery. It could be serious, Linda."

Linda's forehead wrinkled as she felt her mother-in-law's pain. "I'm so sorry. Jim will be upset when he hears, and I'm sure he'll want to fly out to Ohio right away."

"I was hoping he would. And you and Jimmy, too, if you can get away."

Linda nodded, even though she knew Marian couldn't see her. "As soon as I hang up, I'll see about getting some plane tickets. Jim will call you tonight and let you know when we'll arrive in Millersburg; then you can give him more details on Bob."

"Okay." Marian sniffed and blew her nose. "There's one more thing."

"What's that?"

"I know from your letters that you go to church and believe in God. So if you could offer a prayer on Bob's behalf, I'd really appreciate it."

"Of course. I'll call our church and get it put on the prayer chain, too."

"Thanks. See you soon."

Linda hung up the phone with a sense of frustration because she didn't have any idea where Jim was working today. She wouldn't be able to speak to him until he came home, whenever that might be. She could, however, purchase their plane tickets and pray for Jim's dad.

❦

"I picked up the mail, Elizabeth," Abby said when she entered the cozy log house after her walk to the store. "There's a letter for you, too, Edna. I think it's from your daughter."

Edna took the letter, and Abby handed Elizabeth the rest of the mail. Then she went to the loft to put away her jacket, scarf, and gloves. When she returned, she found Edna sitting at the kitchen table, shaking her head, and staring at the letter she had received.

"What's wrong? It's not bad news, I hope," Abby said with concern.

"All three of my granddaughters are down with the chicken pox, plus Gretchen has the flu. Looks like I'm gonna have to return home as soon as possible, because my daughter could surely use some help."

Abby nodded. "I'll run down to the store and use their phone to see about getting us some train tickets."

"There's no need for you to go, Abby," Edna said, pursing her lips.

"What do you mean, there's no need? I thought you were afraid to travel by yourself."

Edna folded Gretchen's letter and stuck it inside the band of her apron. "I think I'll be fine on the train now that I've done it already."

Abby leaned on the cupboard, wondering what she should do. Truth be told, she wasn't ready to return to Pennsylvania, but would it be right to stay on without Edna? She'd only met Elizabeth a few weeks ago and hesitated to ask if she could stay longer.

Elizabeth spoke up as though she could read Abby's thoughts. "I'd be happy if you stayed on awhile, Abby."

"Really? You wouldn't mind?"

"Not at all. I'd like the opportunity to get to know you better."

Edna smiled. "I'm glad that's all settled." She

nodded at Abby. "Now if you want to run to the store again to use their phone, I'd be much obliged if you'd book me a ticket home."

Chapter 31

I still can't believe you booked us a flight into Akron-Canton without bothering to check with me first." Jim released the tray in front of his seat on the plane and grimaced. He dreaded going to Ohio again. What if Linda wanted to extend their stay and drive to Pennsylvania in order to tour Amish Country? They hadn't seen much of it the last time they were there, and she'd been after him to go back ever since. And what if someone from Jimmy's Amish family spotted him and Jim ended up behind bars on kidnapping charges?

Linda looked at him and frowned. "Do you have to keep bringing this up? Ever since you got home last night, all you've done is complain about the trip. If I didn't know better, I'd think you didn't want to see your dad."

"It's not the trip I'm upset about. It's the fact that you planned everything without my knowledge." Jim glanced over at their son, asleep in his seat next to the window. "Before we adopted Jimmy, you left everything up to me, but in the past year or so you've gotten pretty independent."

"Do you see that as a bad thing?"

"It is when you usurp my authority."

She folded her arms and stared straight ahead. "I was not usurping your authority. I did what needed to be done because you weren't there to do it."

"Humph!" Jim snapped the tray shut. Where was that flight attendant? It had been at least ten minutes since she'd said she would be serving a snack, and he could really use a drink.

"Don't you realize how important it is to see your father before he goes into surgery?" Linda asked. "What if he doesn't make it? What if—"

"He will make it. He has to, Linda. Mom couldn't survive without Dad."

Linda turned to look at Jim again, and her face softened. "I know you're worried about him, but all the worry in the world won't change a thing. What Bob needs is prayer, and I've been doing that ever since I talked to your mother on the phone."

Jim squeezed his fingers into a tight fist, until his nails bit into his flesh. "Right. Like prayer is going to change anything."

"It can, and it has."

"Yeah, whatever." He blew out his breath. "I don't see why you and Jimmy had to come along on this trip. Our son should be in school, not thousands of miles from home, mingling with strangers."

Linda's forehead wrinkled. "That's the silliest thing I've ever heard you say. Jimmy's only in first grade, so if he misses a few days of school, it won't be the end of the world. Besides, your parents aren't strangers. They've been out to visit us several times since we adopted Jimmy."

He shrugged. "You're right, as usual."

"This isn't about being right." Linda reached for his hand. "Your parents are my family, too. I want the three of us to be there to offer support as they go through this ordeal."

Jim leaned his head against the seat and closed his eyes. *Guess I'm worried for nothing. Even if Linda decides she wants to tour Amish Country in Pennsylvania, all I have to do is say no. I'll just tell her there are plenty of Amish in Ohio we can see. I know I'm being paranoid when I worry about someone finding out the truth of Jimmy's heritage. Just like with that woman at the fitness center who mentioned to Linda that Jimmy reminded her of an Amish child she used to know. It was irrational for me to think the woman knew the Amish boy I took.*

Jim drew in a deep breath and tried to relax. *I need to remember that Jimmy's not a one-year-old baby anymore. His Amish family or anyone who knew him back then could probably look him right in the face and not even know it was their child.*

⚬⚬

Abraham's boots crunched through the gravel as he headed to the small outbuilding Matthew used for his woodworking shop. The two of them had both been busy lately and hadn't said more than a few words to each other. He figured a good visit was long overdue. Besides, there was something specific he wished to discuss with his eldest son.

Inside the shop, Abraham found Matthew bent over a table, sanding a mahogany quilt hanger. "Got a minute?"

Matthew looked up and grinned. "Sure. Always have time for you, Papa."

Abraham removed his black felt hat and hung it on a wall peg near the door. "Fannie says you didn't come in for breakfast yesterday morning. She figured you'd gone into Paradise to work at the quilt shop, but she and the boys stopped by there, and

Naomi said you hadn't been in."

Matthew blew some dust off the piece of wood he was sanding. "Had some errands to run in Lancaster, so I hired a driver and we grabbed a bite to eat at a fast-food restaurant on the way."

"Ah, I see." Abraham took a seat on a sawhorse sitting a few feet away. "Mind if I ask what kind of business you were tendin' to?"

"Just ordering some supplies and checkin' out a few furniture stores to see what's selling well."

"You thinkin' of adding more to your line than just quilt racks and hangers?"

Matthew nodded. "Yep."

Abraham glanced around. "This building's not very big. How you gonna fit a bunch of furniture inside?"

"Thought I'd work on one piece at a time, then take 'em to the quilt shop and try to sell 'em there."

"You're becomin' quite the businessman these days, ain't it so?"

"I'm workin' on it." Matthew's eyes twinkled. "I think I've found what I've been lookin' for all these years, Papa. Never did enjoy workin' in the fields, and the feel of wood and sandpaper under my fingers brings me much pleasure."

"I know what you're saying, son. Workin' at the store wasn't my idea of fun, but bein' back in the fields is like honey on my tongue. Sure am glad Norman's brother-in-law, Willis, came to work for me after you gave up farming completely."

"Jah, it's good he was able and willing, Papa," Matthew said with a nod.

Abraham chewed on the inside of his cheek as he contemplated his next words.

"You got somethin' else on your mind, Papa? You're lookin' kind of thoughtful there."

Abraham grunted. "Guess you know me too well."

Matthew straightened. "Why don't you just say whatever it is that brought you out here? I have a feelin' it's more than just a friendly visit."

"Well, truth be told, I've been wonderin' about something."

"What's that?"

Abraham left the sawhorse and moved to stand beside his son. "I'm a little concerned because you spend so much time alone."

Matthew rubbed his forehead. "Don't know what you're talkin' about. I live in the same house as you, and I'm around the family a lot."

"Not anymore. You spend most of your waking moments out here or in town at the quilt shop."

"And when I'm there I'm around customers, so I'm not alone."

Abraham gave his beard a couple of sharp pulls. This conversation wasn't going nearly as well as he'd hoped. Maybe he should be more direct with Matthew instead of thumping around the shrubs. "Okay, let me give it to you straight. I'm worried because you don't have a steady girlfriend." He shrugged. "For that matter, as far as I know, you've never had more'n a few dates since you turned sixteen and got your courtin' buggy. I know you're kind of shy around women you don't know well, but most men your age are married and have several kinner by now."

Matthew's forehead wrinkled. "There's a reason for that, Papa. I haven't found the right woman yet."

Abraham released a puff of air and tapped Matthew on the shoulder. "How hard have ya been lookin'?"

Matthew's hand fluttered, like he was batting at an annoying fly. "Ah Papa, do I have to go lookin' for a wife? Can't I just pray about it and let the good Lord bring the right woman when the time's right?" He sobered. " 'Course, maybe I'm not cut out for marriage or raisin' a family."

"Puh! That's plain *eefeldich.* Of all the silly ideas. Of course you're cut out for it. You're a good man with a lot of love to give a wife and a brood of kinner." Abraham shook his head. "Maybe you're just too picky. Have you thought of that?"

"Maybe so, but I won't settle. Not for anything."

"Don't expect ya to settle. Just make a little more effort, that's all. Surely there has to be someone you could become interested in."

Matthew's face turned crimson, and he moved swiftly back to his workbench.

Abraham followed. "There is someone, isn't there?"

"Maybe, but she don't know I'm alive."

"How do you know that?"

"Because she only thinks of me as her big brother." The red in Matthew's cheeks deepened, and he started sanding the piece of wood again, real hard.

Abraham smiled. *Ah, so it is Abby my son's come to care for. Who else would be looking on him as though he were her brother? Better not say anything though. No point embarrassing Matthew more than I already have. Truth be told, Abby and Matthew would be good for each other, but I guess that's not my place to be sayin'.*

"Well, I'd better head up to the house for some lunch. Fannie's probably wonderin' what's keepin' me." Abraham turned for the door and grabbed his hat off the wall peg. "You comin', son?"

"In a few minutes."

As Abraham headed up to the house, his brain swirled with ideas. . .things he might do to get Abby and Matthew together. Of course, she would have to come home before anything could happen.

∞

Abby stood at the end of Elizabeth's driveway, waving good-bye to Edna. She'd been picked up by the same English driver who had met them at the train in Whitefish when they first arrived in Montana. Abby couldn't believe how quickly she had been able to get Edna's train ticket. Coming here, they'd only purchased one-way tickets, since they weren't sure how long they would be staying, and those had been bought several days in advance.

"Shall we go inside and have a cup of hot tea?" Elizabeth asked, touching Abby's arm.

"Jah, that sounds good."

As they started up the driveway, a multitude of doubts tumbled around in Abby's mind. Should she have let Edna go home by herself when she knew how the woman felt about traveling alone? Was Abby really staying because Elizabeth was lonely, or had she made this decision because of her own selfish needs? She'd never felt like a selfish person until she'd come here. In fact, she'd always looked out for others before thinking of herself.

Elizabeth draped her arm over Abby's shoulder. "Edna's gonna be fine, and you did the right thing by stayin' here." She grinned, and the dimple in her left cheek seemed to be more pronounced than usual.

"I hope so."

They entered the house and removed their wraps, then headed to the kitchen. Elizabeth turned on the back burner of the propane stove, and Abby took two empty mugs and a couple of tea bags down from the cupboard.

"Would ya like some banana bread to go with the tea?" Elizabeth asked.

"That would be nice."

A few minutes later they were both seated at the table with steaming cups of raspberry tea and a plate of moist banana bread set before them.

"Edna tells me you're quite a quilter," Elizabeth commented.

"I. . .uh. . .used to be." Abby took a sip of tea, hoping their conversation would take another direction.

"Edna also told me about your quilt shop burning and how your future husband tried to rescue some of the quilts but perished in the fire."

Abby swallowed the tea in her mouth and nodded. This was the first time this subject had come up since she'd been here, and she was afraid if she spoke, she might break down and cry. Just think ing about the fire that had destroyed her dreams made her feel weepy. Talking about it was nearly unbearable.

"How long ago did it happen?"

"Right before Thanksgiving," Abby mumbled.

"And you're still grieving as though it were yesterday. I can see the sorrow in your eyes and hear the anguish in your voice."

Abby nodded. "I wonder if the pain will ever go away."

Elizabeth reached across the table and patted Abby's hand in a motherly fashion. "Of course it will. This kind of grief takes time to get over."

"I understand that you lost your son and husband in a car accident," Abby ventured to say.

"That's true. It happened two winters ago, when the vehicle they were riding in skidded on a patch of ice. The English driver's car smashed into a truck traveling in the opposite direction, and only the truck driver survived the crash."

Abby shook her head. "How awful for you. I can't imagine how it would feel to lose two loved ones at the same time."

"It was difficult, and it took me a good while to get over the hurt and to stop askin' God why He'd taken my husband and boy." Elizabeth's dark eyes filled with tears, and Abby's did as well. "But life goes on, and 'I have learned, in whatsoever state I am, therewith to be content.'" She smiled. "That's found in the book of Philippians, chapter 4, verse 11."

Abby nodded.

"God allowed the accident that took my husband and son, and it's not for me to question why or spend the rest of my days grievin' over what can't be changed. I have chosen to get on with the business of living and have found a purpose for my life again."

Abby leaned forward, her elbows resting on the table and her chin cupped in the palm of her hands. Elizabeth's calm voice was like a strong rope tying Abby fast when she had no strength left to hold on. "What purpose have you found?" she asked.

Elizabeth pushed her chair away from the table. "I can best show you that." She scurried from the room and returned a few minutes later carrying a cardboard box that she placed on one end of the table.

Curious to know what was inside, Abby left her chair and came to stand beside Elizabeth. "What have you got in there?"

Elizabeth lifted the flaps on the box and withdrew a partially made Log Cabin quilt in hues of beige and brown. Abby's heart clenched. How could she ever get over the pain of losing Lester when there seemed to be quilts everywhere, reminding her of the loss she had endured?

"I don't claim to be the best quilter in the world," Elizabeth said, "but I like the work, it keeps my hands busy, and I've found a good reason to do it."

Abby tipped her head. "Oh? What's that?"

"As I'm sure Edna has told you, our community has an annual auction in June."

Abby nodded.

"One of the biggest things we auction off is the quilts. In fact, we receive many quilts from women in other Amish communities. Ten percent of the proceeds goes to help support our school." Elizabeth pursed her lips. "If my son had lived, he would have gone to our one-room schoolhouse for his learnin'. I find great pleasure in knowing the quilts I have worked on all winter help support our school so other Amish kinner can learn to read, write, and do sums." She paused as her fingers traced the edge of the quilt. "Up until this year, I was teaching at the schoolhouse regularly, but when I had a bad bout with the flu, Myra Lehman took over. After I got better, I decided to let her finish out the school year."

"Looks like you still keep busy though," Abby said, nodding at the quilt.

"Jah."

Abby glanced at the cardboard box and spotted another quilt inside with the Tumbling Block pattern done in various shades of blue. "Are you working on more than one right now?"

"I can't take credit for this one," Elizabeth said. "I found it in a thrift shop in Tacoma, Washington, while I was on vacation with a couple single ladies in our community." She smiled. "We went there to see Mount Rainer and what's left of Mount St. Helens."

Abby noticed right away that the quilt was small, probably made for a baby, and she felt a sharp prick of emptiness as she studied it. Reaching out to touch the covering, her eyes filled with unwanted tears. *Lester is gone and so are my plans to be married. I will never have any bopplin, so there will be no need for me to make a quilt such as this. Elizabeth might have been able to set her pain aside and find meaning in life, but I don't see how that could ever happen for me.*

Chapter 32

"Come in, come in. You look exhausted," Fannie said as she opened the back door for Edna.

"Jah, just a bit." Edna removed her black shawl and draped it over the back of a chair. "Things have been pretty hectic at our place this past week."

"I can only imagine." Fannie nodded toward the kitchen table. "Have a seat and tell me how your granddaughters are doing."

"Much better now. Gretchen is over the flu, and the girls aren't feeling nearly as sick."

Knowing her cousin's taste for mint tea, Fannie poured them both a cup and handed one to Edna. "Does that mean they don't need your help now?"

Edna took a sip of tea before answering. "I still plan to check in from time to time and see if there's anything Gretchen needs me to do. But for the most part, I'm back in my own cozy little home, makin' head coverings and workin' on other things for people who don't have the time to sew."

Fannie added a dollop of cream to her tea. "Are you wishing you could have stayed in Montana longer?"

"Not really. I think it's best that Abby spend time with Elizabeth alone, and I didn't even have to come up with a reason to leave early. God worked everything out, and I'm sure if anyone can get through to your daughter, it's my dear sister-in-law."

"I pray that's so, and I hope it happens soon." Fannie sniffed. "Even though I often felt that Abby was taking over too many of my responsibilities, I do miss her and wish she was home with us right now."

"You missin' her company or all the help she gave you?" Edna asked with a wink.

Fannie chuckled. "A little of both. I've been praying every day, asking the Lord to heal Abby's heart and send her home with a joy for living."

"I'm sure she'll return when she feels ready, and I know the Lord wants only the best for Abby."

The piercing wail of a baby's cry halted Fannie's reply. She sighed. "Guess one of the boys is awake and wantin' to be fed. He probably needs to be diapered, too." She pushed her chair aside and stood. "I'd better tend to him before he gets the other brother howlin' like crazy."

"Want me to come along? I can change one babe's windel while you nurse the other."

"Jah, sure. That would be appreciated. We can visit while Titus and Timothy take turns eating."

"Sounds good to me." Edna rose from her seat. "I never seem to get in enough visiting, Cousin."

⧆

As Abby headed down the lane toward the mailbox, she reflected on the church service she'd gone to yesterday with Elizabeth. It was much the same as the ones she attended in Ohio and Pennsylvania, but there were fewer people, since this was a smaller community of Amish. The house where they met was much different, too, being made of logs and set among so many trees. The people had been friendly during the light meal afterward, and Abby had been pleased to spend a little time visiting with Myra Lehman, who reminded her a bit of Rachel.

I wonder how my dear friend from Ohio is doing these days, Abby mused. *I haven't heard from her in some time. Of course, I haven't been good about keeping in contact either. Truth is, I haven't been much of a friend to anyone since Lester died.*

Abby thoughts returned to yesterday's church service, and the words of Isaiah, chapter 43, verse 2, that one of the ministers had quoted, popped into her head: *"When thou passest through the waters, I will be with thee; and through the rivers, they shall not overflow thee: when thou walkest through the fire, thou shalt not be burned; neither shall the flame kindle upon thee."* Abby grimaced. *I feel as though I've been through the fire, but I've been burned so badly my wounds will never heal.*

Sometimes when Abby was alone in her room at night, she closed her eyes and tried to imagine what it must have been like for Lester during the last moments of his life. In her mind's eye she put herself in the scene, hugging him and being consumed by the flames together. The thought of dying in the arms of the man she loved seemed more pleasant than living a life without him.

"Lester should not have died alone," she moaned. "He shouldn't have perished on account of me."

Abby's thoughts went to the colorful quilt Elizabeth said she had purchased at a thrift shop in the state of Washington. *A year ago I thought I'd be making plenty of baby quilts in the days ahead.*

Some would be for Lester and my kinner, and others would be given to family members who were blessed with children.

She drew in a deep breath, determined to focus on something else. As she neared the mailbox, she heard the flutter of birds in the trees nearby and caught sight of a clump of yellow crocus. Spring was almost here, and this used to be her favorite time of year. Since Lester died, no time was her favorite. She barely noticed the changing seasons.

She pulled the mailbox flap open. *I will not give in to tears. Crying won't change a thing, and neither will dwelling on the past.* She thumbed quickly through the stack of mail and noticed a letter from her mother.

Abby leaned against a tree and tore open the letter. She missed Mom, her little brothers, and all of Abraham's family. Even so, she wasn't ready to return to Pennsylvania just yet.

Focusing on the letter in her hand, Abby read it silently.

> *Dear Abby,*
>
> *I hope this finds you well and enjoying your visit with Elizabeth. Edna made it safely home and said she wasn't the least bit afraid. Can you imagine my outgoing, silly cousin afraid of anything? It wonders me that she doesn't travel all over the place, the way some folks do when their family is grown.*
>
> *She's been busy caring for her granddaughters who have the chicken pox and her daughter who is down with the flu,*

and I think she enjoys being needed.

I'm sorry to say that Bishop Swartley passed away a few weeks ago, so there's been another funeral in our community. You'll never believe who the lot fell on to take his place—Jacob Weaver. Abraham's been saying for years that he thought Jacob would make a good bishop, and now it's actually happened. Jacob seems fine with the idea, but I'm not sure how his wife and kinner are taking all of this. Guess it will be quite an adjustment for everyone in the family.

Mary Ann and I dropped by the store the other day. (Jah, Abraham kept the boys by himself for a few hours.) When I was there, Naomi mentioned the auction that would be held in the Rexford Amish community in June. I'm not sure if you'll still be there by then, but even if you're not, I thought it would be good if I sent some quilts to auction off. If you'd like, I could box up the ones Lester rescued from your quilt shop in Berlin and send those, too.

Tears welled up in Abby's eyes. Would it help to get rid of those quilts? Maybe putting them up for auction was a good idea. It would be like burying her past once and for all. She swiped a hand across her damp cheeks and sniffed. "Guess I'll head back to the house and answer Mom's letter."

∽

"Do you really think we should be leaving so soon after your father's surgery?" Linda asked Jim as they drove away from Millersburg in their rental car.

"We've been here a week, Linda, and you heard what the doctor said. Dad's recovering nicely."

"I know, but—"

"We need to get home. I talked to my foreman yesterday, and he's lined up another set of apartments for us to paint."

She sighed. "I was hoping we could have a little vacation time before we head back. Maybe spend a day or two touring the area and seeing some of the Amish again."

Jim pointed out the front window. "There's one now. See the Amish buggy ahead of us?"

From his seat in the back of the car, Jimmy piped up, "What's an Amish buggy, Daddy?"

"The Amish are a group of Plain people living much like the pioneers used to," Linda said, before Jim could respond. "They drive carriages pulled by horses, and they don't use electricity in their homes."

As they drove around the horse and buggy, Linda glanced over her shoulder to gauge her son's reaction. Jimmy had his nose pressed against the window, and when a young boy at the rear of the buggy waved, Jimmy giggled.

"We haven't been anywhere but at the hospital and your parents' house since we came here, Jim. Couldn't we at least take time to stop in Berlin so I can go into that little shop where we bought the quilt for our bed?" Linda pleaded.

"No."

"Why not? We don't have to be at the airport for several hours, and I'd like to see about buying a couple of quilted throw pillows or maybe a wall hanging." When Jim made no reply, she added,

"I promise it will only take a few minutes."

"I suppose if I don't stop, I'll have to hear about it all the way home," he grumbled.

Linda smiled. "Thank you, honey."

A short time later, they pulled into the town of Berlin. Jim found a parking place near a drugstore and informed Linda that she could walk to the quilt shop while he went inside to get some aspirin.

"I'll take Jimmy with me," she said.

Jim shrugged. "Yeah, okay."

Jimmy scrambled out of the backseat and hopped onto the sidewalk, and Linda took hold of his hand. "We'll meet you back here in half an hour," she called to Jim.

"Don't be late." He sauntered up the walk toward the drugstore, rubbing the back of his neck as he went.

"How come Daddy's so cranky?" Jimmy asked.

"I think he's got a stiff neck, and I'm sure he's worried about Grandpa," she replied.

"Is Grandpa gonna be okay?"

Linda gently squeezed his hand. "The doctor said if he does everything he's supposed to do, he should be fine."

"I'm glad."

"Yes, so are we."

As they reached the end of the block, Linda halted. She thought Fannie's Quilt Shop was on this corner, just across the street, but it wasn't there. All she saw was a vacant spot next to another store. "That's odd."

"What's wrong, Mommy?"

"Nothing, Jimmy. I think maybe I'm on the wrong street." Linda looked to the left, then back to the right. Even though it had been several years since they'd been here, many things looked familiar. *Where is that quilt shop?*

A middle-aged woman stepped out of the gift shop next to the vacant lot, and Linda walked up to her. "Excuse me; I'm looking for someone who's familiar with this area who could tell me where Fannie's Quilt Shop is located. Are you from around here?"

"I'm from New Philadelphia, but I live close enough to shop here often, and I'm well acquainted with many of the local stores. Fannie's was right there," the woman said, motioning to the empty lot. "The shop burned to the ground right before Thanksgiving." She clucked her tongue. "Such a shame it was, too. All but a few of the quilts were lost, and a young Amish man died trying to rescue the rest."

Linda sucked in her breath. "Oh, that's so sad. What about Fannie, the woman who owned the shop? Was she inside when it caught fire?"

The woman shook her head. "From what I've been told, Fannie moved to Pennsylvania some time ago. Her daughter, Abby, took over the quilt shop, but she was away helping her mother, who'd given birth to twins."

"I bought a quilt from Fannie several years ago, and I was hoping to buy a couple of pillows." Linda stared at the empty lot with a feeling of regret. "I wish she was around so I could offer my condolences."

"Actually, it's Abby who's to be pitied. She and the young Amish man were engaged to be married, so the loss of her store was devastating for more than one reason."

Tears welled up in Linda's eyes as she considered how Fannie's daughter must have felt when her boyfriend died trying to save her quilts. She thought about Jim and wondered if he would do anything that heroic on her behalf. *Not that I'd want him to die for me. It would just be nice to know that he loved me that much.*

"I guess we'd better head back to the car, Jimmy," Linda said, shaking her thoughts aside. She glanced down, and panic gripped her like a vise. Jimmy was gone.

Chapter 33

Linda looked up and down the street, hoping for some sign of Jimmy, but the only children she saw were two small Amish boys standing beside a black buggy parked up the street a ways. She cupped her hands around her mouth and screamed, "Jimmy! Jimmy, where are you?"

Nothing. No sign of her son anywhere.

Where could he have gone? He was here a minute ago, standing right beside me while I spoke with that woman coming out of the gift shop.

Linda's heart thumped fiercely, and she placed both hands on her chest while drawing in a deep breath. *What if someone has kidnapped my boy? I should never have let go of his hand or taken my eyes off him for even a second. What am I going to tell Jim?* She breathed in and out slowly, trying to calm her nerves. *Think, Linda, think. Don't panic. Maybe Jimmy walked back to the car and is with his daddy right now.*

She whirled around and dashed up the sidewalk.

&

Jim was just coming out of the drugstore when he spotted Linda running toward him. Jimmy wasn't with her, and he figured the boy had already gotten into the car.

As Linda drew closer, he noticed that her

cheeks were pink and several strands of blond hair had come loose from her ponytail.

"Jimmy's missing," she panted. "I called and called but he didn't answer."

"What? He can't be missing, Linda. He was with you."

She let out a deep moan. "I know that, but when I got to where Fannie's Quilt Shop used to be and realized it wasn't there anymore, I asked a woman coming out of a gift shop about it, and—"

Jim held up one hand. "Slow down. Just tell me what happened with Jimmy."

"I'm trying to." Linda blinked and swiped at the tears running down her cheeks. "Jimmy was standing beside me when I started talking to the woman about the fire that destroyed the quilt shop, and when I looked down, he was gone."

"He's probably in there." Jim motioned to their rental car several yards away.

"How could that be? You locked the car before you went into the drugstore, remember?"

Jim's heart began to pound, matching the escalating throb he had felt in his head for the last hour. "Jimmy couldn't have gone far, Linda." He tried to keep his voice calm, even though he felt like he could jump right out of his skin. "Maybe Jimmy saw something in one of the store windows and went inside to check it out."

"Oh, I hope that's the case."

"You search the stores on this side, and I'll look in the ones over there," he said, motioning across the street. "Let's meet back here in twenty minutes."

"What if we still can't find him?" Linda grabbed Jim's arm and squeezed it so tight he felt her fingernails dig into his skin.

"Then we'll look on the next block, and the next, and the next, until we do find him."

Her chin quivered. "Maybe we should call the police."

"No. Absolutely not. He hasn't been missing long enough for that."

She sniffled. "We'd better start looking then."

Jim bolted across the street, fear gnawing at his stomach. As much as he hated to admit it, there was a possibility that Jimmy had been kidnapped. He knew how easily it could be done.

A cold chill spiraled up Jim's spine. *Am I being punished for taking Jimmy from his Amish family? Is this how they felt when they discovered he was missing?* He shook his head and darted into the first store. *No, I did that family a favor. They had too many kids and no mother. Linda wanted a baby, and I gave her one. Besides, we've given Jimmy a good home, and through that ad in* The Budget *I notified his Amish family that he was okay.* Reason, mixed with guilt and gut-wrenching fear, threatened to suffocate him. *I wish I knew how to pray.* He lifted his gaze. *Dear God, if You're up there, please help me find my boy.*

Half an hour later, Jim returned to their vehicle, without Jimmy. His hands trembled as panic swelled in his chest and left him short of breath.

A few minutes later, Linda showed up, but Jimmy wasn't with her either. "I didn't see him in any of the stores, and the people I asked said they hadn't seen a little boy matching Jimmy's description," she said tearfully. "Oh Jim, what are we going to do?"

"Let's move to the next block." It was the only thing Jim could think to do, short of calling the police. And that would only be done as a last resort. He grabbed Linda's hand, and they'd just started up the street, when he halted.

"What's wrong? Why are we stopping?"

"Look!" Jim pointed to an Amish buggy parked on the other side of the street. Three little boys had their heads sticking out the back opening. Two wore straw hats, and one child, who sported a Dutch-bob, wore no hat at all.

"Jimmy!" Linda hollered. "Oh Jim, he must have been playing with those Amish boys the whole time."

Jim could only nod, as words stuck in his throat. Relief turned his muscles to jelly. Their son was one of the children wearing a straw hat, and if he hadn't been able to see Jimmy's yellow sweatshirt, Jim would have sworn the kid was actually Amish.

He is Amish, his conscience reminded him. As quickly as the thought came, he dashed it away.

Linda raced across the street, with Jim on her heels. She rushed to the open buggy and leaned inside. "Jimmy! Oh, I'm so glad to see you, honey."

Before Jimmy could respond, Jim shook his finger in the child's face and shouted, "What do you think you're doing? We've been searching everywhere for you. Don't you know how scared we were when we couldn't find you?"

Jimmy's dark eyes filled with tears. "I just wanted to play with these boys, Daddy. They're Amish. Can ya tell?"

Jim blew out his breath with an exasperated groan. "Take that hat off and get out of the buggy right now!"

"You don't have to be so harsh," Linda said, reaching inside to take Jimmy's hand. "Come on, sweetie. You need to come with us now."

Jimmy removed the straw hat and handed it to the towheaded Amish child. "Here ya go. Thanks for lettin' me play in your buggy."

The two Amish boys waved and said something in Pennsylvania Dutch, while Jim lifted his son to the ground.

"You scared me when you disappeared," Linda said, leaning down and stroking Jimmy's cheek. "Please don't ever do that again."

"We need to get to the airport." Jim glanced at his watch. "Or we're going to miss our plane."

As they walked back to their car, Linda glanced over her shoulder. "Those two little Amish boys are sure cute, aren't they, Jim?"

"Yeah, I guess so."

"If it weren't for Jimmy's yellow sweatshirt and short hair, he would have looked like he was one of them, don't you think?"

Jim merely shrugged and kept on walking. There was no way he would admit to Linda that he'd thought the same thing. And he certainly wasn't about to tell her that the boy they'd supposedly adopted from the state of Maryland was actually an Amish child whose real family lived in Lancaster County, Pennsylvania.

∽∼

Abby took a seat at the kitchen table, prepared to write Mom a letter. When she'd returned from the mailbox, she had spoken with Elizabeth about her mamm's request to send some of her quilts for the auction in June. Abby also mentioned that she would like to auction off the remaining quilts from her shop in Ohio and said she hoped it might help her put the past behind her. Elizabeth agreed that it was a good idea. Now Abby needed to let Mom know so she could set the wheels in motion.

"Does this mean you'll still be here during auction time?" Elizabeth asked as she pulled out a chair and took the seat opposite Abby.

Abby nodded. "If you don't mind me staying that long."

Elizabeth waved her hand "Not at all. In fact, I'd enjoy the company as well as the help."

"I'll be happy to help you and the other ladies in the community fix the meal you'll be serving to those who attend the auction, but I'd rather not have anything to do with the quilts," Abby said with a lift of her chin.

Elizabeth shrugged her slim shoulders and smiled. "I wouldn't want you to do anything you're not comfortable with."

"Danki."

"So, now," Elizabeth said, pushing away from the table, "what should we have for lunch? I can get started on it while you write your letter."

"Are you sure you don't mind? I can help with lunch and write to Mom later on."

"Don't mind a bit. You keep on writing till you're done." Elizabeth grinned. "I thought maybe later this afternoon we could take a bike ride over to the Lehmans' place. Myra and you seemed to get along pretty well the other day, and I'm thinkin' the two of you might like the chance to get better acquainted."

"That sounds nice, but I haven't been on a bicycle since I was a young girl. I doubt I could still ride."

"Oh, sure you can. Once you've learned how to ride a bike, you never forget." Elizabeth stared across the room with a faraway look in her eyes. "I remember how my little brother and I used to ride our bikes back in Indiana where we grew up. We had some of our best visits when we rode into town to do errands." She smiled. "I think next to walking, riding a bike is the best way to travel, because you're able to see more scenery along the way. In a buggy you have to keep the horse in line and make sure you stay on your own side of the road."

"Do you have more than one bike?" Abby asked.

Elizabeth nodded. "I've got my own, plus the one my husband used to ride. I'll let you take mine, since you haven't ridden in a while. You might have trouble with the bar in the middle of the man's bicycle."

"That's nice of you, but—"

"Now I insist."

"Jah, okay. I'll give it a try."

❧

Naomi had just gotten her girls down for a nap and was planning to go over the receipt ledger when Lydia Weaver and her youngest daughter, Leona, entered the store.

"Wie geht's?" Naomi asked.

"Doin' fine, and you?"

"Other than being awfully tired, I can't complain."

"I've got some finished quilts out in my buggy," Lydia said, her blue eyes twinkling. "Me and my two oldest daughters recently finished several, so they're ready to sell in Fannie's quilt shop." She glanced around the room. "Thought maybe if Caleb or Matthew was here, I could talk 'em into bringing the boxes inside the shop for me."

"Caleb's getting one of our horses shoed, and Matthew's laboring at home in his woodworking shop."

"Guess I can manage on my own then." Lydia chuckled and pushed a strand of light brown hair back into her bun. "I loaded the quilts by myself, since Jacob and Arthur had already left for their paint job before I decided to come into town. So if I could get the boxes into the buggy, I'm sure I can get 'em back out."

"I'd be happy to unload them for you," Naomi offered. She stepped down from her wooden stool and started for the front door, but the sound of her youngest daughter's wail halted her footsteps. "Ach! There goes Susan. I hope she doesn't wake her sister."

"Can I play with the boppli?" Leona asked. "I could keep her company while you and Mama bring in the quilts."

"I guess that would be all right." Naomi glanced at Lydia for her approval. Leona was almost ten years old and seemed quite capable.

Lydia nodded and headed for the door.

Naomi reached under the counter and handed Leona a small, faceless doll. "If you give this to Susan, I'm sure she'll settle right down."

Leona took the doll and scampered off toward the back room.

"Be careful you don't wake Sarah," the child's mother called after her.

"I won't."

Naomi and Lydia stepped onto the front porch and down the steps. A few minutes later, they stood at the back of Jacob Weaver's market buggy.

"Have you heard anything from Abby lately?" Lydia asked, shielding her eyes from the sun.

"Had a letter from her a few days ago, and she seems to be doin' okay."

"When's she planning to come home?"

Naomi shrugged. "Don't know. Fannie seems to think she'll stay on at least until June, which is when the Amish community near Rexford holds its annual auction."

Lydia reached into the buggy and picked up the first box, and Naomi lifted the second one out.

"Sure would be nice if Abby decided to run the quilt shop for Fannie when she gets home," Lydia commented as they started for the store.

"I'm not sure Abby will ever work around quilts again. She's still grieving for Lester and the loss of her quilt shop. So far, nobody's been able to get through to her."

Lydia clicked her tongue. "It's such a shame when someone as young as Abby loses a loved one and can't come to grips with it." Her forehead creased as she shifted the cardboard box in her hands. " 'Course, I'm no expert on the subject of grief, since life has been pretty good to me and Jacob these twenty-two years we've been married."

"Guess nobody knows how they would handle things until it happens," Naomi said.

"That's for certain sure."

They had reached the porch, and Naomi leaned one edge of the box against the side of the store as she reached out to grab the handle on the screen door. She held it for Lydia, but the woman nodded for her to go ahead. Naomi had only taken a few steps when she halted. "Was in der welt—what in the world?"

In the middle of the floor sat two little girls with chocolate on their faces and various size candy wrappers surrounding them. It was a comical scene, and Naomi didn't know whether to laugh or cry.

"Ach, Leona," Lydia scolded, "I thought I could trust you not to get the baby up, and what's all this with the candy now?"

The child stared up her mother, and tears quickly filled her green eyes. "I couldn't get Susan to quiet down, and when Sarah woke up, she asked for some candy."

"Jah, well, that didn't give you the right to give her any, and especially not the boppli. She's too young to be fed chocolate."

"I figured she was hungry."

Naomi bent down and scooped Susan into her arms, then she grabbed hold of Sarah's hand. "I'd better take these two into the other room and get them cleaned up. When I come back, we can see about setting out those quilts."

"Jah, okay."

I sure hope the rest of this week goes better than today, Naomi thought as she and the girls headed to the back of the store. *For I surely don't have the energy to deal with much more.*

Chapter 34

Abby couldn't believe how well she had adapted to riding a bicycle again. For the past two months she'd been pedaling all over the area, visiting her new friend Myra, making trips to the country store, and going for rides simply for the enjoyment of spending time alone in the beautiful woods. Her depression had lifted some, but she still blamed herself for Lester's death, and even though Elizabeth kept coaxing Abby to make a quilt, she flatly refused.

"I can't believe the auction is only two days away," Abby said to Elizabeth as they rolled out pastry dough for some of the pies that would be sold to those attending the big event. "Don't know where the time has gone since I first came here to visit."

"Time does seem to move along rather quickly." Elizabeth smiled. "I've enjoyed your company and will miss you when you're gone."

Abby stared at the floor. She wasn't sure she wanted to return home. Being in this small Amish community was like a quiet respite.

"You're welcome to stay on even after the auction," Elizabeth was quick to say. "I'm sure I speak for others in our community when I say we'd be glad to have you stay here permanently."

Abby smiled. "That's nice to know, but it wouldn't be fair to my mamm."

"If you returned home, would it only be to please her?"

Abby pondered Elizabeth's question before she answered. Truth be told, she had spent most of her life trying to please her mamm, especially after Dad's death. It wasn't that Mom had asked Abby to make sacrifices. The two of them had always been close, but Abby had felt a sense of obligation to her mother that went beyond simple respect or willingness to help out. She'd been trying to fulfill her promise to her daed and had given up a lot in the process of trying to please Mom and see that her needs were met. Even now Abby wondered if she'd been selfish for staying here so long. Her mother had told her several months ago that Dad's request didn't mean Abby should be so self-sacrificing and put her own needs on hold. She'd also been reminded that since Mom was married to Abraham now, it was his job to look out for her.

"I'm feeling confused about things," Abby admitted. "I miss my family and want to be near them, but I've enjoyed being here with you, too."

Elizabeth nodded and measured out some lard as she prepared to make another batch of dough. "For now let's concentrate on gettin' ready for the auction. When that's behind us, you'll have time to decide what you want to do."

"That's true, and we do have a lot to get done before Saturday morning."

"I'm thinking about putting that small quilt I found awhile back into the auction," Elizabeth said. "There's not much point in me hanging on to it, because unless God brings another man into my life soon, it's not likely I'll need a baby covering. I'm not gettin' any younger, ya know."

Abby grinned. "You never know how things will go. Look at my mamm. None of us expected her to marry again, much less become the mother of twin boys at her age."

Elizabeth clucked her tongue. "Poor Fannie. I can't imagine raisin' a couple of zwilling at any age."

"The twins can be quite the handful, but they're sure cute little fellows."

"I'm sure they are."

Abby sobered. "I hope Mom is managing okay without my help. She relied on me pretty heavily for a time."

"What do her letters say about how she's gettin' along in your absence?"

Abby grabbed the rolling pin and flattened the mound of pie dough in front of her. "Says she's doing fine, but then my mamm's never been one to complain."

"And how's your stepsister these days? Didn't you mention that she said in her last letter that she's pregnant?"

Abby nodded. "Naomi and Caleb have two little girls, and I think they're hopin' for a boy this time."

"Say, I've got an idea," Elizabeth said excitedly. "Why don't I give you the baby covering? You can present it to Naomi, if you like. I'm quite certain it's an Amish quilt, and I'd like to see it go to someone who would appreciate it."

"I suppose I could take it to her, and I'd be happy to pay you for it."

"I wouldn't think of takin' your money," Elizabeth said with a wave of her hand. A dusting of flour from her fingers drifted to the countertop, and she chuckled. "It'll be my gift to your new niece or nephew."

Abby smiled. "All right then. I'll take the quilt to Naomi whenever I decide to go home."

∾

Linda walked slowly down the hospital corridor. She'd discovered a breast lump last week and had gone to the doctor for a thorough exam. This morning she'd had a mammogram in the hospital's diagnostic lab. Depending on the results, she might be faced with a biopsy. *Oh Lord,* she prayed, *please don't let this be cancer.*

Linda thought about Jimmy and how much he needed her. He'd turned seven two months ago and wasn't ready to be without his mother. She thought about Jim and how it might affect their marriage if the lump was cancerous. He had so little patience with her anymore, especially when she was sick or emotionally wrought. Would he want to be saddled with a wife who had serious health problems? *And what if I were to die before Jim finds the Lord as his Savior? I want our son to grow up knowing Jesus, and if Jim remains set against religion, he probably won't see that Jimmy goes to church or receives any religious training.*

Linda drew in a deep breath and tried to relax. She knew she was worrying about things that hadn't even happened. *Please calm my heart, Lord, and if this does turn out to be cancer, then all of us will need Your help in the days ahead.*

"You're lookin' awful tired these days," Fannie said, when she discovered Naomi bent over an empty shelf in the store, swishing a dust rag back and forth.

Naomi looked up and wiped the perspiration from her forehead. "I do seem to tire more easily with this pregnancy than I did with my other two. Guess it's because I have a lot more to do now than I did before."

Fannie gave Naomi a hug. She had come to care deeply for the young woman and hated to see her working so hard when she obviously didn't feel well. "Why don't you bring the girls over to our place each morning on your way to work? That way you won't have so much responsibility here at the store."

Naomi smiled but shook her head. "I couldn't ask you to watch my kinner. You've got your hands full takin' care of your own two active boys."

"They can be a handful at times," Fannie admitted. "But while Nancy's still working as a maad for Anna Beechy, now that Mary Ann's out of school for the summer, she's home most of the time. That young girl has been a big help to me lately, and I'm sure she wouldn't mind helpin' care for your girls."

"You really think so?" Naomi straightened and reached around to rub her lower back.

"I do. Besides, Sarah and Susan would be good company for Timothy and Titus." Fannie chuckled. "Might keep 'em occupied so Mary Ann and I could get more chores done around the house. I may even find more time for quilting."

"Did you leave the twins with Mary Ann this afternoon?"

Fannie nodded. "Jah, they were both sleeping soundly when I decided to come to town, so I figured she'd have no problem with 'em while I was gone."

"It's good for you to get away once in a while."

"It does feel kind of nice." Fannie shifted from one foot to the other. "What do you think about my offer to watch the girls?"

"I'll speak with Caleb about it as soon as he gets back from his dental appointment," Naomi said. "If he has no objections, maybe we could bring the girls by next Monday and see how it goes."

Fannie smiled. "Sounds good."

"Did you come by for anything in particular?" Naomi asked. "Or did you stop to check on the quilt shop?"

"Both. I need some sewing notions, but I wanted to see how many quilts are in stock right now. If we're running low, I might have to ask a few more women to do some quilting for us." Fannie nodded toward her shop. "Now that it's summer, things can get busy when the tourists start comin' in."

"That's true, even here in the store." Naomi headed to the quilt shop, and Fannie followed. "Have you heard anything more from Abby?"

"I got another letter from her last week, and she mentioned that the auction will be held this Saturday. I'm guessin' my daughter's been helping the women in the community get the food ready that they plan to sell that day."

"From what Abby said in her last letter to me, it

sounded like they'll have to feed at least a thousand people."

Fannie nodded. "I'm hopin' once Abby sees our quilts auctioned off, she'll be ready to come home. I miss her something awful."

"I'm sure you do. I'll be glad when Abby's back in Pennsylvania, too."

Fannie let her hand travel over a stack of queen-sized quilts. "I'm beginning to wonder if I should just sell the quilt shop and be done with it."

Naomi frowned. "Why would you want to do that? I thought you loved quilting."

"I do enjoy making quilts, but I have no desire to drag the boys into town every day and try to run this place by myself."

"We need to keep praying about the matter," Naomi said. "I'd hate to see the quilt shop close."

Fannie shrugged. "If Abby returns and still refuses to work here, then I'll probably be forced to sell."

∞

Linda glanced at Beth, who sat behind the wheel of her compact car. "Thanks for driving me to my appointment this morning. It was easier to have the biopsy done knowing you were waiting for me in the other room."

"I was praying, too." Beth tapped the steering wheel with her fingertips. "I still don't understand why your husband couldn't take time off to be with you. Surely he must realize how serious this could be."

"Jim doesn't care about anyone but himself," Linda said, as the bitter taste of bile rose in her throat. *I will not give in to tears. It won't change a thing.*

"I can see why you're frustrated, but we need to be patient and let the Lord work in Jim's life." Beth's voice was low and soothing, and in that moment, Linda almost believed her.

"What if this turns out to be cancer?"

"Then you'll do whatever the doctor suggests." Beth reached over and squeezed Linda's hand. "Our whole church will be praying for you."

"What scares me more than the disease is wondering what will become of Jim and Jimmy if I should die."

"Let's trust the Lord and take things one step at a time. The results of the biopsy could be negative, and then you will have been worried for nothing."

Linda nodded as tears blurred her vision. "I know I should trust God more, but sometimes it's hard, especially when I don't get answers to my prayers."

"God always answers," Beth said with a note of conviction. "Sometimes it's yes, sometimes no, and sometimes He says to wait. Regardless of how God answers, we must accept it as His will."

"I know," Linda murmured.

"No matter how this turns out," Beth said with an encouraging smile, "we'll get through it together . . .you, me, and our heavenly Father."

Chapter 35

Abby sat on a backless wooden bench inside the quilt barn, observing the auctioneer as he hollered, "The bid's at three hundred dollars for this Lone Star quilt. Do I hear four hundred?"

In the row ahead, an English woman's hand shot up as she lifted the piece of cardboard with her bidding number on it.

"Four hundred dollars. Do I hear five?" The bidding went on until the Amish man finally shouted, "Sold at seven hundred dollars!"

Abby was amazed at how many quilts hung inside the tent. What seemed even more astonishing was the number of people who had crowded into the area to watch the proceedings or bid on a quilt or wall hanging. She recognized the quilt being bid on now and leaned forward. It was one of her mamm's, and she figured the king-sized covering with various shades of blue would go for a tidy sum. She wasn't disappointed. It sold for nine hundred dollars. The other quilt her mother had sent was queen-sized, made in the Dahlia pattern with hues of maroon, pink, and white. Soon it was also gone—sold for seven hundred and fifty dollars.

Abby's spine went rigid when the two young Amish women standing on the raised platform held up one of her quilts—a Double Wedding

Ring pattern, with interlocking rings made from two shades of green on a white background.

Tears stung her eyes as she thought about her and Lester's wedding plans and the quilt she'd been working on before she left Ohio. If she had finished the quilt and they'd gotten married as planned, it would have been covering their bed right now. All that remained of Abby's previous life as a quilter were the four double-sized quilts about to be auctioned off.

Her heart clenched when the auctioneer shouted, "Sold for six hundred dollars!"

The Amish women held up the second quilt Abby had made. This one was designed in the Distelfink pattern, which had been a favorite among the English who'd come to her shop in Berlin. In short order, it was sold for five hundred dollars.

Tears trickled down Abby's face, and a sob worked its way up her throat. *Oh Lester, I loved you so much. You sacrificed your life to save my quilts, and I gave you nothing in return.*

The third and fourth quilts were then bid on and sold, and Abby swayed as a wave of nausea coursed through her stomach. She'd hoped that seeing her quilts auctioned off would bring release, but it only added to her grief. She stood on trembling legs and pushed her way through the crowd. Outside, she rushed behind the barn where her bicycle was parked. She needed to be alone— to go somewhere and find a quiet place to sit and calm down.

Abby pedaled across the open field, dodging the throng of people shopping at the various booths and weaving in and out of parked cars until she found her way to the main road. She kept the bike moving faster, taking her farther and farther away from the noisy auction and those painful memories of her beautiful quilts.

By the time Abby reached a turnoff for Lake Koocanusa, she was panting for breath. She braked and let her feet drop to the ground, then sat motionless, staring at the vast body of water below while she fought to gain control of her swirling emotions.

A hawk soared overhead, and Abby caught sight of a turkey hen and her chicks stepping out of the brush. The darker leaves of the trees surrounding the lake contrasted with the lighter bottle-green grass growing nearby. It was quiet and peaceful, which was just what she needed right now.

Feeling a need to be closer to the lake, Abby guided her bike slowly down the hill, following a narrow trail and being careful not to get her long dress caught in the bushes. When she reached the bottom, she noticed a young English boy sitting on a boulder with a fishing pole. He appeared to be alone, for she saw no one else in sight. Not wishing to disturb the child, she took a seat on one of the downed trees.

Clasping her hands around her knees, Abby lifted her face to the sun. She tried to pray, but no words would come. A verse of scripture popped into her mind. It was 1 Peter 1:7, one Elizabeth had shared with her that morning: *"That the trial of your faith, being much more precious than of gold that perisheth, though it be tried with fire, might be found unto praise and honour and glory at the appearing of Jesus Christ.*" That was the second verse about fire Abby had heard since coming to Montana, and she wondered if God might be trying to tell her something. Abby knew her faith had been tried, but she felt as if her trials had done nothing to bring honor or praise to the Lord.

If only I could know peace and happiness again. If I could just be free from the overwhelming guilt I feel because of Lester's death. If only my life had some meaning.

Splash!

Abby's eyes snapped open.

"Help! Help!"

She jerked her head to the left, and her breath caught in her throat. The little boy she'd seen fishing had obviously fallen into the lake, and he was in trouble.

Abby scrambled off the log and jumped into the lake, giving no thought to the clothes she wore. Her father had taught her and Harold how to swim when they were little, but she hadn't gone swimming in several years. Even so, she soon discovered that, like riding a bike, she hadn't forgotten what to do in the water.

The boy continued to fight as he flailed his arms. His head bobbed up and down in the water. Abby reached out and grabbed the edge of his shirt, pulling him closer to her. She wrapped her arms around his chest, but the child floundered around as he fought to remain afloat.

"Calm down. Don't panic. I've got you now." Abby hoped he would soon relax, for if he kept thrashing like this, they might both drown. "Dear God, help us!" she shouted above the boy's screams.

The child went limp, making it easier for her to swim while she pulled him to shore. A short time later, they both lay on the grassy bank, the boy coughing and sobbing, Abby gulping in deep breaths of air. She was aware that her kapp was missing, her bun had come loose, and a clump of soggy hair pushed against her shoulders. Her dress was soaked, and so were her sneakers, but she didn't care. The child was safe, and that was all that mattered.

The boy stared at her with brown eyes, huge as chestnuts. "You. . .you saved my life."

She smiled. "What's your name?"

"Peter. I live up the hill."

"I'm Abby, Peter, and I think I'd better take you home."

He hiccupped on a sob. "Mama's gonna be real mad, 'cause she's told me never to come to the lake by myself."

Abby's heart went out to the child, but she knew what had to be done. "My bicycle is parked up the hill. We can ride double. How's that sound?"

Peter nodded, and she helped him to his feet. "I think I lost my pole," he whimpered.

"A fishing pole can be replaced, but you can't. Your mother will be happy to know you're okay."

Sometime later, with Peter riding on the handlebars in front of her, Abby pedaled into the boy's yard. A young woman with dark brown hair worn in a ponytail rushed out of the log home and onto the driveway. "Peter! Where were you, and why are your clothes all wet?"

"I. . .I went fishin', and I fell into the lake when a big one grabbed hold of my line," the child answered.

Peter's mother lifted him from the handlebars and hugged him tightly.

"I heard the splash and realized he was in water over his head and couldn't swim," Abby said.

The boy's mother stared at Abby. "Who are you?"

"Abby Miller, and I—"

"She jumped into the water and saved me, Mama," Peter interrupted, as his mother set him on the ground. "I would've drowned if she hadn't come along."

Abby's cheeks warmed as Peter threw himself into her arms. "I'm glad I was there," she whispered.

Peter's mother gave Abby an unexpected hug. "I'm Sharon Beal, and I thank you for saving my son."

"You're welcome."

"Why don't you come into the house and dry off? You're probably cold."

Abby shook her head. "I'm all right."

"At least let me get you a towel."

Abby glanced at her dress. She'd wrung it out the best she could, but it was sopping wet and stuck miserably to her skin. "Jah, I'd appreciate a towel."

Sharon patted her son on the head. "Run into the house and get some towels for you and Abby."

"Okay." Peter hesitated a moment, offered Abby a toothless grin, and scampered away.

"You were in the right place at the right time; there's no doubt in my mind," Sharon said to Abby. "God was watching out for my boy and brought you along at the exact moment it was needed."

Abby stared at the ground, puzzled by the woman's remark. Had she really gone to the lake because God had ordained it? If that were so, then why hadn't—

"Are you okay? You seem troubled."

Abby lifted her gaze to meet Sharon's. "I was wondering why God would send me to rescue Peter but let the man I was supposed to marry die."

Sharon tipped her head as a look of confusion clouded her dark eyes. Before Abby could explain, Peter came running toward them with a towel draped around his neck and another one in his hands. He handed the second towel to Abby. "Here ya go."

"Thank you."

"Now run inside and change into some dry clothes," his mother said.

Peter bounded off again, offering Abby a quick wave before he departed.

"Before my son came out, you said something about the man you were supposed to marry dying," Sharon said. "Do you mind if I ask what happened?"

Abby rubbed the towel briskly over her arms and legs. She didn't know why she felt compelled to tell this near stranger about the fire that had snuffed out Lester's life, but she found herself pouring out the whole story. "If I'd only realized that the dream I kept having was a warning and returned to Ohio sooner, Lester might still be alive," she said with a catch in her voice.

Sharon's forehead wrinkled. "Is that how you see it?"

Abby nodded.

"Ecclesiastes 3:1 says, 'To every thing there is a season, and a time to every purpose under the heaven.' " Sharon touched Abby's arm, and Abby felt warmth and comfort. "I believe God allows us to experience certain things in life that help us grow and learn to rely on Him. Even if you had returned to Ohio sooner, the fire might still have destroyed your quilt shop, and you could have been the one killed. Or perhaps both you and Lester would have perished."

Abby trembled as a rush of emotions spiraled through her body. "I've often wished I had been burned in the fire. It would have been better to have lost my own life than to have endured the pain of losing the man I loved."

Sharon slipped her arm around Abby's shoulder. "If you had died in the fire, you wouldn't have come to Montana. And if you hadn't come here, you would not have been at the lake this afternoon to save my boy."

"I. . .I guess you're right." Abby drew in a deep breath and released it slowly. "I've spent these last seven months feeling sorry for myself, wallowing in guilt, and trying to drown out the past by working so hard, when I should have been trying to deal with things."

"It's all right to grieve, Abby, but you must remember that the Lord is near to those with a broken heart. It says so in Psalm 34:18. All you need to do is call out to Him, and He will give you comfort, whether it be through His Word, by helping others, or in something as simple as a child's touch."

"Thank you," Abby said tearfully. "I've strayed so far from God these past several months, and I surely needed that reminder."

The two women hugged again, and Abby handed the wet towel to Sharon. "I must be going now or my friend Elizabeth will wonder where I am."

"Good-bye, Abby, and may God bless you in the days ahead."

As Abby pedaled her bicycle toward the auction barn, the verses of scripture Peter's mother had shared played over and over in her mind. Seeing her quilts auctioned off had put an end to the reminder of her quilt shop, but it had not put an end to the pain of losing Lester or lessened her guilt. But a few simple passages from the Bible and the kind words of a grateful mother had helped Abby see the truth. For the first time since Lester's death, she was glad to be alive.

Abby drew in a deep breath, savoring the clean mountain air. She noticed the budding wildflowers growing along the edge of the road and joined the birds in song as they warbled a happy tune from the trees overhead. Jah, it was wunderbaar gut to be alive!

A car whizzed past, and Abby gripped the handlebars, moving her bike to the edge of the road. *Guess some things aren't so different even here in the woods.* She glanced at a covey of quail running into the bushes, and smiled, refusing to let the speeding motorist spoil the moment. She could hardly wait to tell Elizabeth all that had happened after she'd left the quilt barn. Surely her new friend would share in this joy. Abby thought about Mom and the rest of the family waiting in Pennsylvania. *I'll send them a letter right away.*

Abby's attention was drawn back to the road when she heard a noise, and two female deer stepped out of the woods. She swerved to keep from hitting them, but her back tire spun in the gravel and she lost control. The last thing Abby remembered was the trunk of a cedar tree coming straight toward her.

Chapter 36

A bby moaned as she squinted against the ray of light streaming into the room. Her head ached, her vision was fuzzy, and nothing seemed familiar. *Where am I?* She tried to stretch and winced when a throbbing pain shot through her leg. *Oh! What's happened to me?*

"I'm glad you're finally awake. You've been in and out for the last couple of days."

Abby didn't recognize the woman's voice. She turned her head and blinked at the middle-aged woman with short auburn hair who stood beside her bed. She wore a nurse's uniform. "Wh–where am I?" she rasped.

"You're in the hospital. You were brought to Libby by ambulance late Saturday afternoon."

Abby tried to sit up, but the dull ache in her head prevented her from doing so.

"Better lie still," the nurse instructed. "You've had a serious concussion, and your leg is broken." She touched Abby's arm. "From what I was told, you took quite a spill, so it could have been a lot worse."

Abby squeezed her eyes shut, trying to remember what had happened. Saturday morning she'd gone to the auction and had watched her quilts being auctioned off. Then, unable to bear the pain of it all, she had ridden Elizabeth's bike down to the lake. There'd been a little boy there. He'd fallen into the water, and she'd rescued him. When Abby took Peter home, his mother had shared some verses of scripture and words of wisdom, helping her realize that life did have meaning.

And last, Abby remembered getting back on her bike and heading toward the auction. There were two deer on the road, and—

Her eyes snapped open. "I skidded in some gravel and must have hit a tree."

The nurse nodded. "That's what the paramedics figured had happened, although you were unconscious when they arrived."

"Who found me, do you know?"

"A man and woman who were driving to the Amish auction spotted you lying alongside of the road. They called 911 on their cell phone, and after the ambulance arrived, they drove to the auction and told someone what had happened."

Abby curved her fingers under her chin. "Oh my! Elizabeth must be so worried. She probably wonders why I never came back and doesn't know where I am."

"Elizabeth King?"

"Jah."

"I guess with the description the English couple gave to the people in charge, they were able to figure out it was you who had been hurt. Elizabeth is here now in the waiting room."

Abby drew in a deep breath. "Can I see her?"

"Certainly. I'll send her right in." The nurse left the room, and a few minutes later, Elizabeth entered with a worried expression on her face.

"Oh Abby, I'm so glad you're going to be all right." She rushed to the side of Abby's bed. "When the doctor told me you'd had a concussion, I was terribly worried."

"The nurse said my leg's broken, too."

Elizabeth nodded and took a seat in the closest chair. "What were you doing out there with my bike?"

"I. . .I decided to go for a ride."

"But I thought you were going to help me and the other ladies serve the meal after you'd watched some of the quilts being auctioned off."

"I had planned on that."

"When it came time to get things set out, you were nowhere to be found, but it wasn't until later that I really began to worry."

Abby's eyes filled with tears. "I'm sorry for causing you worry."

"It's you I'm concerned about." Elizabeth reached for Abby's hand. "What made you decide to go for a bike ride?"

"I had hoped if my quilts sold, it would put an end to my past and make me feel better."

"Did it?"

Abby shook her head. "I felt worse, and the only thing I could think to do was get off by myself for a while." She went on to tell Elizabeth about the boy who had fallen into the lake and how she'd saved him. Then she relayed what Peter's mother had said when she'd taken him home and how the woman had helped her see things more clearly. "I was planning to share this with you when I got back to the auction, which was where I was heading when I ran into a tree."

Elizabeth's eyes watered, yet she smiled. "I'm glad you've come to grips with the past and are ready to face the future."

"Sharon reminded me that if I hadn't come to visit you, I wouldn't have been at the lake Saturday afternoon to save her son." Abby brushed her tears away. "God showed me some other things, too."

"Such as?"

"All this time I've been feeling guilty for not returning to Ohio sooner, and thinking I could have spared Lester's life, when I should have been trusting God and allowing Him to heal my pain." She paused and moistened her lips with the tip of her tongue. "Peter's mother was right. If the fire hadn't happened at my quilt shop, I never would have come to Montana. I realize now that even if I had been there when my shop caught fire, I might not have been able to talk Lester out of going in. It was an accident—one I wish hadn't happened, but it did, and—" Abby couldn't go on. Her voice broke on a sob.

"God used you in a mighty way when you saved that boy from drowning. I'm happy you've decided to trust Him again, and I know He is, too." Elizabeth plucked a tissue from the small box on the nearby table and blew her nose. "I know Edna and your mamm will be glad to hear this good news, too."

"Do they know about my accident?"

Elizabeth nodded. "When I heard what had happened, I used a friend's phone to call your stepsister's store in Paradise. Naomi said she would get word to your mamm and the rest of the family."

"I'm ready to go home to Pennsylvania,

Elizabeth. I mean, as soon as I'm able to travel."

"I figured you might be."

"I don't know what the future holds for me, but I want to do something worthwhile—something that will help others and let them know God cares for them."

Elizabeth reached into her purse. "I wonder if you might be interested in this."

"What is it?"

"It's some information I recently received from a friend who lives in Indiana. Some of the women in her community are making quilts to send to people in Haiti, where there's a need for warm blankets."

Abby thought about what Elizabeth had shared. Until Saturday afternoon, she'd given up on the idea of quilting again. But now she was being offered the opportunity to make quilts and give them to others who had so little. She was certain it was what God wanted her to do.

∞

"What do you mean, you're going to Montana?"

"You heard me. I'm going there as soon as Abby gets out of the hospital and feels up to traveling." Matthew looked at Naomi as if she'd taken leave of her senses, but she thought it was he who was talking crazy.

"Shouldn't it be someone else's responsibility to go after Abby?" she questioned.

He leaned across the counter until his face was a few inches from hers. "Think about it, Naomi. Fannie can't go; she has the twins to care for. Abraham, Norman, Jake, and Samuel are in the middle of plantin' the fields. And you—well, you're in no condition to go anywhere now that you're in the family way again. Besides, you've got two little girls and a store to look after. I'm the only one with the time to go."

Naomi smiled. "So I've been right all this time, jah?"

"Right about what?"

"You're in love with Abby, and don't deny it, because I see the light shinin' in your eyes."

"What light's that?"

"The light of love."

Matthew's ears turned pink, and the color spread quickly over his face. "I've told you before. Abby thinks of me only as her big brother."

Naomi shrugged. "That could change."

He grunted and took a step back. "We'd best wait and see how it goes."

"You're still willing to go after her, even though you don't know if there's a future for the two of you?"

"Jah. She needs me."

Naomi skirted around the counter. "Matthew Fisher, you're a wunderbaar man."

∞

Jim stared into his cup of coffee and tried to focus his thoughts on the paint job his crew was scheduled to do. But no matter how hard he tried, he couldn't keep his mind on work. Linda's hurtful expression and slumped shoulders when he'd come home Friday night had made him feel like a heel. *She's upset because I didn't go with her when she had the biopsy. She thinks I don't care.*

He pushed his chair away from the kitchen table and stood. *I do care. I just couldn't go, and it wasn't my job keeping me away, like I told her. I can't let Linda know how scared I am that she might have cancer. What would Jimmy and I do if she were to die?*

Jim glanced at the clock above the stove. It was almost six thirty, and he needed to get on the road. Today's paint job was in Renton, a good hour away if traffic was heavy on the freeway. He'd thought about waking Linda before he left and apologizing to her. But she and Jimmy usually slept in now that he was out of school for the summer, and Jim didn't want to disturb her. *I should have apologized this weekend, but I couldn't seem to get the words out. Maybe I'll leave her a note.*

Jim opened the rolltop desk in one corner of the kitchen and pulled out a sheet of paper and a pen. He hurriedly scrawled an apology, said he would bring home pizza for dinner, and left the note on the kitchen table. At least now he could go to work without feeling so guilty.

Chapter 37

Linda hung up the phone and sank to the couch as shock waves spiraled through her body like a spinning top. The pathology report wasn't good. The doctor said there was a cancerous mass in her left breast and he wanted to schedule Linda for a mastectomy as soon as possible.

She squeezed her eyes shut, and tears rolled down her cheeks. "Oh Lord, help me deal with this. Give me strength in the days ahead, and no matter what happens, please help my faith to grow stronger."

"Mommy, why are you crying?"

Linda's eyes snapped open. She didn't know Jimmy had come into the living room. For the last hour, he'd been upstairs playing. She sniffed and swiped her hand across her damp face. "Come sit beside me so we can talk."

Jimmy did as she asked and snuggled against her side. "Are you mad at Daddy? Did he yell at you again?"

"No, Jimmy." How could she tell her boy the truth without frightening him? And shouldn't she let Jim know what the doctor said before she told Jimmy anything about her going to the hospital?

"Why were you crying, Mommy?"

She kissed the top of his head. "I'll explain

things after your daddy gets home."

"Okay."

Jimmy scooted away, but she reached out to him. "Don't go yet. I'd like to ask you something."

"What?"

"It's about Sunday school."

He grinned. "I like my teacher, and Allen and I always have fun during playtime."

"I'm glad." Linda fingered the edge of her Bible lying on the table to her right. "Will you promise to keep going to church, even if Mommy can't go?"

Jimmy's eyes were wide. "How would I get there if you didn't take me?"

She swallowed hard, afraid she might break down in front of him. "I'm sure Allen's mother would be happy to pick you up."

His forehead wrinkled. "Why can't you keep takin' me to Sunday school?"

"I. . .I will, Jimmy, for as long as I'm able." She moistened her lips with the tip of her tongue. "I just meant that if Mommy got sick and couldn't take you, I'd want you to go anyway."

Jimmy nodded soberly. "You're not sick, are you, Mommy?"

Linda drew a deep breath, praying for the right words. "Why don't the two of us go into the kitchen and see about having some lunch? We can talk about this later. How's that sound?"

"Can I have chicken noodle soup?"

"Yes, of course." Linda leaned over and kissed Jimmy's cheek. *Oh Lord, please give me many more years with this precious boy.*

∾

"Are you excited to get home?" Matthew asked Abby as they rode in the backseat of their English driver's van, heading for Abraham and Fannie's place.

"Jah, I surely am. I never could have made the trip alone, and I appreciate your comin' to get me."

"I'm glad I could do it." He grinned at Abby, and her eyes flitted from his firm, full mouth to his serious brown eyes. The thick, dark hair covering his ears gleamed in the sunlight, and for the first time since she'd met Matthew, Abby realized how handsome he was.

"You've been kind to me the whole way here," she said, taking the apple Matthew had just handed her.

"It's easy to be kind to someone as sweet as you." Matthew looked straight ahead, but Abby noticed that his ears had turned slightly red. He embarrassed easily. She'd discovered that soon after moving to Pennsylvania.

She hesitated before responding to his last statement, not sure how she should interpret the words. Could it be that Matthew saw her as more than a little sister? If so, why hadn't he said anything to let her know? He was probably just speaking kindly in a brotherly way, the same as he always had. Still, if there was a chance that. . .

"On the train we talked about lots of things," Abby said hesitantly, "but there's one thing I didn't tell you."

"What's that?"

"Even though I will always have memories of Lester with me, I'm ready to move on with my life."

Matthew's eyebrows shot up so high they disappeared under the brim of his straw hat. "Oh?"

She nodded. "I know that when the time is right, someone will come into my life who will love me as much as Lester did, and I shall love him in return."

Matthew shifted in his seat. "Uh. . .Abby. . . I hope I'm not speakin' out of turn, but I was wonderin'—"

She reached over and touched his arm. "What were you wondering?"

He glanced at her, then looked quickly away. "Do you. . . uh. . .think you could ever be interested in someone like me?"

The rhythm of Abby's heartbeat picked up, and she shifted on the seat beside him. "Jah, I believe I could."

Matthew's face broke into a wide smile, and he reached for her hand, sending unexpected warm tingles up her arm. "I won't rush you into anything, because I know you've still got a lot of healin' to do, but I would like the chance to court you whenever you're ready."

She nodded. "I'd like that, too."

The van pulled into the Fishers' graveled driveway, and Matthew jumped out. He came around to help Abby down, then handed the crutches to her.

Abby's heart swelled with emotion. "I'm so excited to see everyone." She nodded at her suitcase, which their driver, Walt Peterson, had taken from the backseat. "I've got something to give Naomi for that boppli she's carrying."

Matthew chuckled. "Caleb's hopin' for a boy this time. Guess he feels a bit outnumbered with only girls around their place."

Walt set their suitcases on the front porch and said good-bye.

Matthew helped Abby up the steps, and they

were almost to the front door when it swung open and a chorus of voices shouted, "Welcome home!"

"And I'm ever so glad to be here," Abby said in return.

Mom, Abraham, Mary Ann, Nancy, Jake, Samuel, Norman, and his wife, Ruth, all crowded around, but Mom was the first to hug Abby. "Come inside and have a seat. You must be exhausted."

Abby nodded. "It was a long trip, and my leg's beginning to throb."

Abraham took Abby's crutches and helped her over to the couch. After she was seated, Matthew pulled up a footstool and slid it under her leg.

"How much longer will ya have to wear that thing? It looks mighty heavy," Mary Ann said, leaning over to study Abby's cast.

"Three more weeks." Abby reached for her mother's hand as Mom took a seat beside her. "Where are the twins? I'm anxious to see how much they've grown."

"They're upstairs taking their afternoon naps, but it's nearly time for them to wake up," Mom replied.

"Mary Ann and I will go fetch them." Nancy grabbed her younger sister's hand, and they raced out of the room.

"Will Naomi and her family be over soon?" Abby asked.

Mom nodded. "They plan to stop by after they close the store for the day. I invited them to have supper with us."

"I'm glad. It will be nice to have the whole family together again."

Abby spent the next half hour answering

questions and offering explanations about Montana, the Amish auction, how she had saved the little boy from drowning, and her bicycle accident. "I'm happy to say that soon after my cast comes off, I'll be ready to take over your quilt shop." She smiled at her mother. "That is if you still want me to."

Mom's eyes shimmered with tears, and she sniffed a couple of times. "I'd like that very much. It's truly an answer to prayer."

"I'm hoping to enlist the help of several women in our community to make quilts that will be sent to needy people in Haiti. Elizabeth told me about the special project," Abby said.

"That sounds like something a group of women are doing over near Strasburg, where Edna lives." Mom pursed her lips. "Only I believe they're sendin' their quilts to Africa."

Mary Ann and Nancy entered the room carrying Titus and Timothy. But Abby didn't mind the interruption to the conversation. She was happy to see her little brothers, who had grown so much in her absence. "Bring those precious boys here so I can love on them a bit," she said, motioning for the girls to come over to the couch.

"Be careful now," Abraham said with a chuckle. "Titus and Timothy have more energy than five other boys their age, and we don't want 'em bumpin' that leg of yours."

Mom waved her hand. "Oh Husband, how you exaggerate." She reached for Titus and plunked him in Abby's lap, then took Timothy and seated him between her and Abby.

Abby kissed and hugged on the boys awhile;

then Ruth asked Mom if it was time to start supper. Mom agreed but was reluctant to leave Abby.

"Ah, she'll be fine by herself," Jake said with a snicker. "Probably would enjoy bein' away from all the noise for a while."

Abby shook her head. "I don't mind the noise one bit."

"I'll take the twins outside to sit on the porch swing." Abraham gathered up his sons, while Mom, Ruth, and the girls headed for the kitchen.

"I think the rest of us ought to go outside, too," Matthew said, looking at Norman, then Jake, and finally down at young Samuel. "Abby needs some quiet time before the rest of the family arrives, don't ya think?"

"I'm okay, really," Abby spoke up.

"Even so, it would make me feel better if you rested awhile."

"Yes, Dr. Matthew," she said with a smile.

He grinned, like he was pleased with himself, and carefully lifted Abby's injured leg, helping her to lie on the couch. "Close your eyes, and we'll let you know when Naomi and her family arrive."

Abby settled against the pillows with a sigh. It was ever so nice to be home.

∽

"It's good to see you again, Abby. You were surely missed," Naomi said. Supper was over and the two of them had come to the living room for a visit.

"I'm glad to be here." Abby nodded at her suitcase, sitting near the woodstove. "Would you mind bringing that over to me? I've got something for you."

"You didn't have to bring me anything."

Abby smiled. "Actually, it's more for the boppli you're carrying."

"I see." Naomi placed the suitcase on one end of the couch, and Abby scooted closer to it. She snapped the lid open and lifted the baby quilt, holding it out to Naomi. Naomi stood staring at the quilt with a puzzled expression. Finally, with shaky fingers, she reached out and took it, examining each little square and touching every corner. Tears streamed down Naomi's cheeks, and she sank into a chair near the couch. When she lifted one end of the quilt and pressed it against her cheek, her whole body trembled.

Concerned, Abby wondered if giving the baby covering to Naomi had been a bad idea. "I was hoping you would like the little quilt."

Tears coursed down Naomi's cheeks. "Oh, I do, Abby. I just need to know where you got it."

"Elizabeth gave it to me. She said she'd found it at a thrift store when she and some other women from her community were on vacation."

"Where was it, Abby? Did she tell you where they had gone?"

Abby sat trying to recall what Elizabeth had said about the trip. "I think it was somewhere in the state of Washington. Why do you want to know, Naomi?"

"Because this was my little brother's quilt."

Abby leaned slightly forward, unsure of what her stepsister had said. "What was that?"

"This quilt belonged to Zach. Our mother made it for him before she died."

"But how can you be sure it's the same quilt?"

Naomi held up the covering. "See here, there's

a small patch that doesn't fit the Tumbling Block pattern. The quilt got caught in Zach's crib rails one morning, and I was in such a hurry I didn't do a good job patching it." She slowly shook her head, and more tears fell. "I would recognize this anywhere. It's Zach's, I know it is."

Abby gasped. "Do you know what this means?"

Naomi nodded. "It means my little brother must be living in the state of Washington somewhere." She stood and began to pace in front of the woodstove. "I've got to tell Papa about this. He needs to know Zach is still alive."

Abby opened her mouth to protest, but she closed it again. Finding the quilt was no guarantee that Abraham's son was still living. For that matter, the fact that Elizabeth had found the quilt in Washington didn't mean Zach was there. Whoever had kidnapped the boy could have sold the quilt or thrown it out. It might have passed through many hands before it ended up in the thrift store.

How do I say this to Naomi without upsetting her further? If I'd known this little covering was going to cause her such pain, I would have left it with Elizabeth. As the words flitted through her head, Abby quickly changed her mind. *The quilt is a link to Naomi's missing brother, maybe an important one. Who am I to dash away any hope Naomi has of seeing Zach again?*

Naomi started for the front door, and Abby figured she was heading for the barn where the men had gone after supper. Her hand touched the doorknob, but suddenly she whirled around. "I can't show Papa the quilt. Not now. Maybe not ever."

"Why not?"

"He's been through so much over the years, I won't see him hurt again. This would only get his hopes up." Naomi flopped back into her chair, draping the quilt over her knees. "Even if Zach is living out West, we have no idea in which city or who his kidnapper is. Zach's not a baby anymore either. He would be seven years old by now. Why, he could walk right up to us and we probably wouldn't even know it was him."

"I'm sorry for upsetting you," Abby apologized. "Maybe it would have been better if I hadn't given you the quilt."

"No, no, I'm glad you did." Naomi buried her face in the quilt. "It might be hard to understand, but holding this actually brings me comfort."

"Are you sure about not telling your daed?"

Naomi stood. "Someday, maybe. For now I'll keep it in my boppli's room as a reminder that somewhere my little bruder is still living among the English and I need to keep praying for him."

Abby nodded. "I'll be praying, too."

"I'm going to the kitchen to get a paper sack to put the quilt in, so none of the others will see it."

"Do you want to put it back in my suitcase for now?"

"That's a good idea." Naomi placed the quilt inside the suitcase, shut the lid, and then hurried from the room.

A few seconds later, Matthew showed up. "Whew, it's still mighty warm out there. Looks like we're in for some hot weather." He wiped the perspiration from his forehead and smiled at Abby. "Before this summer's over, you might wish you had stayed in Montana, where it's cooler."

"I don't think so." She patted the cushion beside her. "Have a seat."

He grinned, and his ears turned pink. She had embarrassed him again, but that was okay. The fact that Matthew blushed so easily was part of who he was, and she rather liked it.

"How'd you like to go on a picnic with me one day next week?" he asked, lowering himself to the couch. "That is, if you're feelin' up to it."

"I'd like it fine, and I'm sure I'll be feeling well enough to go." Abby chuckled. "Of course, you'll probably have to bring a chair for me to sit in. It might be easy enough for me to drop to the ground, but gettin' back up would be a lot harder."

Matthew reached over and took her hand, giving her fingers a gentle squeeze. "Why don't you let me worry about that?"

Abby leaned against the sofa cushions and sighed. *I know my faith has been tried and withstood the flames. And regardless of what happens with Zach, the Fisher family, or between Matthew and me, I'm confident that God will see us through.*

Discussion Questions

1. Abby Miller was a self-sacrificing daughter. What were her reasons for being so giving? Are Christians always supposed to set their own needs aside in order to minister to others? Is there such a thing as being too self-sacrificing?

2. Abby believed that the recurring dream she had was a warning of what was to come. She blamed herself for Lester's death and felt that if she had heeded the dream warning, he would have been spared. Do you believe that God ever warns us of coming events through our dreams? How would you respond to a recurring dream you felt was a warning?

3. Was Abby's self-recrimination over the fire in her quilt shop justified? Was she really the one to blame? If not, who was at fault, or was it merely an accident?

4. What motivated Jim Scott to get rid of Zach's Amish baby quilt? Did his guilt over the kidnapping lessen because he gave the quilt away? What is God's answer for our guilt?

5. Linda Scott changed in many respects during this book. How did she change, and what brought about those changes? How did Jim deal with the changes he saw in his wife?

6. When Abraham Fisher's wife gave birth to twins, he made the comment that God had taken away one son and given him two. Do

you believe God was responsible for the disappearance of Abraham's son, Zach? Or did God merely allow it to happen? Can you think of an incident in your life when God allowed something bad to happen but healed your grief with something good?

7. How did Naomi deal with the loss of her little brother? Was she justified in feeling that her father had forgotten about Zach when his sons were born? Was Naomi right to confront him on this? Is it always better to let others know the way we feel about things?

8. In order to deal with the pain of her loss, Abby drove herself to work harder and avoided most social situations. What are some ways people choose to deal with the pain of a traumatic event? Is there a right or a wrong way? How does God want us to deal with painful situations?

9. What do you think would have happened if Fannie had insisted that Abby return to her quilt shop in Ohio sooner? Was Fannie right to feel guilty when Abby lost everything?

10. How did saving a young boy's life change Abby's perspective on things? Do you believe God directs us to be in certain places at certain times? Or do you feel that everything happens by coincidence or because of our own choices?

11. When Abby gave Naomi the quilt that had once been Zach's, Naomi decided to keep it from her father because she didn't want to upset him or get his hopes up. Is it ever right to hide the truth from someone because we are trying to protect them?

12. What did you learn from Abby's experiences in *The Quilter's Daughter*?

13. Are there any positive aspects to the Amish way of life that you could incorporate into your own life?

About the Author

New York Times, award-winning author, Wanda E. Brunstetter is one of the founders of the Amish fiction genre. Wanda's ancestors were part of the Anabaptist faith, and her novels are based on personal research intended to accurately portray the Amish way of life. Her books are well-read and trusted by many Amish, who credit her for giving readers a deeper understanding of the people and their customs. When Wanda visits her Amish friends, she finds herself drawn to their peaceful lifestyle, sincerity, and close family ties. Wanda enjoys photography, ventriloquism, gardening, bird-watching, beachcombing, and spending time with her family. She and her husband, Richard, have been blessed with two grown children, six grandchildren, and two great-grandchildren.

To learn more about Wanda, visit her website at www.wandabrunstetter.com.